The DUNGEON

THOMAS McDONALD

To order additional copies of this book, contact:
Bookwhip
1-855-339-3589
https://www.bookwhip.com

The DUNGEON

PROLOGUE

The woman from the newspaper ran over to Leroy and threw her arms around his neck, giving him a big kiss on his lips. She exclaimed, "I got it all! I got it all! I got it all on film! I took pictures of everything. I'll get to be a reporter now. I always wanted to be one. Thank you, thank you, I love you.

Leroy grimly said, "Please don't print the one with the woman."

"Oh, I have to. It's so romantic."

Leroy murmured, "I don't think the Captain will like it. It's not proper police procedure."

Ashley walked over to stand with Leroy while paramedics gently carried the dead cashier from the bank. Leroy said, "what a waste, She was just a young girl with her whole life ahead of her."

Ashley said, "at least you got the killer. That should count for something."

Ashley gave Leroy a dazzling smile. "Well, now that you have killed all the bad guys and kissed all the girls, can we go home now?"

CHAPTER ONE

The police station in Garland was about the same as all other Police Stations. Leroy sat in his car and watched the traffic going in and out of the Police Station. Well here he was, a small town boy in the big city. This was his new home. He got out of his Ford Thunderbird and walked to the entrance. It was the same car he had in high school. He thought about times he had raced it. He had never lost a race.

Leroy walked into a large room of mass confusion. He looked around and saw a nameplate with Sergeant O'Malley on it. He walked over to the desk. He said, "Leroy Cooper reporting for duty, sir." The Sergeant looked up and gave Leroy an inspection. "Well, we got a new recruit all spit and polish." Leroy looked the Sergeant over. He looked like he had been around the block too many times. He looked old and tired with his hair almost white. "Welcome to Dallas. I'll see if the Captain is in." Sergeant O'Malley walked over to a closed door marked Captain on it and knocked.

"Come in."

"We have a new recruit checking in, sir."

"Send him in." Captain whispered to himself, good we need more men. They were always short on men.

Sergeant O'Malley said, "You can go in now and good luck, you will need it."

As Leroy walked over to the office, he wandered what the Sergeant had meant by the remark. He would find out. Leroy walked into the office and stood at attention in front of the cluttered desk. The office was a mess.

He said, "Leroy Cooper reporting for duty, sir."

"At ease Cooper, sit down and give me your file."

Leroy handed him his file. Captain Curry opened his file and scanned over the pages. "You got good marks at the Police Academy except for the firing range. You passed, but with low scores."

"Sir, I can explain that. A 38 Police issue isn't my kind of firearm."

Captain Curry laughed, "Most all the new recruits say that. What is your choice of a firearm?"

"A Colt 45, sir." "And you don't miss with it?"

"No sir, I don't."

"Good, I'll keep that in mind if I ever need a sharpshooter, but right now I need to get you a partner for training and get your gear issued to you. We are short on men like most police stations. We get by the best we can with what we got. Crime is at an all- time high. You will start on patrol in the morning. Now let me see who I can team you with." The Captain studied the roster.

"Let's see now, I'll team you with Corporal Ashley Lewis. She has been with us for five years. She knows the area and streets by heart. She works traffic, school zones, and parking tickets. She takes care of a lot the small crimes. We like her and don't want her to get hurt. We wouldn't want our recruit hurt right away either," laughed Captain Curry.

"Is that all, sir?"

"For now, I'll see you at seven in the morning, in the briefing room. Turn right when you leave the office and it is all the way down the hall."

"Thank you, sir. I'll be here."

"Oh by the way Corporal Ashley shot a sharpshooter on the range."

Leroy had rented a small one bedroom, one bath apartment close to the police station. He hated long drives to and from work. He stopped at a mom and pop grocery store around the corner and stocked up on food and beer.

Leroy parked his car and carried his groceries into his apartment. He put his groceries away and decided to take a shower before he finished unloading his car. He showered and put on shorts and a t-shirt. He went back out to his car to finish unloading. He got his two bags and his radio. A radio was all the entertainment he had, but that could change. There was a good looking woman standing across the hall from his door.

"Hi, I'm your neighbor Ann Mitchel. Do you need any help?"

"If you can get my beer that's all I have left." Ann came out to the car and got the beer. "Boy, do I like your car. What kind is it?"

Leroy replied," It's an older Ford Thunderbird. I got it while I was still in high school." They slowly walked back to Leroy's apartment.

"I saw you when you were still in uniform, you looked great." Ann thought now why did I say that? He will think it is a come on. She blushed red as Leroy looked her up and down from her head to her toes. He liked what he saw. Ann had on red short-shorts and a white shirt tied between her breasts. She wasn't wearing a bra. He could tell her breasts were firm by the way they pointed out. She was only about five feet two inches tall with long black hair.

She had all the curves in the right places, green eyes like a cat and lips that begged to be kissed. Leroy stared at her and she stared back. Leroy broke eye contact first.

"Thanks for the help."

"You're welcome."

"My name is Leroy Cooper and I just arrived in Dallas. I have been lost ever since I got here. Dallas is so big."

Ann laughed, "Most people are the first time in Dallas. Here let me help you with a bag while you unlock the door."

"Thanks for your help again." They went into his apartment and put the bags down. As Ann put her bag down she had to bend over showing her nice firm breasts. Her female scent teased his senses and he stared at her as she rose back up. Leroy had an instant erection. He turned his back, but Ann had already seen his fly rise up. She smiled and could feel her wet panties. Her juices were flowing. What was wrong with her? She had to leave, this guy was causing her body to heat up and she didn't want to embarrass herself.

Leroy said, "Would you like a beer?"

"No, thank you. I have to go, but I'll take a rain check." Sparks were flying between them as Ann left and they both knew it wasn't over.

Leroy showered and went to bed, but he couldn't sleep. He was restless and tossed and turned in his sleep. He thought about tomorrow and his first day on the police force. What would it be like on the streets of the big city? There was so much crime going on all the time. Would he back down when the chips were down? He had never been tested with real life situations. He finally went to sleep, but he dreamed about the hot little number next door. His dreams were XXX rated.

Ann had the same problem. She dreamed he was kissing her and they were both naked. She opened her legs for him and he slammed into her. He rode her hard until she had a climax. She woke up in an empty bed. It was morning too soon.

Leroy walked into the briefing room and looked around. It was almost full, but he wasn't late. He saw a tall blonde with a nice slender body and a regulation police haircut. She was as tall as Leroy.

Ashley saw Leroy and walked over to him. "Good morning. I'm Ashley Lewis and I believe I am your new partner."

"Hi, I'm Leroy Cooper and I'm glad to meet you." They shook hands.

"Do you have a problem working with a woman, one that out ranks you?"

"No, not at all," he lied. He was hoping to be placed with a man, one with a lot of experience.

"Leroy, I will always have your back." She read him like a book.

They sat down for the day's briefing. Sergeant O'Malley took the podium.

"We have a long briefing today, lots of bad guys and bad girls." He passed out a long list. "This is your list of outstanding warrants. The hookers are working the streets again. There are still a lot of drugs being sold on our streets. Put a stop to it! We have a new recruit with us. His name is Leroy Cooper and his partner will be Corporal Lewis. Good luck Cooper."

Ashley and Leroy picked up their gear and headed for their patrol car. Ashley glanced at Leroy, "Well another day and another dollar."

"Our car is number seven," Ashley said.

"Has it been lucky for you?"

"Well yes, so far I haven't had a dent in it." Things were about to change, She had Leroy with her. He was always in trouble of some kind.

The morning was quiet, except for giving a few citations for speeding, running red lights or stop signs. Ashley said, "It's about lunch time so let's get some food." She pulled into a fast food place across from the First National Bank.

Leroy observed an old black Ford left running, parked to the side of the bank. "Are you coming?" asked Ashley.

"Hold up a minute. Something doesn't look right at the bank." They stared at the bank.

"I don't see anything wrong, murmured Ashley. Leroy tensed as he watched the driver of the old Ford. The driver was very nervous, glancing to the bank door and back ahead, he was looking over at the Police car.

"There's a robbery in process, call it in."

"Leroy, are you sure you know what you are talking about?"

"No, but it's better to be safe than sorry."

Ashley called in and the dispatcher replied, "I don't have anything from the bank to indicate any trouble."

Leroy got out of the car and reached in his bag in the back seat. "What is going on?" asked the dispatcher.

"My partner is strapping on what looks like an old west fast draw holster with a big gun in it" Shots were fired in the bank.

"I'm on it. The alarm just went off here at the station. Help is on the way," said the dispatcher.

"Ashley cut that get-a-way car off. Be careful. I'm sure he is armed."

"What are you going to do?"

"I'll take care of the rest."

"Shouldn't we wait for backup?"

"Too late," Leroy started slowly walking toward the bank entrance.

"Parked a couple of cars down from the Police car, a Dallas newspaper employee, Katherine Stewart, watched Leroy. She wasn't a reporter yet, but she had always wanted to be one. And now was her chance. She always carried a camera with her. Katherine jumped out of the car and started snapping pictures. She had heard the shots fired in the bank.

All hell was about to break loose.

Leroy stopped and spread his legs in a gunfighter stance. He flexed his hands and relaxed, he was ready for action. Two men came out of the bank, followed by a third man dragging a young woman with him.

Ashley yelled, "Police, put down your guns."

The two men answered with a volley of gunfire from automatic weapons. Ashley ducked as bullets slammed into the police car.

"Hey punks, that's no way to treat a lady Police Officer," shouted Leroy.

Both men turned their attention back to him. Leroy's hand went for his gun and he shot the man to his left before he could get off a shot. The second man fired, but in a hurry and not close enough. Leroy dropped the second man with one shot. Both men were dead before they hit the payment.

"Get out of my way," yelled the third man, "or I'll kill the woman." The woman was screaming her head off. "Shut up lady."

"Give it up, you saw what a Colt 45 can do," argued Leroy. The man glanced over at his fallen men, but he didn't give in. He looked at his get-a-way car and back at Leroy. He started to drag the woman, keeping her in front of him as he made his way toward the car. Ashley burned rubber as she aimed her car in front of the get-a-way car to cut him off.

Leroy shouted, "Lady, tilt your head to the left." As she tilted her head, Leroy with his arm extended took a shot. The bullet hit the man in the head knocking him backwards to the payment. His last words were "Who was that guy?" and he was dead. The woman fainted and fell on him.

Ashley cut off the get-a-way car, but the man stuck a gun out the window to fire at her. Leroy fired just in time before he got a shot off. The Colt 45 almost took the man's arm off. He sat there in shock as Ashley got out of her car to take care of him.

Leroy holstered his weapon as he walked over to the woman that fainted and tried to wake her up. She had blood all over her clothes where she had fallen on the robber. She was gorgeous. His face was only a couple inches from her face. Leroy couldn't resist twining his fingers in her long hair. Now their lips were only an inch apart. Leroy murmured, "What the heck." He kissed her. Her body tensed and her eyes flew open. She said softly, "What are you doing?"

"I was trying to wake you up, you fainted."

She was utterly fascinated by this man holding her in his arms. "Kiss me again. I'm not totally awake yet." Leroy kissed her again without hesitation, while she curled her arms around his neck. She kissed him with deep heated passion. When they came up for air, Leroy helped her to a standing position. She looked down at her clothes. "Oh, I'm a mess. I got to get cleaned up. Thank you for saving my life."

"My pleasure," Leroy replied.

Police cars and an ambulance filled the parking lot. Police converged on the crime scene. Two policemen ran a tape around the crime area, one picked up the money bags and the other picked up the weapons. He inspected the automatic weapons. He said, "Their weapons are better than any that the Police have. We should find the dealer and buy from him." The paramedics took care of the robber's arm and put the three dead men in body bags. They left for the hospital with a Police car to escort them.

Captain Curry came out of the bank and faced Leroy. "What happened in the bank, sir?" Leroy inquired.

Captain Curry's face looked like stone. "They killed a woman cashier when she set off the alarm. The last man you shot killed her when he saw her push the button. You didn't hear me say this, but I'm glad you killed the sorry bastard." He looked Leroy over, gazing at the Colt 45 on his hip. "I see you used your own weapon and hit what you aimed at."

Leroy replied, "Yes sir, I did."

"You and Corporal Lewis did a good job. However why didn't you wait for backup?"

"There wasn't time, sir."

"You and Corporal Lewis take the rest of the day off. I'll see you in the morning with your full report." Leroy planned to leave the kissing part out.

The woman from the newspaper ran over to Leroy and threw her arms around his neck, giving him a big kiss on the lips. She exclaimed, "I got it all! I got it all! I took pictures of everything. I'll get to be a reporter now. I always wanted to be one. Thank you, thank you, I love you!"

Leroy grimly said, "Please don't print the one with the woman."

"Oh, I have to. It's so romantic."

Leroy murmured, "I don't think the Captain will like it. It's not proper police procedure."

Ashley walked over to stand with Leroy while paramedics gently carried the dead cashier from the bank. Leroy said, "What a waste. She was just a young girl with her whole life ahead of her."

Ashley said, "At least you got her killer. That should count for something."

Ashley gave Leroy a dazzling smile. "Well, now that you have killed all the bad guys and kissed all the girls can we go home now?"

Leroy laughed, "Yes we can. The Captain gave us the rest of the day off." They walked over to their car. Leroy said, "My side of the car is full of holes."

Ashley tossed him the keys. "You drive. I'm too far out of it to drive. I have never been in a shootout before. My husband is going to kill me when I get home. He doesn't like me being a cop. We've only been married a year." Ashley was babbling all the way back to the Police Station. "Where did you learn to shoot like that? How could you just stand there with them shooting at you? How could you shoot that man while he was holding that woman in front of him?"

Leroy laughed, "I told her to tilt her head," as if that would explain everything. Leroy got in his car and waved bye to Ashley. "See you later and don't worry your husband will get over it. He loves you and doesn't want to see you hurt." As Leroy drove away he realized he didn't know Ashley was married. He was real glad he wasn't married to a cop. He didn't know if he could take it. Well, he didn't have anyone to marry anyway. Leroy slowly parked his car and started toward his apartment. He walked slumped over and he was dead tired. He needed a shower and some sleep. He looked up and saw

Ann running toward him, "I saw what happened at the bank. It has been on television and radio all afternoon. You sure look tired."

"I'm very tired," replied Leroy.

""Poor baby, come along with me and I'll make you feel better." Ann took his hand and led him into her apartment.

"Well so much for a shower and sleep," sighed Leroy.

Ann said, "You take a shower while I fix some food and drinks. After you eat you will feel better." Leroy wasn't so sure about that. He had never killed anyone before. The only thing that kept him from falling apart was the fact that they had killed a girl in cold blood while in the bank. She was only doing her job as she was trained to do. The alarm had already been set off so why kill the girl? Leroy felt sick, for the girl, but not for the coward that killed her. She was married with three children, what a waste. He pulled off his clothes and stepped into the shower. He only turned on the cold tap. He needed something to bring him back to life.

Leroy walked into the kitchen with only a towel around his hips. "I need to go across the hall and get some clothes."

Ann stared at the half naked man in her kitchen. She saw broad shoulders, slim hips, black curly hair on his chest and a face that needed some loving. Twining her fingers together she itched to slide her fingers into his wet hair. Was that the hair on his chest or the hair down below? She was having thoughts as she stared at the towel and wished it would fall off. She wanted to see what was under the towel. Ann shouldn't be thinking thoughts like that. What was wrong with her? It had to be lust. She was confused. She took a deep breath, "sit down, the food is getting cold."

"Are you sure you don't want me to get some clothes on?"

"Yes, now eat."

Leroy ate chili dogs, fries and a coke to drink.

Ann stared at Leroy. It would be fool-hardy to get involved with a cop and the danger of his job, but her body was hot. He could put out the fire. Leroy thought he knew what she was thinking. He stared back at her.

Leroy could smell her female scent and knew that she was hot, ready to make love. She was nervous and nibbled at her lower lip. Her lips parted and slowly licked her lips with her tongue. That action almost made Leroy lose it. He wasn't sure how much longer he could play games.

They stared at each other. Leroy asked, "Have you made up your mind?"

"Yes I have," Ann whispered.

Ann reached up between her breasts and untied her shirt. It was the same shirt and short-shorts she was wearing the first time he saw her. She pulled the shirt off and dropped it to the floor. Leroy stared at two perfect mounds with spots in the middle, not too big, not too small, but just right. Leroy had an immediate erection.

Ann walked over and jerked the towel away from Leroy, then let it drop to the floor. Ann smiled noncommittally, "Did I do that?" She pointed at his huge tool.

"Yes and what are you going to do about it?"

She took his hand and pulled him toward the bedroom. "Come with me and find out." Standing by the bed, Leroy pulled her into his arms. They fit perfectly together. Ann could feel arousal against her soft belly. She could see desire and hunger in his eyes.

Leroy said softly, "Last chance to back out. Are you sure about this?"

Her heart hammered against her ribs. "Yes." Ann responded, her fingers moving to his face tracing the lines and then running her fingers over his face. Ann covered his mouth with hers. Her tongue plunged deeply into his mouth tangling with his tongue. She clung to him as sensation after sensation of heat overwhelmed her body.

Leroy pulled away and broke the kiss. He kissed the curve of her neck while holding her around the waist. He lowered his head and started down her body. His tongue found a hard nipple and nipped it. Then he took the other nipple and sucked on it like a baby. Ann moaned and arched her back against him.

Moving lower he pulled down her shorts, followed by her panties. He parted her thighs, then her womanly lips, then slid a finger in and found she was wet and ready. Leroy thrust his tongue deep into her heated body. Ann bucked toward him. She put her hands around his head and tried to pull him deeper. She moaned as wave after wave of pleasure brought her to a climax. She fell back on the bed sweating and trembling, her body jerking with contractions caused by reflux action. Moving above her, she opened her thighs inviting further intimacies, her hips rose to meet his incoming thrust. He thrust deep into her soft hot body. She moaned as her hips rose to meet each thrust. Leroy slammed harder and harder trying for deeper penetration into her body. He was trying to put out the fire. She started to squeeze with her muscles and Leroy knew she was going to have an orgasm again.

They both had a climax at the same time and Leroy fell on her chest flattening her breasts. Leroy started to pull out, but Ann clung to him. "Not yet, it feels so good." He lay on top awhile waiting for her to come back to earth. They were still connected. Her muscles were still milking him dry.

Finally, Leroy rolled to his side with her back to him and pulled her back to him spoon fashion. They were satiated from making love and dosed off to sleep.

About three in the morning, Leroy woke up with a big erection with his hand on a nice firm breast. The nipple was peaked. His erection was close to her damp folds. Leroy slowly entered her until she had it all. He laid still and waited for a response from Ann. He didn't have long to wait before her inner muscles curled around his length and started to squeeze. He pulled almost out and thrust slowly back in all the way. Ann arched her back to meet each thrust. Ann came first, but Leroy was right behind her. Wrapped in one another's arms, both of them spent, they went back to sleep.

The next morning, Leroy slipped out of bed, gathered his clothes and went back to his apartment. After a shower and shave he was wide awake and ready to take on another day. He got dressed for work.

Leroy stopped on the corner at the mom and pop grocery and deli. The owners, John and Marie, were a nice old couple. Marie got him coffee and donuts. "Thank you, Leroy. It is on the house."

"How did you know my name?"

"Everyone knows your name." She handed him a newspaper. Bank robbery fouled was the headlines on the front page. The robbery was laid out in pictures as it happened. The last picture was Leroy kissing the woman.

Marie said, "I think it is just like in the movies. You kill all the bad guys and get the girl."

Leroy quoted grimly, "I don't think my boss will see it that way." Leroy started for the door. "Thanks for the coffee and donuts."

Marie replied, "You're very welcome."

What a nice little old lady thought Leroy. He met Ashley in the hall on the way to briefing. He said, "Would you go in with me?"

Ashley grinned at him, "Chicken."

"Yes, I am."

All hands turned as they entered the briefing room. Leroy wanted to turn around and run back out the door. Ashley said softly, "Take it like a man."

Everyone said, "Dirty Harry arriving!"

It made Ashley mad that they were teasing Leroy. She stopped with fire in her eyes as she scanned the room. It got quiet all of a sudden. Ashley said, "I can't believe this. I have been a cop for five years and nothing like this ever happened. How many of you boys and girls would have faced three robbers, two of them with automatic weapons? Please raise your hands." "Um-hum, I thought so.

"That's enough, take your seats," said Sergeant O'Malley. He went through the normal briefing for the day. After briefing, Sergeant O'Malley told Corporal Lewis and Leroy, "Fill out your reports from yesterday and report to Captain Curry's office.

"Yes sir," they replied.

They left the briefing room and went to their desk that they shared. Ashley typed the report as they put the report together. Finished, they both signed the report.

"Ok Corporal Lewis since you are senior, how about you take the report into the Captain while I wait out here for you."

"No way, Harry. Now, why did I say that? I'm sorry."

Leroy laughed, "You to."

"I'm sorry. I don't know why I said that." Ashley said, "Come on, I'll hold your hand and not let the bad old Captain get you." They both laughed as Leroy walked in the open door still holding Ashley's hand. He let her hand drop like it was a hot potato.

Gruffly, Captain Curry said, "What are you two laughing about?"

"Corporal Lewis was telling me a joke sir."

Captain Curry slid a newspaper in front of them. Hand me your report. You can read the newspaper while I read your report."

The pictures were staring at them. Leroy glanced at Ashley, "You take a good picture." Ashley put her finger on the picture of Leroy kissing the woman. "So do you," she couldn't keep from grinning at him.

Captain Curry said, "I don't like what happened yesterday, but you stopped a robbery and probably saved that young woman's life. If they had gotten away they would probably have raped her then killed her. They were wanted for rape and a lot more charges. The problem is the public will say too much force was used."

Leroy protested, "Sir, those punks would have killed anyone who tried to stop them."

"Did you have to kill three of them?"

"Sir, those men are like a wounded bear, the bear keeps coming until you kill it or it kills you." Leroy had made his point.

"Ok, you two get out of here. Please don't kill anyone today."

"Yes sir."

Ashley said, "You drive. With your hands on the wheel, you can't shoot anyone."

"No, but I could run over someone."

Ashley grinned and then started to laugh. "Leroy you are a nut case." He looked at her and laughed.

It was afternoon and they had very little in the way of excitement. As they were turning right on Belt Line when a black Ford ran a red light and slammed into the front of the driver's side of the Police car. The black Ford didn't slow down, but increased its speed. Leroy spun the police car in the direction the black Ford was going, burning rubber, lights flashing, and siren wailing. He gave chase.

"Ashley, are you ok?"

"I think so, just shook up a little." Ashley called in a hit and run. "I'm on it." The dispatcher asked, "What was hit?"

Ashley replied, "We were and now we are in pursuit of the suspects." Ashley started giving street names as the chase continued. Leroy grimly said, "If that car isn't stopped soon, someone is going to get killed."

At that very moment, the black Ford ran a pickup off the road. Speeds of the chase reached eighty miles an hour. Next he ran a car off the road. Ashley glanced out her window as they passed. "That was a little old lady driving that car."

"That's it, I've had enough," said Leroy. They said they were setting up a road block ahead. The black Ford slowed down and turned down a side road, So Much for the road block. The Ford ran another car off the road. Leroy grabbed the mike from Ashley. "This suspect is running people off the road. We are going to take him down." Leroy pulled in close. "Ashley, take out a tire."

"I don't know if I can. Are you sure we should do this?"

"Just do it!" replied Leroy.

Ashley pulled out her 38 pistol, took aim and fired. She missed. "Keep firing," instructed Leroy. She took aim and started firing at the tires again. One, two and the third hit a tire. The black Ford lost control, hit a parked car, catapulting over the car, crashing on its side and sliding to a stop. Leroy came to a quick stop. He and Ashley were out of their car, with their guns drawn. Ashley warned, "Get out of the car with your hands up." A young kid stuck his head out. "Please don't shoot."

The windshield had popped out when their car hit the parked car. The crawled out through the opening.

"Face down on the payment," ordered Ashley. She handcuffed him while Leroy for other heads to appear. They ended up with four. They were all young, seventeen to eighteen years old and all drunk. Leroy handcuffed the other three while they waited for backup. When the backup arrived the Policeman, Sam asked, "Harry, where are all the bodies?"

"Very funny," replied Leroy.

"Well, since you did all the work we'll take them to the station for you," said Sam.

"By the way, it looks like you need a new car."

"Why?" It's just now getting broke in with holes on the side and caved in on the other side," asked Ashley. They all had a good laugh.

Sam said, "You know who we are taking in don't you?"

Ashley sighed, "Yes, poor little rich kids. The driver is a councilman's son. We call them the untouchables. They think they are above the law.

Leroy said, "I don't care if it is the mayor himself, if he was endangering lives I would take him in."

Sam said, "I see you don't know politics in the police force yet."

"No, but I guess I'll learn soon enough."

"Ashley said, "We will take two of kids and you take two."

"Okay by us, let's move them out," Sam replied.

After the young men were booked and their reports filed, Ashley said goodbye to Leroy and went home.

On the way home Leroy stopped at the mom and pop grocery to get some food from the deli. Marie asked, "How was your day?"

Leroy replied, "Not too good. We put some little rich kids in jail. The driver was a councilman's son. That will cause a big problem."

"Why should it?"

"Some people think they are above the law." Leroy pointed to what he wanted from the deli. Marie filled his order for him. Leroy asked, "How much damage?"

"You don't pay."

"Yes I do, I'll be eating out here regularly. I live just around the corner." Marie didn't want him to pay, but Leroy made it clear he would pay for everything but coffee.

"Thank you, Leroy."

"You are very welcome."

Ann was waiting for Leroy as he got out of his car. He said, "What did you do to your hair?" It was several different colors.

"I dyed my hair. Don't you like it?"

"It's different."

Ann frowned, "You don't like it."

"Yes I do," he lied.

Leroy looked tired. "Come with me and I will make you forget how tired you are," Ann suggested. She gave him a cold beer and led him to her bedroom. Leroy sat on the bed drinking his beer as Ann began a striptease dance. She slowly took off her shirt. She wasn't wearing a bra as usual. Next, she unbuttoned her shorts and eased them over her hips letting them drop to the floor. Ann stepped out of them with only skimpy lace panties on. She walked slowly over to Leroy.

Leroy had a big lump in his throat and his mouth went dry. "Take it off, take it all off," mumbled Leroy.

"No you don't lover. It's your turn to strip for me." She reached for his beer and sat it on the night stand. Ann pulled him to his feet and sat down on the bed. "Ok now it is show time. Show me what you can do. Take it off, take it all off," laughed Ann. Leroy stared at her like she was crazy. "Come on now, play like you are a male stripper and think how good making love to me will be after you dance for me. It will make me hot and horny."

I can do this thought Leroy. Leroy started to rotate his hips while removing his shirt, gun belt, shoes, socks, pants and his last item his shorts. His peaked erection stood out for all to see.

Ann liked her lips. She giggled, "My, my, my, who are you going to beat to death with that club?"

Leroy grinned, "You I hope." He dropped to his knees as Ann rose up so he could slide her panties off. Leroy stared at her cat. "What happened to your black cat?" Her cat was now green with a tattoo which read, keep off the grass. Ann giggled, "Isn't it cool?"

"Yes, just different, I like it," Leroy lied again.

Ann spread her legs and smiled at Leroy. He slammed into damp folds of her soft flesh. Ann locked her legs around him and the muscles in her green cat put the squeeze on. He was almost ready to come. "Get off, don't come yet, hold on," whispered Ann. Leroy pulled out and rolled over. Ann shifted position until she was astride him. She reached down and guided him into her hot damp place. Ann giggled, "I want to be on top for this climax. I want to ride that big tool until it dies." She rode him hard, having climax after climax until Leroy finally went limp. Ann rolled off exhausted, content as a kitten. She curled up next to Leroy and went to sleep. Leroy laid there awhile and stared at the ceiling. He replayed their lovemaking. It had been savage. Ann had never missed a stroke. She gave as good, as she got. She was good. Leroy finally drifted off to sleep.

At midnight, Ann's alarm clock went off. She reached over and turned it off. Leroy was wide awake. "What was the alarm for? Do you have to go to work?"

"No"

"What then?"

"You have to go back to your apartment."

"Why? What's going on?"

Ann looked at him with a shy expression. "My boyfriend is coming home from a trip."

Leroy felt sucker punched. "Say what, did I hear you right? You have a boyfriend?

"Yes and he is a biker."

"You are talking a big man and a big bike?"

"Yes, I'm sorry."

Leroy couldn't believe what was happening. "Why did you have sex with me?"

"I liked the uniform," Ann giggled.

"Time to go home," Leroy jumped out of bed, picking up his clothes and headed for the door. He said, "Well, it was fun while it lasted."

"We had good sex," Ann giggled.

"Yes, we did."

One o'clock, Leroy was still wide awake, ticked off and staring at the ceiling. He was confused. He thought she liked him. After a short time, he realized what had happened. She was using him for sex since the boyfriend was out of town. When they were together making love, love was never mentioned. It was case of lust and good sex. As Leroy went to back to sleep his last thought was I hope she doesn't tell her boyfriend about me.

Leroy met Ashley in the briefing room. She glanced at him, "What happened to you, bad night or a good night and who was she?"

"Yes and no, don't ask."

She was curious, but let it drop for now.

Captain Curry called Ashley and Leroy into his office after briefing. He slid a newspaper in front of them. "Looks like you two have a champion in the newspaper office."

Leroy said, "I don't know anybody at the newspaper."

Captain stared at him. "Yes you do. She is the woman that kissed you in front of the bank. She is now a reporter. The report she made on the robbery and pictures landed her the job."

Leroy and Ashley scanned the newspaper. "My kind of girl, she doesn't pull any punches," said Leroy.

The newspaper article said three young men sometimes to as those that above the law because of their social class were arrested for speeding, failing to stop for police, running cars off the road and resisting arrest. This was a good job by our Police department. Keep up the good work and we need more Police officers like you. This report was written by Katherine Stewart.

Captain Curry said, "I have already had calls from high up. Poor little rich kids, sometimes I hate this job. They won't get but a small slap on the hand, if anything.

Leroy said, "It's not your fault the system is screwed up."

"Is that all, sir?" asked Ashley.

"No, there's more. They want you off regular patrol, if you get my drift."

Leroy said, "I get the picture."

"You will work school zones and places where nothing ever happens. Stay low and out of sight until this blows over. I'm sorry about that."

"No problem, sir.

Ashley, you will be assigned a new partner and get a new car. Leroy will drive the old car until our shop has time to repair it. It will probably be a few weeks. The shop is a little behind."

Ashley asked, "If it is okay with you sir, I would like to stay with Leroy."

"Are you sure that's what you want?"

"Yes sir, I like being with him. I feel like I'm alive and I know Leroy is dangerous to be with, but he gets the job done. I know I can count on him to always have my back and he would do anything to keep me safe."

Captain Curry stared at Ashley like she had lost her mind. "You know what we call a Policeman like Leroy, don't you?"

"Yes sir, he's called a maverick, he breaks rules and most of the time makes his own rules. He doesn't go by the rule book, but I still want him as my partner."

"You won't be on regular patrol, so you will keep the old car and be assigned with Leroy. You will get all the easy assignments, for now."

" Thank you, sir."

"I hope I don't live to regret my decision."

Leaving the office, Ashley looked back and smiled at the Captain. "We'll see if we can stir up some action."

Leroy laughed, "I bet we will."

Captain Curry sighed, "I hope not, it would be nice to have one quiet day."

Ashley parked their car close to a school zone. She said, "If they see the police car, they will slow down and we will have a nice quiet day."

"If you say so," he replied. Leroy got out of the car and took the radar gun with him. "Just in case." He smiled at Ashley.

Standing at the crosswalk, Leroy smiled at the little boys and girls as they crossed the street. A small boy stopped and stared at Leroy. He said, "My daddy said you are Dirty Harry. Is it true, do you kill people? Are you really him?"

Leroy smiled at the little boy, "No, I'm not Dirty Harry, but sometimes people call me that."

"Do you kill people?"

The school bell sounded and all the kids ran for the school. Leroy watched the little boy run away. He was saved by the bell. A new sports car pulled up and stopped. "Hi officer, we are good little boys today."

"Good, keep it that way."

They laughed as they drove off. Ashley said, "Let me guess, little rich boys with a new car."

"How did you guess?"

CHAPTER TWO

"You had a strange look on your face as you watched them drive off. What were you thinking about?"

"I was remembering back when I was their age and all the stunts we pulled."

She said, "You were a bad boy."

"Yes, I guess you say I was," admitted Leroy. He laughed, "I got in trouble all the time. One day with a bunch of guys, we were driving too fast down an old dirt road, when a turkey ran across the road in front of us. Punky slammed on the brakes."

It was close to Thanksgiving. Punky said, "Catch the turkey and we can have a feast." They caught the turkey and carried him with them. Who was going to cook the turkey? They didn't have any idea at the time. We were just a bunch of crazy kids, having fun. It was a stupid idea.

Ashley said, "Did you cook the turkey?"

"No, we didn't get that far. The funny part was one of the guys had a nickname of Sheriff." Punky said, "I can see the headlines now, turkey rustlers captured, Sheriff in with the rustlers."

Ashley laughed at the story. Leroy said, "It wasn't so funny the next day. The turkey rustlers were captured. Our parents had to come to get us and they were not happy campers. All of us were grounded for a very long time. One nice thing happened the Sheriff didn't let them book us."

"By the way, who was Punky?" asked Ashley.

"You don't want to know. He was the one always getting us in trouble. But, guess what?"

"He is a doctor now?"

"No, but Punky is in the United States Navy. He is an officer and a pilot. He is in Pensacola, Florida, Saufley Field, taking advanced flight training. Punky will be flying aboard the carrier U.S.S. Lexington."

Ashley was curious about the rest of the guys that were always in trouble. "What about the other boys? Or I say men, what happened to them?"

"Let me see now, Mike Love is married and has a ranch where he trains horses for the movies and runs cattle. I believe he has a kid also. His wife Linda was due when I left. Rex Johnson is here in Dallas and single at the time. He is an electronic engineer for Texas Instruments.

Gary Mitchel is floating around at this time. He doesn't have a clue what he wants to do with his life. Punky is a maverick like me. It would be fun to watch him in the Navy. He doesn't like to take orders, like me.

Ashley started the car. She said, "It's time to earn our paychecks." The rest of the day was slow and boring. They only wrote a few minor tickets.

Leroy finally got his answering machine the day before. He had several calls when he got home. Rex Johnson had called from Texas Instruments and wanted to get together for a night out. His mother called to check on him. She was worried about all the violence. She wanted him to quit and go back to college. Mike Love was checking on him also. He had heard about the bank robbery. He even had a call from Punky, the troublemaker himself, what's happening in the big city of Dallas. Leroy called the ones he could reach. He would call the others later.

Six months later.

Captain Curry called Leroy and Ashley into his office. "It's finally over. Starting Monday you will be back on regular patrol, with a new patrol car."

"That's good news, thank you sir," said Ashley.

"Since you two have been on light duty, crime has gone up. Robbery has gone up twenty percent. Car theft is up by ten percent and missing persons by ten percent. The odd thing is every time we have a missing person, their car is never found. It is always a fancy new car and the driver is a young girl. I don't like the looks of that. I hope it's not what I think it is. We don't have a body, yet."

Ashley said, "I hope we don't start finding bodies."

Homicide is working on it, but so far they haven't found a lead."

"You have a list of names and cars that are missing. Keep a close watch for them. We need a break, something that will get things rolling."

Ashley replied, "Yes sir, we will do our best."

"Have a nice weekend. It will probably be your last one off for a long time."

When Leroy got home, he had a message on the answering machine. Leroy, this is Katherine Stewart from the newspaper. Would you give me a call at home? Leroy wandered what she would want with him. Well, might as well find out. Leroy dialed the number she left on his answering machine. On the second ring, Katherine picked up.

"Hi, this is Leroy Cooper returning your call. How may I help you?"

Katherine's heart skipped a beat. What caused that? This was a business call, wasn't it? Katherine said, "I was wandering if I could come over and get an interview from you?"

"Fine with me, I just need to go to the grocery store. I am out of everything."

Katherine said, "I'll be there in about an hour."

"Ok, I'll see you then. By the way, don't you need my address?"

"No, I have it."

"How did you know my address and phone number?"

She said, "I've got a friend at the Police station."

"Ok, I'll see you shortly."

Leroy was going to walk, but he needed a lot, so he decided to drive. Katherine picked up her purse and camera. Never leave home without it, she joked about her camera. Maybe she could jet a naked shot of Leroy. Now why did she think of that? She suddenly felt warm all over. What was wrong with her?

Katherine didn't know Leroy. She had taken pictures of him and wrote stories for the newspaper, but that was all, well almost all. A little voice said, "What about the kiss?" She closed her eyes, daydreamed about the kiss, it had been in front of the bank after the hold up. Katherine had been so excited about taking pictures that she had forgotten about the effect it had on her.

When they touched, it was like an electric shock. She had walked away in a daze. Katherine thought it was all the excitement going on at the time, but now she wasn't so sure. She was curious now. She wanted to kiss Leroy again and see what effect it had on her. Katherine wanted to know if the kiss had the same effect on Leroy as it had on her. Maybe she should just mark it up to plain old lust. She hadn't been with a man in a long, long time. Did he look good in a Police uniform? It was always something about a man in uniform that turned the girls on. Katherine got in her car and took off to Leroy's apartment.

Leroy parked in front of the grocery store and went in. He went up and down aisles picking up items he needed. Leroy, when finished, went to the register to check out.

Marie kept her head down as she checked him out, which wasn't right. Leroy glanced to his left where a large white man was standing, staring at him. Leroy asked. "Where is John?"

Marie said, "He is taking a nap."

Leroy said, "I'm sorry, I forgot my coffee." He came back with his cup of coffee.

Marie glanced up at him. "That will be fifty cents for the coffee."

Leroy reached for his wallet. Leroy said, "Sorry, I'll be right back. I left my wallet in the car. As he was walking out he glanced back and could see the man talking to Marie. He could see the fear in her eyes. She was trying to keep from crying. Leroy thought back to what Marie had said and her actions. It hit him, John was taking a nap and she had looked down. John had to be on the floor behind the counter.

Leroy walked to the driver side of the car. He reached in the back seat and pulled out his Colt 45. He strapped on his fast draw holster and tied the tie to his leg. He slid the Colt 45 into the holster. Leroy thought he had better check the load. He pulled the 45 and checked the load. It was fully loaded. He slid the 45 back into his holster.

Katherine pulled up beside Leroy, "What's going on?" she asked.

"There is a robbery in process at the grocery store, call it in. Get back as soon as you can."

She said, "I'm on it." Katherine had a citizen band radio in her car. She made the call to the police station.

Leroy started walking back to the store. Katherine said, "Aren't you going to wait for backup?"

He glanced back, "No, it may be too late. I'm going in."

Katherine's heart was banging against her ribs as she watched a story unfold. Leroy glanced back before he entered the store. She gave him a thumb up to let him know backup was on the way. Katherine parked her car and grabbed her camera.

Leroy wished Ashley was here to cover his back. She would be reaching for her gun to cover his back. He had Katherine covering his back with a camera. He should wait for backup, but then he would have a hostage situation on his hands. Surprise was on his side and he was going to use it.

Time was wasting. He entered the store. Leroy had on shorts, a t-shirt, flip-flops for shoes and a Colt 45 on his side. He looked stupid and probably was for the not waiting for backup.

The man didn't see the gun on Leroy's hip until he got to the counter and turned to face him. He took the man by surprise. The man stared at Leroy like he was some kind of a fruit cake. Leroy said, "Marie Is John back there?"

"Yes, he is on the floor."

"Get down there with him."

Marie ducked down behind the counter. She said, "Watch out. There are two of them."

Leroy said, "I am the Police. You can do this the easy way, or the hard way, that's up to you." The man laughed at Leroy. "What are you, some kind of gunfighter or just a nut case?"

Leroy said, "There's one way to find out."

The man said, "Joe, are you in place?"

"Yes, I am," came from the front of the store.

The man by the counter started to raise his weapon. "We take the hard way." His shot went wild, but Leroy's Colt 45 sounded like a cannon, as the bullet hit the man in the chest. Leroy hit the floor rolling, a move that took the man up front by surprise. He fired over Leroy, going over the counter and hitting the wall. Leroy's bullet as he rolled and fired, hit the man in the left shoulder. Leroy shouted, "Give it up."

"Never," The man fired at Leroy on the floor, sending concrete chips flying. Some of the chips went into Leroy's left arm. The bullets went on striking the counter. Leroy fired again. His bullet hit the man in the head slamming him back through the plate glass window. The man was dead by the time he hit the pavement.

Katherine was as fast with a camera as Leroy was with a gun. She shot a picture as the man came through the plate glass window and one of him lying on the payment. Katherine crept up to front door and eased inside. She started taking pictures as fast as she could click the camera.

Marie stood up from behind the counter. She asked, "Is it over?"

Leroy replied, "Yes, it's over, thank God. How is John doing?"

Marie looked down at her husband on the floor. "Not too good. They beat him up real bad. John wouldn't give them the combination to the old safe. I tried to get him to give it to them, but he wouldn't. He is a stubborn old man. He would never give me the combination because he was afraid something like this would happen."

Leroy asked, "Katherine did you call for an ambulance?"

She glanced at him while still shooting pictures, "Yes I did."

At that moment, Police stormed into the store. Two paramedics followed close behind them. One checked the robber, he said, "This one is dead."

Marie said, "Over here, my husband is on the floor behind the counter."

The other paramedic said, "The one out front is also dead. I'll call for the meat wagon." After the paramedics made sure he was stable, they took John to the hospital.

The meat wagon came and took the bodies away.

Katherine snapped pictures of Leroy and Marie. Marie was treating Leroy's arm for cuts. Katherine smiled at Leroy. He said, "Yes I know. It's part of the story." They stared at each other. Leroy liked to look at Katherine. He wandered if she liked to look at him. Sparks were flying between them.

Leroy's pants suddenly became too small. He turned away for fear she would see the effect she was having on him. Too late, Katherine noticed his fly rise. She blushed, beet red.

Katherine said, "I got to go to the newspaper office and write this story, but I still want to do the interview."

"It's ok, I understand, we can do it some other time."

She wanted very much to be with Leroy, but duty calls. Katherine said, "How about you come over to my place tomorrow night and I will cook for you? How long has it been since you had a home cooked meal?"

"A very long time," he replied.

"Well, it's on for tomorrow night and will seven be ok with you?"

"Sounds good to me, it's a date, I'll be there."

Katherine smiled and hurried out the door. Two of the Police with Leroy barricaded the window until it could be replaced. Leroy said, "I'll come down to the station in the morning and file a report."

"Ok, then we will be on our way. By the way, we like your uniform." They laughed on their way out to their Police car.

Leroy said, "Marie that was smart of you to make me pay for the coffee."

She smiled at Leroy, "Thank you for being here." Marie gave him a big bear hug.

"You're mighty welcome and you call me anytime you have trouble. I live just around the corner."

The crime scene cleared up, Marie locked the door after helping Leroy with his groceries. Leroy said, "I forgot my coffee. Oh well, it will be cold by now."

Marie laughed at Leroy as she headed for her car. She went to the hospital. Leroy went back to his apartment. He was exhausted. He took a shower and went straight to bed, but he couldn't go to sleep. He stared at the ceiling replaying the robbery in his head. He didn't like killing people. What could he have done differently? What was wrong with people that make them do, bad things. The old saying, the devil made me do it, Leroy didn't buy it.

As Leroy stared at the ceiling, an image appeared before his eyes, a very pretty image, of Katherine Stewart. He thought back to the time, in front of the bank, when she had kissed him. It had been like touching two hot electric wires together, sparks flew. Katherine was short and had to put her arms around his neck, to pull his head down so she could kiss him. She was petite, only five feet two inches, had a nice tan, short black hair and green eyes. She wore a short dress, which showed off her slim legs, high heel shoes, which made her look taller than she was. Leroy could see her bright smile. He was going to have to take a closer look at Miss Stewart. OH, it may not be Miss, it could be Mrs. He didn't know, but he was going to find out.

Leroy was off on Saturday, but he still had to go to the Police station and file a report from last night. Some of the police that worked the crime scene with Leroy were in the office. They came over and crowed around him while he typed his report.

They were curious about everything. How did you know there was a robbery in progress? How did he get his gun? Why had he shot the one robber two times? How did the reporter know about the robbery?

Leroy finished his report, signed it and laid it on the desk for them to read. He said, "When all of you finish reading my report, would you put it in Captain Curry's in basket?"

"We will, Harry." Leroy's muscles tensed, then relaxed, guess he would have to go by the nickname, like it or not. As he was leaving, one of the policemen called him, "Leroy, you have a phone call."

He took the phone, "This is Leroy. How may I help you?"

Ashley accused, "What are you trying to do, get yourself killed?"

"No, I hope not. I would sure like to have had you there with me to cover my back. Katherine, the reporter, covered my back with a camera."

Ashley laughed, "I bet that made you feel real safe."

"You bet, like a target on my back."

"Oh, when did you get on first name basis with the reporter? How did she happen to be there when the robbery went down?"

"There's nothing going on. She was on her way to my apartment when she caught me at the grocery store. She called in the robbery."

"And why was she going to your apartment?"

"Katherine was going to interview me."

"What in the world for?" Ashley asked.

"I don't know," hedged Leroy.

Ashley giggled, "Sounds like monkey business to me."

Leroy said, "I'll see you Monday. I'm going to check on Marie at the grocery store." Leroy picked up a few things at the store, items he didn't need. He wanted to check on Marie and John. He asked, "How is John doing?"

Marie said, "They think he will be coming home by Monday."

"That's good news."

The plate glass window had been replaced, the store was cleaned up and everything was back to normal. It was back to business as usual. Marie set a large cup of coffee on the counter in front of Leroy. "Thank you for last night. I hate to think what would have happened to John and me if you hadn't come by. They would probably have killed us just for a very small amount of money."

"I'm glad I was here and if you need me I'm just around the corner." He gave her his phone number. "Call me anytime, day or night."

Leroy took a nap and woke up to the phone ringing. His mom was on the line, worried as usual. "Mom, I'm alright. I only got shot three times."

His mother went off on him, no sense of humor. "I want you to quit the Police force and go back to college."

"Mom, I'm not sure I want to go back to college. If I become a lawyer, I would be defending the scumbags I put in jail."

"But son, you would be making big money, you could get married, have a home and a family."

Leroy had all he could stand for one day. His mother would go on and on. "Mom, I got to hang up, I got a date."

He showered, shaved, dressed in faded jeans and a red short sleeved shirt. Leroy grabbed a bottle of red wine and left for Katherine's apartment. He was fifteen minutes late when he rang the doorbell.

Katherine opened the door. "Come on in, dinner is almost ready."

Leroy said, "Sorry I'm late. I couldn't get my mother off the phone."

She slanted a look at the strong profile, what a hunk. The room seemed to get smaller. Katherine had on white shorts and a red t-shirt. She was barefoot. Leroy was six foot one, which made him nine inches taller than her. Katherine looked up at Leroy. "I feel at a disadvantage, you are so tall."

"I like it like that." Katherine blushed red."

Leroy gave her the bottle of red wine. "Come on in the kitchen and sit down while I finish dinner."

Leroy remarked, "Dinner sure smells good." It had been a long time since he had had a good meal, usually he ate fast food.

Katherine smelled something better than food. She could smell Leroy's masculine scent and a touch of after shave. Her body responded to him. She was hot and nervous. She looked at Leroy and he didn't look much better. Katherine was trying to get her body back in control. They were like two high school kids on their first date. If they were in a car, they would fog up all the windows with their hot breath.

Katherine put dinner on the table. She had made a pot roast with potatoes, onions and carrots. She had made a large tossed salad to go with the roast. "I have French and Ranch dressing to go on the salad. I made apple pie for dessert with ice cream to go on it. I made tea or we can have wine. We can eat inside or outside," Katherine was babbling.

Leroy held up his hands. "Stop it!" Katherine stopped and stared at Leroy. "Come here." Leroy stood up and opened his arms. He gave her a slow coaxing smile. Swept by reckless desire, she went into his arms. He was so tall, that she had to look up to see his face. Leroy studied her eyes, he saw hot desire, fear, uncertainty about what to do, but she didn't back off. She stared at Leroy. He watched her mouth, his eyes turned dark. Was he going to kiss her? Her dad said he wasn't going to let her until she was thirty years old, little Katherine was only eight years old, but going on sixteen. Katherine asked, "Do you like kids?"

That caught Leroy totally off guard. He hedged, "Yes I guess, I had never thought about it."

""Well I love kids."

"Let's eat before the food gets cold." They sat down and started to eat. Katherine said, "May I start the interview?" She was still rattled by the way Leroy affected her. She had never felt like this before. She had to get control of her body before she made a fool of herself.

Leroy said, "I'm ready on one condition. I get to ask you a question for each one you ask me."

"I object. I'm the one giving the interview."

"I like you Katherine and I want to know all about you."

"Are you going to get personal?"

He glanced up and down her body, giving her a very sensual once-over. Katherine's heart skipped a beat, her breasts became heavy and her nipples became hard as marbles. Leroy said, "It all depends on you. You ask the questions first, if you get personal, then I will get personal."

Katherine had never been in this position before, but she didn't want to back out. She wanted to know all about Leroy. She wet her lips with her tongue. She could do this. She said, "Here we go."

Leroy smiled at her like a cat that just ate the family bird. She knew she had been had. Katherine said, "My first question, where were you born?

"I was born in a small town called Boonville, Texas."

"Did you grow up there?"

"Yes, I had a normal growing up, went to school, and played football, but not good enough to get a scholarship. I was an only child and my mom and dad were great. See, I don't have any hang-ups from a bad childhood.

"Why did you want to become a Policeman?"

"When I was a kid and we were playing games, I was always the good guy, so I guess I still want to be the good guy and catch all the bad guys."

Katherine wanted to get personal. She wanted to know the good stuff. "Did you date in high school?"

"Yes, but I played the field. I didn't want to go with just one girl. It was more fun that way."

Katherine said, "I thought as much, you look the type." It was starting to get good. "Did you have sex in high school?"

"Doesn't everybody?" Leroy asked.

"You didn't answer my question."

"Yes, many times."

She blushed, "Did you know what to do or were you winging it?"

"I went to a whorehouse in LaGrange, Texas called the Chicken Ranch with my friends and was taught by some good looking girls, that could drive a guy crazy in a minute." Leroy looked into her eyes, "I could teach you all the tricks."

"No thank you, but her body said yes. She said, "Just one more question, do you have a girlfriend here in Dallas?"

"No, I had one for a very short time, but she dumped me."

"Why did she dump you?"

"Leroy admitted grimly, "She had another boyfriend that she didn't tell me about. He is a big biker. I have to look up to him and I'm tall."

Katherine laughed, "Now that's a good one."

"Now it's my turn," grinned Leroy. Katherine knew it was payback time. He started out easy on her. "Where were you born?"

"Here in Dallas."

"Did you grow up here?"

"Yes, my Mother died when I was fourteen. Dad raised me and my sister. We loved her very much. It was extremely hard on Dad. At times he would sit for hours and just stare at the walls, but slowly he came out of it."

"I'm sorry about your Mother. It was a bad age for you. You were at the age you start looking at boys and you needed a Mother to talk to."

Katherine said, "You were right there. Dad tried to talk to me, but he didn't know what to say, so he finally gave up. I was on my own."

"Why did you become a reporter?"

Katherine smiled, "I think I have always wanted to be a reporter. When I was just a kid, Dad bought me a small camera. I would take pictures and write stories about the pictures. When I was in high school, I was on the staff for the school paper. I loved it. I covered all the sport events. I wanted to do personal, you know the juicy stuff, but the school wouldn't let me."

Leroy smiled at Katherine and said, "Now it's time to get personal. Did you date in high school?"

"I didn't date very much?"

"Why didn't you date?"

"I was too busy trying to make good grades." It was hard for Leroy to believe that one. She was just too good looking not to date.

"Did you have sex and lose your cherry in high school?"

Katherine became very quiet and nervous. She couldn't look him in the eye. She blushed red and looked away. She hedged, "Do I have to answer that?"

"You know the rules. I had to answer your personal questions."

She gave him a murderous look. "I don't want to do this."

Leroy took her hand in his. Heat ran up her arm and down her body making her hot. Leroy said, with a serious expression, "Tell me, I need to know. I got to know, it's driving me crazy not knowing." She knew he was teasing her to make her relax and it was working.

Katherine giggled, "Ok, I was sixteen when Jeff, one of the football players gave me a good line. I fell for it hook, line and sinker. I lost my cherry in the back seat of an old Buick. He didn't take his time and it hurt. He got what he wanted and got off."

Leroy said softly, "He was a jock, what did you expect? He was only thinking of himself. You never had a climax have you?"

"No, I have never had a climax." That one completely shocked Leroy. Embarrassed, she said, "After that he never asked me out again."

"What! Was he crazy?" He couldn't believe she didn't have lots of guys chasing after her. "You were a looker. Was the guy blind?"

She looked painfully at him. "I was a little homely back then, or just plain."

"Ok, I didn't know you back then, so I can't say one way or the another, but now you are a beautiful young woman and will turn heads everywhere you go."

She looked at Leroy with tears in her eyes. You really know how to build a girl up. "Was it a line?"

Leroy replied, "I don't do lines. I talk straight except when I am teasing."

Katherine blushed, "Thank you, you just made my day." If it was a line he was giving her, it was working and she was falling for it, hook, line, and sinker, again. Oh well, such is life.

"Do you have a boyfriend now?"

"No, I haven't had time to date since I have been working at the newspaper. Since my bad experience in school, I guess I haven't wanted to try and date again."

Leroy smiled, he liked her answer. He was beginning to like Katherine or maybe more than just like her. He didn't want to go there yet. "One last question, you didn't ask me here for an interview for the newspaper, did you?"

After a long hesitation, Katherine finally gave him an answer. "No, I didn't."

Why did you call me over?"

"I wanted to get to know you without being too forward. I didn't think you would catch on."

Leroy smiled, "I want to know you to. Now, when do we go on our first date?"

Katherine said, "You are a fast worker. I don't know you that well."

Leroy replied, "Life is too short to waste a minute of it."

"You are serious about dating, aren't you?"

"You bet I am." They talked on into the night. He said, "It's getting late, I had better go." Katherine was relaxed and didn't want the night to end. She could never remember spending time with a man and enjoying it so much.

Leroy stood up to leave. Katherine said softly, "Don't go, you are off Sunday aren't you?"

Yes, but what about you?"

"I don't have to go in until the afternoon. I got to write an article on crime in the city, but it shouldn't take long."

He glanced at Katherine, "What would you like to do?" That left it wide open. She could see his eyes turn black with desire, or was it lust. It suddenly got hot in the room, or was it her that was hot? Her bra seemed to be getting too small for her breasts, her nipples strained to get out. She needed something cold to cool off. "Would you like something to drink?"

Leroy replied, "Anything that's cold."

She asked, "Why don't we watch old movies on television?"

"It sounds good to me. I have always liked old movies, especially cowboy movies with John Wayne. He has always been my favorite star."

She said, "I'll make some popcorn, we have to have popcorn while watching the movies."

Leroy moved over to the couch and sat down. He called, "Do you need any help?"

She instructed, "You can get the glasses and the wine." Katherine made popcorn, brought it in and sat it on the coffee table. She turned on the television and found an old movie, staring Clark Gable. She sat down beside Leroy. They ate popcorn and sipped on wine. After her second glass of wine, Katherine laid her head on his shoulder, relaxing as she leaned into him, wanting more contact. She turned her head and looked up at Leroy. He looked down into her eyes, desire, arouse and nerves shown, and more he couldn't make out. He knew she was hot and wanted him. He wanted her just as bad.

"I still want that kiss," he confessed. She responded by twining her arms around his neck. Leroy lowered his mouth to hers. He played with her lips until she opened to him. He slid his tongue slowly into her mouth. He teased her by running his tongue around until she responded with a shy touch of her tongue to his. Her nipples harden against his chest.

Leroy pulled her closer flatting her breasts, with her hard nipples digging into his chest. He started to stroke her mouth with his tongue. He would slide his tongue deep into her mouth and then slowly pull out. Katherine moaned and arched into him. A little voice in her head said stop before it was too late. She was already in over her head, she didn't want to stop, her body demanding more.

Leroy slid his hand under her t-shirt and cupped her breast, making her moan again. He pushed back breaking off the kiss. "No," she moaned.

Leroy asked, "Do you mean no, or no don't stop?"

"No, don't stop."

He pulled at the bottom of her t-shirt as she raised her arms, so he could pull the t-shirt over her head, letting it drop to the floor. He reached for the front catch on her bra, pulling the bra off and letting it fall to the floor. Her breasts were free, firm, soft skin, standing straight out, with peaked nipples, waiting to be touched. He stared at her "Your breasts are perfect." Leroy reached to cup a breast and play with the nipple. He lowered his head and sucked on a nipple, while playing with the other nipple with his thumb and forefinger. She arched against him wanting more. Her body was on fire, she wanted him to put out the fire before she burned up.

He slid lower, kissing on her body as he went, until he reached her shorts. He released the catch and pulled down the zipper, sliding her shorts over her hips, letting them drop to the floor. Katherine was wearing black lace panties. Leroy glanced up at her as if asking permission to go on. She sighed, "Yes, don't stop, go for it." The little voice in her head said, too late now.

Leroy slid her panties off. He touched her damp folds with his finger. She was wet and ready for him. He lowered his head between her thighs, as she opened her legs for him. Inhaling her female scent, he slowly slid his tongue into her soft folds. Katherine put her hands around his neck and arched her back against him. He slid in and out with his tongue, until she was whimpering and her body was quivering.

He knew it wouldn't be long until she had a climax. He wanted her to have a good experience at making love, so he would let her have her first orgasm. He slammed into her with his tongue, while holding her by her hips. She squeezed with her muscles around his tongue, as she had her first orgasm, ever.

He then moved up her body and kissed her. Leroy put his leg in between her thighs and she opened her legs for him. He said, "I want to be in you."

Katherine was just coming back to earth from her climax when Leroy entered her. She relaxed her muscles so she could accommodate him not having sex since high school, she was very tight. Leroy slowly dove deeper and deeper, until she arched her back, completely taking all of his erection. He was still, letting her get familiar with his size, since he was large.

She relaxed and Leroy began to move, slowly at first, then picking up speed as he slammed into her heat. She clung to him, her body clamoring for release. "Give it to me faster and deeper."

Katherine threw her legs around Leroy, arching her back to meet each thrust. She felt her hot folds clench around his manhood. Leroy slammed into her one last time, as Katherine climaxed. She squeezed Leroy hard and he came deep inside her. Leroy slid off her. They curled up together spoon faction. They were both exhausted and fell asleep in seconds.

Leroy opened his eyes slowly, trying to remember where he was. He thought last night had been a dream, but he was naked and his hand was resting on a bare breast. They were like two spoons curled together. Katherine was still asleep. Leroy had a big hard on. His erection touched her damp folds of her passion heated flesh. He thought, well, he would just have to wake her up.

As Leroy slowly entered her, Katherine woke up. "Oh, you feel so good in me. What a way for a girl to wake up now give me all of it." Leroy didn't have to be told a second time. He slammed into her hot folds, making her go crazy, her body throbbing for release.

"Time out, I want all of you in me." Katherine rose up with her fanny in the air. "OK, now give it all to me and don't hold back." Leroy rose up on his knees, grabbing her hips, and he gave her a fierce stroke going very deep, slowly pulled out, before slamming back in. He rode her hard until she started to quiver, being close to a climax.

Katherine squeezed Leroy's erection with her inner muscles, calling his name as she went over the edge. He gave one more tremendous lunge and went over the edge with her. Leroy eased out of Katherine and fell over on his back. She turned over on her side facing him.

She was sated and content. Catherine whispered, "I wish we could stay in bed all day." Leroy turned over and they stared at each other, both of them still naked. He gazed into her eyes and saw passion, contentment, something he couldn't make out, maybe love. She turned away and got out of bed. "I'm hungry." She put on her robe and went to make breakfast, while Leroy got showered and dressed. Katherine made coffee, cooked bacon, eggs, and toast. Leroy came in and set the table for her. While they ate it was silent. Leroy said, "Are you regretting last night?"

She was silent for a moment. "No, it's just that I feel so vulnerable at this time. I should have stopped last night, but I couldn't and didn't want to. It was heaven on earth, you making me feel like a desirable woman. You must think I am a wanton woman and very easy.

"Never, I think we have a very strong attraction to one another."

Katherine had more than a strong attraction, I think I am falling in love, but she didn't tell Leroy, it was too soon, or good sex, whatever.

Leroy said, "I better leave so you can get ready for work." Katherine walked him to the door. He pulled her into his arms and kissed her. "Thanks for breakfast, it was good."

"You are welcome. You can come over anytime and eat." She shyly looked up at him. "About last night, it was incredible, now I know what it really was like to make love."

Leroy kissed her again, "Me too, and I'm glad that you were finally able to know what a climax was really like. I'm glad that I was the first one to make you climax."

Leroy was lazy when he got home, taking a long nap. When he woke up it was dark. He was hungry enough to eat a horse. He fixed a huge ham sandwich, some potato chips and a cold beer to drink.

Later, he turned on the radio to listen to the news and weather. As usual, the news was bad, another small bank had been robbed by five white males and a large amount of cash was taken. They made a clean getaway from Police, the car which was found a few blocks away had been reported stolen by the owner. The Police have no leads at this time. The sports came on, but Leroy didn't pay them much attention since he wasn't into sports, except for shooting his Colt 45 to stay in practice. The weather next day would be hot, around ninety degrees, but he had to go back to work.

He decided to call Rex Johnson. He called and they talked about old times. Rex wanted to know if Leroy was seeing anyone at this time. "I haven't dated anyone since I got to Dallas," which wasn't a lie, but he left out his times with his next door neighbor, Ann Mitchell and the newspaper reporter, the good looking Katherine Stewart, which just thinking about her gave him a hard on.

Leroy changed the subject, "And who are you going with this time?"

Rex didn't think Leroy was telling him everything, but he let it go for now. "I'm going with anything with a skirt on. You know I like to play the field and you are the one who taught me how. Remember our trips to the Chicken Ranch, now those were the good old days." The girls were out of this world. They could make you come in one minute flat or drag it out until you wanted to scream.

Leroy thought about it, "Yes it would be fun if we could go back in time and do it over again, but the Chicken Ranch is closed. I heard Marvin Zenler kept after them until they were forced to close down."

Rex said, "That sure sucks, that was such a good cathouse."

Well, we could talk all night, but we both have to go to work tomorrow, so call me when you want to go out on the town."

"Ok, good night to you and don't work too hard."

Another day, another dollar, thought Leroy as he entered the briefing room. All eyes were on him as he sat down by Ashley. Ashley looked around, "Well, you have done it again, but you did a good job of saving that old couple."

Sergeant O'Malley came in for the briefing. "We've got a big problem all over Dallas. Car theft again is on the rise, but with something different. When the new car is stolen, we have a missing person report to go along with it. We need to find one of those cars so we can find out what happened to the girls. I hate to even think it, but I think sooner or later we will be finding bodies. You have handout sheets for the rest of the items. "At this time I would like to say, Leroy, a job well done. You saved an old couple and took two scumbags off our streets. And don't worry about the things our public will say about too much force." The Sergeant came over and shook Leroy's hand, followed by the rest of the Policemen.

"That was nice," said Ashley, "And no more Dirty Harry jokes."

Leroy said, "Yes, and look at our new patrol car."

"Well, since this is your day for being good, I'll let you drive, Harry. I couldn't resist," laughed Ashley.

"Your time is coming and payback will be sweet." They got in their new car, ready to go on patrol, but there was a large sign on the dash which stated, take care of our new car. Leroy said, "What does that mean?"

"The car repair crew likes the cars to stay in one piece, not destroyed like our last car."

Leroy started the car and pulled out into traffic. He glanced over at Ashley, "Time to stir up some action."

She stared at Leroy, "Couldn't we have one nice quiet day?"

He laughed, "Think how boring it would be."

A bright red Ford Mustang crossed in front of them at a light, moving at a high rate of speed. "We got our first fish." Leroy said as he gave chase.

"Leroy, we are not fishing."

"Sure we are, depends how you look at it, better than saying, there goes our first ticket." Leroy pulled in behind the Mustang, turned on his lights and touched the siren. The Mustang pulled over to the curve. Ashley said, "You chased her down, you write the ticket, while I run the plates for any wants."

"But it's a young girl. Wouldn't it be less embarrassing for her if you gave her the ticket?"

"Yes, but you will make more of an impact on her. Maybe she won't do it again."

Leroy started writing out a ticket for fifteen miles over the speed limit. He finished and handed it to her. "Sign on the X, please."

"I'm getting a ticket? How do you know how fast I was going?"

Leroy replied, "You were caught on radar going forty five in a thirty mile an hour zone."

She complained as she signed the ticket. "My mother is going to kill me when sees the ticket." She couldn't understand why he gave her a ticket, with her giving him a good skin show. Blushing she pulled her skirt down. She thought he must be gay.

"Let me give you a little advice. What you did could have gotten you into a lot of trouble. There are bad cops that would have taken that as an invitation to swap sex for a ticket and then what would you have done? Hookers do that all the time."

"I would have said no."

"Then he would have said that you were trying to bribe a police officer. Do you get the picture?"

"Yes sir, but Mom said she never got a ticket when she showed some skin."

"Well, I suggest you have a talk with your mother and give her the same advice I just gave you. Have a nice day."

Ashley asked, "What took you so long? I was about to call for backup," she laughed.

"I was giving her some free advice that may keep her out of trouble."

Ashley sighed, "You were giving her advice on how to stay out of trouble and must I remind you that you are always in trouble."

Leroy grinned, "Now that wasn't nice to say about me."

"Yeah right, it fits you to a T."

Leroy pulled back out into traffic and started cruising. They pulled over several drivers for minor violations like a broken tail light, expired inspection stickers, and missing parts, like side mirrors.

Ashley suggested, ""How about we break for lunch? It's been a long time since breakfast."

"Would you like to have fast food? Is McDonald's alright with you?"

"Sure, it sounds good to me."

Leroy pulled into McDonald's and parked. They went inside to eat and take a break. While they were eating, a girl was cleaning tables next to them, when she recognized Leroy.

She said, "I know you, you kill all the bad guys and I think you use too much force."

Ashley quoted grimly, "If this place is ever robbed and we make the call, if a robber takes you hostage, we'll just stand by and let him take you. He will probably rape you and then kill you. Is that alright with you?

The girl was dumbfounded, cat had got her tongue and she just stared at them. Leroy said, "Well, I guess you gave her something to think about."

Ashley argued, "That girl made me mad, being so stupid. What is wrong with the public? The more you try to help them, the more they call bad cop."

Leroy said, "Time to go back to work." He pulled off a side street and set the radar. They were quiet for most of the evening.

Car seven, we have a large group of bikers in the twenty two hundred block of Elm Drive. Check it out, came over the radio. "Car seven ten four, we are on it." Ashley said, "Turn right and it's about five blocks down, now right and we are on Elm." In the distance they could see bikes, bikes and more bikes.

"What's going on?" murmured Leroy. He pulled up in the middle of the bikes and stopped.

Ashley said on the loud speaker, "Cut your engines, cut your engines now." The bikers killed their engines. They were arguing among themselves.

Leroy asked a big biker, "What's going on?"

He looked at Leroy, "We're lost and it's my fault. I made a wrong turn someplace, now everyone is mad at me."

Leroy asked, "What's your name?"

"Bull because I'm so big."

"And the lady that's with you."

"Her name is Heifer." Now why didn't that surprise him? "What is the name of your gang?"

"It's not a gang. We are just a group of people who like to ride bikes. We all have jobs and work." Leroy found out Bull was a bouncer and Heifer was a waitress in the bar and the others were lawyers, bankers, store owners, plain workers, who like to ride bikes on weekends. There was close to fifty, most bikers riding double with girlfriends or wives.

"We have a big problem, "called Ashley.

"What's up?"

"There is a little girl lost in the woods along a creek a few blocks from here and the dispatcher wanted to know if we can respond. There is a big car pileup taking most of the officers and firemen. They want to know how many people we will need for the search."

"Tell them we are on our way and will let them know as soon as we can." Looking at Bull, Leroy said, "You heard the call. Now I'm going to ask a big favor of you."

"If you will help us, I will give you an escort out of Dallas to a big truck stop where you can get food and gas."

"What do you want us to do?"

"Go with us and help us find the little girl before it gets dark."

"Bull turned to the other bikers, "What do say guys and gals?" Everyone shouted, "We will do it."

Bull turned to Leroy, "You lead the way and we will follow you." Leroy got in his car and pulled out in front of the bikers. Bull yelled, "Start your engines."

Leroy glanced at Ashley, "I think it's going to get noisy."

She laughed, "You think so?"

Leroy took the lead with all the bikers following him. Ashley pointed to the address on the house and Leroy pulled in front of the house and stopped. The bikers parked up and down the street.

A woman came running out of the house, "My baby is lost," she was crying.

Ashley inquired, "How do you know where she is?"

"I am Mrs. Jones and Sandy, my daughter is six. She likes to explore. There is a small hole in our back fence. I went inside for only a moment to answer the telephone and when I came back out she was gone."

Ashley said, "Tell us what is on the other side of the fence."

"There is a creek and one direction is open, but the other way is woods on either side of the creek."

"Thank you Mrs. Jones, we will take it from here."

"Turning to the bikers, Leroy said, "We will split into groups. I will take the left bank and Bull will take the right side. We need to stay even as we work our way down the creek, so we don't miss her. Ashley, stay here and keep the station up on things. Tell them we have plenty of help and, Ashley, why don't you leak the story to a certain reporter. It will make a good human interest story."

Ashley smiled at him, "Let me guess which one, her name wouldn't be Katherine Stewart, would it?"

He smiled at her, "Could be." They made the hole bigger, as they squeezed through and lined up. Leroy said, "Move out." They started slowly down the creek on both sides.

Ashley made a call to the station and gave a report. "You don't need people, you have about fifty people looking for the little girl, you got them where, bikers?"

Captain Curry was close by and heard part of the report. The dispatcher gave him the rest of the details. "It doesn't surprise me. With those two, you never know what will happen next," Captain Curry said. "I'm going to the scene and see what the situation is at this time. Call me if you need me." Lost kids always took top priority.

When he arrived on the scene, Ashley and Mrs. Jones were out front by the police car. Another car pulled up, a young woman with a camera got out, that would be Katherine Stewart, and another car pulled up with Mr. Jones in it. He hurried to his wife and took her in his arms. Captain Curry walked over to where Ashley was standing. "Any word yet?"

"No sir."

"Let me have the walkie-talkie. Leroy, this is Captain Curry. How is it going out there?"

"Slow sir, but if we speed up we might miss her. The brush is thick."

"You do realize it will be dark soon."

"Yes sir, we have a few flashlights, but not enough."

Time slowly ticked away, dusk dark was close to setting in. They slowly moved on down the creek. Leroy was starting to worry. What if they didn't find her in time?"

It was starting to get dark, but everyone pressed on. They wouldn't give up until Sandy was found. Captain Curry called, "It's getting dark. Do all of you want to take a break, get more lights, and start again?"

"No sir, we will keep going as long as it takes to find her."

Sandy heard them coming close to her. She gave out weak, "Help me, help me, I'm over here." Bull said, "Everyone be still, I think I heard something." Sandy called again. Bull charged over toward the sound. He saw her on the ground by the creek. He went down on his knees beside her. "I can't walk, I hurt my foot." Bull gently picked her up and started out with her. "It hurts so much."

"Leroy, call and tell them we found her and she's going to be alright." Bull hugged Sandy close to his broad chest. "It's going to be alright, you will be with your Mom and Dad in just a little while."

They had a long way to walk out, but they finally saw the hole in the fence. Bull went through first with Sandy. Her mother and father stood back to let everyone through. Katherine took a picture of Bull as he handed Sandy over to her mother.

Sandy said, "Let me down. I need to tell Bull thank you for saving me." Bull went down on his knees to her level. She put her arms around Bull, kissed him on the cheek and said, "I love you, you are my hero." Katherine took another picture.

Katherine walked over to Leroy, "What no kiss this time," She teased.

"Well, I guess you can't win them all."

Katherine stood on tiptoe and put her arms around his neck, pulling him down so she could give him a big kiss. "See you can win them all, if you try. I am so proud of you and Ashley. You two make a good team."

Leroy said, "And to think when we re teamed, I didn't want to be teamed with a woman and now I don't want to be with anyone but Ashley. She takes up for me when they tease me and she will always have my back."

Katherine said, "You know we haven't had a chance to get together since the night we were together. I miss you."

"I miss you too. We are going to have to do something about it."

"When, that's the problem, with our crazy work hours. I've got to run now to get the story in the paper for tomorrow. Thanks for the story, and yes, I know you didn't because of Police rules." Leroy opened his arms and she went into them for a goodbye kiss. As Katherine drove off, a little voice in Leroy's head said, watch out or you will get hooked on that woman. He thought maybe he was already hooked.

Leroy walked back to the crowd. The Jones had sent out for food and drinks for everyone. Ashley and the Captain were talking, so Leroy joined them. Captain Curry said, "Well you two did great finding the little girl, but what are you going to do with all these bikers?"

Ashley said, "No problem. Leroy told them we would escort them through Dallas, out to the truck stop going toward Oklahoma."

"You two think of everything, so I'll head back to the Police station. I'll see you in the morning at the briefing.

Bull came over to Leroy, "We are ready to hit the road if you are." The Jones thanked the bikers, Leroy and Ashley for finding their daughter.

"Time to hit the road," said Leroy. The bikers started their engines, as Leroy pulled out in front of the bikers. With the Police car in front, followed by a long line of bikers, with small American flags flying from the back of each bike, it looked like a parade. When they got on the north side of

Dallas, people started to wave at them and the bikers waved back.

Ashley picked turned on the radio that had picked up on the bikers and the lost child story. The station was playing it up big. It was news for the station and good publicity for the bikers. Leroy said, "I'm glad they picked up on the story." He turned right into the truck stop, as a group of people rushed out of the truck stop. A man waved the bikers in at two pumps. "These pumps are for you. You are very welcome here as long as you like." People gathered around the bikers and talked.

"This made my day," said Leroy.

Ashley grinned, "Well you kissed the girl. Everything is good, so can we go home now?" She teased him all way back to the Police station.

"What is this always wanting to go home? You act like you have something to go home for."

"I do. I got a husband I hardly ever see."

Leroy laughed, "But look of all the fun you have. There is never a dull moment."

"You can say that again. I think he hates you for keeping me out so late. I never seem to get home on time anymore. Tonight I'll be late again."

The bikers waved goodbye to them, as Leroy turned around and headed back to Dallas. They got back to the station late and decided they would do their reports in the morning.

"By the way Leroy, what about that kiss you received from Katherine? That is the second time she has kissed you at the scene. Do you two have something going?"

"I wish, but I don't know how she feels about me, or getting mixed up with a Policeman. It's hard on Policemen's wives and girlfriends. Some women can't take the stress."

Ashley suggested, "Why don't you ask her how she feels about you?" She is a newspaper reporter and that is a stressful job. Maybe she can take the stress."

"I don't want to mess up a good thing." He didn't want to share his sex life with Ashley, but he knew she was like a dog with a bone. She would keep on until she knew all that had happened between him and Katherine. "Ok, so it's a more than friends."

"Uh-hum I thought so, you are having an affair."

Leroy argued, "Ok, I give up, have it your way. I'll see you in the morning.

"By the way, how about coming over tomorrow night for dinner if we get off on time and you can meet my husband."

Leroy replied, "You want me to come over so he can kill me for getting you in trouble and keeping you out late."

Ashley laughed, "Poor baby, I'll protect you."

Leroy looked at his watch, "Your husband is going to be mad, look at the time." It was after ten and they hadn't left the station yet.

On his way home, Leroy stopped off at the grocery store. He wanted to check on John and Marie. John was back at work. He looked as good as new. Leroy hit the deli for something to eat. They were just getting ready to close for the night. He waited until they locked up before he went on to his apartment. As soon as he got inside, he called Katherine. "Did I wake you?"

"No, I just got home. It took me awhile to write the story. Be sure to read it tomorrow, I made Bull a hero. It will make people respect the bikers. Everyone always thinks that all bikers are bad."

"Yeah right, like back in the days of Cowboys and Indians. The saying was the only good Indian was a dead Indian. The big reason I called is Ashley invited me over for dinner tomorrow night and I was wandering if you would like to go along and keep me company?"

Katherine was happy to finally have Leroy ask her out, even if it was only to dinner with friends. She thought about their time spent together in her apartment. Her nipples became hard, her breasts firm, straining at the material of her shirt and she could feel her juices wetting her panties. She wanted Leroy here and in her. Katherine said, "I would love to go."

"Then it's a date. I'll pick you up at seven unless I have to work late and in that case, I'll call you."

Leroy ate supper, took a shower and went to bed, but he couldn't go to sleep. He kept thinking about Katherine, how good she felt in his arms and her soft body against his hard body. He had a tremendous hard on and it was torture to lay there. He couldn't sleep like that, so he got up and took a long cold shower.

The next day at briefing several of the Policemen were told to report to the pistol range and that included Leroy and Ashley. "I hate to go to the Police range," said Leroy.

"Why is that?" asked Ashley.

"I can't hit the broad side of a barn with the 38 pistol. I always barely pass. You will show me up for sure."

Captain Curry met them in the hall. "Look at the write up, the newspaper woman sure made points with me. She mentioned how I came to scene to help out and made sure everything that could be done was being done. Bull, the Jones family and myself had pictures in the paper."

Ashley said, "Good for you sir, you work so hard but never get any praise for it. It's about time you got some praise for your work.

Captain stared at her, "What have you two done that I don't know about?"

"Nothing, sir, we have been good."

"Then you want something."

"Well yes, Leroy could use a big favor."

Captain Curry knew he was being set up, but for what he didn't know. Leroy looked at her and the Captain, he was lost also. "Sir the handbook for police rules states each officer will qualify with the weapon he uses to perform his duties. Wouldn't you say Leroy has performed his most important duties with a Colt 45?"

"Yes, I have to agree he has."

Then he should be able to fire at the range with his Colt 45. Am I right sir?"

Captain Curry said, "Ok little lady, you out foxed me. He can fire with his Colt 45."

Ashley glanced at Leroy and grinned, "Go get your Colt 45 and show everyone how to shoot."

Captain Curry murmured, "Now what have I done?" He thought he had better tag along and see what would happen. He walked up to the instructor in charge of the range and told him it would be alright for Leroy to use his own weapon.

Leroy walked up with his Colt 45 strapped to his leg. He and Ashley took stands side by side. The other officers on the firing line stopped firing and watched as Leroy and Ashley stepped up to firing line. The instructor said, "You can commence firing."

Leroy smiled, "Ladies first."

Ashley pulled her weapon and commenced firing, hitting four bull's-eyes and one in the next ring. She smiled at Leroy, "A little something for you to beat." Her hammer was resting on an empty chamber for safety so she had only fired five shots. She was one of the best shots at the police station. All the officers shouted at Ashley, "Way to go. You put the pressure on Leroy."

Leroy stood in a gunfighter position and relaxed. His hand went for his gun so fast it was hard to see. He fired five times, returning his gun to the holster, hitting the bull's-eye all five shots.

The bull's eye was gone except one little piece that was still hanging. Leroy went for his gun again, no more bull's eye, only a hole where it used to be. The instructor said, "You can't carry six rounds in your weapon."

Leroy explained, "I always carry six, the bad guys always know when a policeman is out of rounds, because of the rules.

I don't go by that rule. It could get me killed, but the sixth round may save my life."

Everyone stared at the target. "I don't believe it," said the instructor.

Captain came over and looked at the target. "Can you do that again?"

Leroy said, "I can try but I don't know for sure."

Ashley said, "I bet he can do it again, any takers?"

Several of the officers didn't think he could do it again. Ashley was covering all bets. Captain Curry said, "You can't gamble out here."

"Sir we will just play like."

"Yeah right and pigs fly."

The target had been replaced and everything was ready to go. Leroy stepped back into position. He loaded his weapon and tried to relax. It was so quiet you could hear a pin drop. His hand went for his weapon, six shots were fired and Leroy dropped his weapon back into his holster. It got very quiet as everyone stared at the target.

Ashley yelled, "Yes, yes, Leroy did it again." The bull's-eye was gone again, with only a hole where it was supposed to be. Leroy looked at Ashley and grinned, "Can we go home now?"

She laughed, "As soon as I collect our winnings from those suckers."

Captain Curry wasn't surprised at Leroy's skill with a gun, not after he saw the reports of his shootouts. They were moving targets, so the still targets were easy. When he looked over at Ashley, she was picking up her winnings. He smiled, Leroy was a bad influence on her. She used to never break a rule, always by the book and quiet as a church mouse. What a pair they made.

Ashley said, "We can go now." She had a wad of money in her hand and was so excited. "What a bunch of suckers."

Leroy asked, "Why were you so sure of your bet, I could have missed."

"It's so simple. I knew if you could hit moving targets while they were shooting at you, still targets would be a piece of cake."

Leroy laughed at her, "You are a nut."

Katherine asked, "Do you want half of our winnings? You sure earned them."

"No you keep them. By the way, do you mind if I bring someone with me to your house tonight?"

"No, you can bring anyone you want to, but I can guess who you are bringing, Katherine."

"Yes, I asked her and she said yes."

"Well good for you. You need a woman in your life."

"I guess you could say that I'm really starting to like that girl, I mean woman."

Ashley grinned at him, "Don't get mad but you are so big and she is so small, you are like Mutt and Jeff together. It is so funny to watch you two kiss. She gets on tiptoe and puts her arms around your neck to pull you down for a kiss."

"Well time to get back to work and hope for a quiet day," sighed Ashley. They cruised around for some time before a speeder passed them. Leroy was driving so he turned on the lights and gave chase.

The car pulled over and a little old lady was driving. Leroy pulled in and stopped. He grinned at Ashley, "Your turn, I'll run the plates. We may have a Maw Barker on our hands. I'll cover your back and call for backup if needed."

"Very funny," Ashley said, as she got out of the car.

She walked up beside the car, "Good evening, may I see your driver license and registration?"

"What for, may I ask? I haven't done anything wrong."

"You were speeding and radar clocked you fifteen miles over the speed limit."

"Well I don't believe in those new fancy gadgets. I think it is just a way to get money out of old people." Ashley knew Leroy was laughing and enjoying every minute of it. "Don't you have anything to do than harass us old people? Why don't you go catch some crooks?" Ashley was starting to get a headache. She could see Leroy grinning ear to ear.

Ashley tried one more time, Could I please see your driver license?"

"Don't have one, they took it, said I was too old to drive."

Ashley groaned, "May I see your car registration?"

"Nope, why do I need a registration if I don't have a driver's license?"

"Good point, I'll be right back."

Leroy said, "I hate to give you bad news but we are going to have to arrest the little old lady. She has a warrant out for her arrest. I called for a tow truck and it should be here shortly."

Ashley sighed, "Now all we have to do is get her out of her car and into the Police car. What is her name?" "The run sheet shows her name to be Betty Adams, address is a nursing home. She has a son that looks after her welfare. I called the station and asked them to try and locate him."

The tow truck pulled up in front of her car and the driver got out of the truck to pick up her car. Ashley said, "We better go get her." Leroy and Ashley walked over to her car.

Leroy said, "Mrs. Adams, could you get out of your car and come with us? Your car is sick and we have to take it in to fix the bad problem, it's not safe to drive, we don't want to see you hurt driving it."

Ashley turned her head to keep from laughing. Leroy was a good con artist. "You will have to help me out of the car." They helped her out of the car and into the Police car. "I need my walker," said Mrs. Adams. Leroy went and got her walker.

Mrs. Adams carried on all the way to the Police station, young people in trouble, drugs everywhere, rapes, sex and robbery. It wasn't like that when she was growing up. People didn't even lock their doors back then. When a young man came to call, he had to come in and meet the father.

They finally got to the Police station and got the little old lady inside. Her son came running up to them. "Mom, where have you been?"

"Oh, I was out for a nice drive until the Police pulled me over."

"Mom, you don't have a car anymore."

"I know. I borrowed one from the nursing home. I'm tired and want to go home."

"I'll see what I can do to straighten this mess out so I can take you home."

Ashley said, "I sure hated to bring in the little old lady. Did you see how everybody looked at us, like the bad cop thing? What was she wanted for?"

"It was car theft, driving without a license, escaping from a nursing home, among other things.

"Wow, can you believe that? I feel sorry for her son trying to get everything back to normal."

"Are we still on for tonight," asked Leroy.

"Sure, I'll go home as soon as we get our reports done." It took a while but they were finally done and they could leave.

"Do you want me to bring anything?"

"No don't bring anything, just bring yourself and Katherine. I am looking forward to meeting her and finding out about her."

"You be nice to her, ok."

Leroy called Katherine as soon as he got to his apartment. "Are we still on for tonight?"

"Sure, I'm looking forward to it."

"I'll pick you up in an hour."

"I'll be waiting."

Katherine searched her closet for something to wear, finally deciding on a neat black dress with a plunging neck line and black high heels to match. She took her clothes off to take a shower. While touching her breast, she dreamed about Leroy and what could happen tonight. Her body became hot all over. Her nipples became hard. She ached for Leroy's touch and more. She took a long cold shower to cool down. Wasn't that what men did when they couldn't get a girl to have sex with them? Katherine took a long time with her makeup. Katherine wanted to knock his socks off and she didn't want to come home alone. She was a wanton woman tonight and didn't care, as long as she got Leroy in bed with her tonight. She looked at her reflection in the mirror and was pleased with what she saw. Her body started to heat up again. She thought she had to cool it, she didn't want to, but she didn't have time for another cold shower.

The doorbell rang and Katherine went to open the door. It was time for Leroy to pick her up. She opened the door and Leroy just stood there staring at her. "Wow," he finally found his voice. Leroy was dressed in jeans and a t-shirt, but he looked great to her. She tried to make out what aftershave he was wearing. She wanted to touch him but didn't want to make a fool out of herself.

Leroy seemed to read her mind, opening his arms for her as she walked into his arms and reached up to put her arms around his neck. No words were needed, they knew what they wanted. He covered her mouth with his, pulling her close against his chest, her breasts crushed between them. He could feel her nipples digging into his chest. When they came up for air, Katherine said, "That's a good way to start our date."

Leroy grinned, "I missed you too. It's been too long since I kissed you."

"You can do it all you want to later, but I guess we better go. Ashley will think we got lost," She giggled.

Katherine locked up and they walked hand in hand to the car. Leroy opened the car door for her and then went around to the driver side. Katherine said, "I like your car."

"It's an old Ford Thunderbird. I had when I was in high school. I guess I should get a new car, but I want to keep it. It's like an old pair of shoes that are broke in good."

Katherine snuggled close to Leroy. She could feel the heat from his body. She laid a hand on his thigh, stroking his inner thigh. She went too far and touched a huge erection. She blushed, her face turning red. "Sorry about that, I didn't know it came down that far." Leroy put his hand over hers. He took her hand and guided it up the full length of his erection.

Katherine could feel it throbbing through the fly of his jeans. "It's so big," was all she could say, she had lost her voice. She couldn't believe she had taken all of him when they had made love the first time, but right now she wanted to take it all again.

Leroy turned right and pulled into the second driveway on his left. The house was a small brick home with trees, flowers and a white picket fence around the house. Ashley met them at the door and ushered them in. Ashley's husband walked in a second later. "Jim this is Leroy, my partner and his date, Katherine. This is my husband Jim." They shook hands.

Ashley said, "Why don't you men go in the den and watch a ball game while Katherine and I finish dinner?"

"Sounds good to me," Jim said as he showed Leroy the way to the den. As it turned out they didn't watch much of the game, but talked a lot. Leroy told him about life in a small town, about starting college to become a lawyer, stopping college to be a Policeman and some of the things about the job.

Jim told Leroy about himself, born in Dallas, lived here all his life, didn't go to college, went to trade school to learn computers. He had a good job with Accenture. Jim laughed as he told how he met Ashley.

"She stopped me and gave me a ticket for speeding and I gave her a hard time all the time she was writing out the ticket. I could see she was mad as a wet hen, but by now I was having fun just watching her. For some reason, I don't know what came over me, I thought I would make her blush, but it didn't."

"What did you do?" asked Leroy.

"I asked her would she have dinner with me tonight at Hooters." She looked at me like I had lost my mind. Ashley smiled at me, ""Why not, what time?" I was in shock for a few minutes. She laughed at me, "Cat got your tongue?" She gave me my ticket, as she got in her cat. "I'll meet you at Hooters at seven and don't be late. Have a nice day." "I sat there and watched her drive off. Boy, had she put me in my place. I didn't think she would show up but I went early just in case she did. At seven she wasn't there and I decided to give her a few minutes."

"At five after seven, she came through the door, wearing a beautiful blue dress, high heels, her long hair streaming down her back. I lost my voice again. All I could say was, "Hi, you look beautiful." She said, "You look great yourself."

"I'm sorry about asking you to come to Hooters, it was supposed to be a joke. I never would have believed you would take me up on it." Ashley laughed, "I guess the joke is on you when you gave a dare and I took the dare."

"We started to date and now here we are married a year now, end of story."

"Jim asked, "What about you and Katherine? Ashley said you first met her at the bank robbery. Have you been dating?"

"No, would you believe this is our first date? I like her and would like to see how she would like going out with a cop. It takes a certain kind of woman to handle going with a cop, with everyday danger."

"Tell me about it. I worry all the time about Ashley but she won't quit. Please take good care of her for me."

"I will do my best to keep her out of harm's way."

"Thanks, that all I ask."

The girls were having a girl talk of their own. Ashley wanted to know about Leroy and her. "Do you like Leroy?"

"I don't know. This is our first date."

"What about him coming over to your house?" The question caught Katherine off guard and she blushed.

"I gave him an interview."

"Why didn't it appear in the newspaper?"

She was busted, "Ok, I did it for myself. I wanted to know all about him."

Ashley giggled, "It pays to be a newspaper reporter."

"How did you and Jim meet?"

"I gave him a ticket," and she told her the rest of the story.

Ashley came in, "Ok, what are you so serious about?"

"The ball game," Jim lied.

"Well dinner is on, wash your hands and come to the table."

Ashley had out done herself, dinner was great. She had cooked a pot roast with potatoes, carrots and gravy. She had a salad and cherry pie with ice cream for dessert. They ate and talked through dinner.

Jim asked, "Katherine how do you feel about going with a Policeman?"

The question caught her by surprise. "I don't know since this is the first time I have gone out with a Policeman. I don't know if I could live with the danger all the time. Jim, how do you handle it with Ashley?"

"Not very good I must admit. I worry about her all the time but I live with it. I wanted her to quit but she loves her job, so it is her decision. She was on the Police force long before we met."

Katherine thought about what Jim had said. She didn't know if she could deal with the danger everyday but she had better start thinking about it. What would it be like to be married to Leroy? She liked him very much or did she love him? She did know she loved being with him.

Ashley said, "Enough shop talk, it's time to play cards or something."

Jim suggested, "How about poker or spades?"

"Spades," responded Katherine. I played spades in high school and loved it. Ashley and I will take on you guys."

Jim looked at Ashley, "No cheating."

"Now you don't think I would cheat do you?"

'Yes, you always try to cheat."

Leroy looked at Ashley. He couldn't believe she would try to cheat. Ashley giggled, "We all have our little hang ups. "I like to try to cheat and get away with it."

Jim went and got beer for the men and wine for the women. They played late into the night. They were having a good time. The women beat the men bad. The men blamed it on Ashley cheating or bad luck at cards.

"It has been fun," said Katherine, "But tomorrow is another long work day and we had better go." They said their goodbyes and walked out to their car. Leroy opened her door for her then went around to the driver side. He started the car, pulled out and headed to her apartment.

Leroy asked, "When we get to your place do I get to come in for a night cap?" She smiled at him, "it depends if you are good or not." Leroy stepped on the gas and hoped he didn't get stopped for speeding. How would he explain that to Captain Curry?"

When Leroy pulled into her driveway, they got out and ran to the door. As soon as she unlocked the door and they were inside, Leroy pushed Katherine against the wall. He reached under her dress, pulled her panties off and gathered her dress around her waist. Katherine had reached for his belt, unzipped his fly and let his pants drop to the floor, followed by his shorts. He picked her up and she locked her legs around his waist.

Leroy kissed her, thrust his tongue deep into her mouth, flattening her breasts with his chest. He could feel her nipples digging into his chest. Katherine moaned, "I want you inside me now." He lowered her slowly as she stretched to take all of him. When he was fully sheathed in her hot trembling body, he didn't move, so she could feel all of him in her. Katherine pushed against him and moaned, "I took it all." She couldn't believe she had done it because Leroy was so big and she was a small woman.

As Leroy thrust into her, she arched her back to try and get deeper. She was burning up and thought she would burst into flames any minute if the fire wasn't put out. "Give it to me faster and harder," she yelled. Katherine squeezed Leroy's organ with inner muscles giving him great pleasure. He slammed into her harder as she squeezed her legs tighter.

Katherine's head was spinning, she had lost control of her body as she bucked up and down, then she was quivering as she had her first climax. She tightened her muscles on Leroy as he pounded home in her hot moistness. He knew he was close to coming so he slid almost out and gave her one final thrust. Katherine had a second climax at the same time and could feel Leroy's seed going deep into her body. "Oh Leroy, it feels so good."

Then a little voice in her head was scolding her, stupid you didn't use any protection. When she finally came back to earth, she remembered she had taken a pill. Leroy slowly lowered her to the floor. He had to hold her up as she couldn't stand on her own. Leroy picked her up and carried her to the bedroom. He said, "Now let's take our time and do it right."

Katherine thought how could it get any better? She said, "It was great the first time. Can you do it again so soon?"

Leroy took her hand and placed it on his tool. "Stroke it slowly."

As Katherine stroked it, she watched it began to grow. She liked the feel of his organ in her hand, liking the power she had to make him big and hard. "Ok I can't take any more or I'll come in your hand."

Leroy removed her dress and bra. Her breasts were full and her nipples peaked. She removed Leroy's t-shirt and put her arms around his waist pulling him to her. Now they were both naked.

Their full length was pressed together. His erection was pressed into her belly. He laid her on the bed and lay down beside her.

He ran his hand between her thighs and spread her legs for him. Leroy ran his hand over her mound, sliding a finger into her folds. Katherine arched her back and moaned. He pulled his finger out. She was slippery and hot. He knew she was ready for him.

Positioned above her, his large erection touching her folds, slowly he lowered himself until he was fully sheathed, then waited for her to relax. She was sore and a little swollen from their first love making. "Do you want me to pull out?"

"No just wait a minute until I stretch a little, you are so big." When Leroy felt her muscles curl around his erection, he started to move in and out slowly. She picked up the rhythm with him and arched to meet him stroke for stroke. They were good together. Katherine pleaded, "Make it last as long as you can. It feels so good." He pounded into her until she was on the edge and then he would slow down. "Your wish is my command." After he took her to the edge two more times she couldn't take it anymore.

"Get off, I want to drive." Leroy thought that was a funny way to put it, but he rolled over on his back and out of her. Her female scent teased his senses and he liked the female sex scent, his erection becoming harder.

Katherine straddled him, grabbing his erection and guided it into her passion heated bed. She started to bounce up and down. She threw her head back and rode him hard. Leroy asked, "What happen to lasting a long time?"

Her body was clamoring for release. "I can't wait any longer, my body is on fire." Katherine slammed down hard, squeezed his erection so hard he couldn't pull out if he wanted to. Leroy felt her juices dripping on him as she had spasm, after spasm and he started coming deep in her. She fell over on his chest, her breasts against his chest, her nipples flat and relaxed. Leroy was still inside her heat. She whispered, "I love you." She said it so low. She didn't think he heard her.

A little voice in her head whispered, now how do you know you are in love? It was the sex that made you say it. Leroy rolled over on his side with his organ still inside her. They bowed their legs and went to sleep spoon fashion.

Sometime during the night, after many times he came in her, he didn't know. His organ died. The alarm clock went off. Katherine reached over and turned off the alarm. "I'm calling in sick."

Leroy hit her with a pillow, "If I can make it up, so can you. I'll make coffee."

Coffee and two mugs were on the table when Katherine made it to the table after a shower. 'Leroy last night was fantastic. How many times did we have a climax?"

"I don't have a clue, because I went to sleep still in you and I know I had at least one more climax. We have to get together more often. We were so sex starved that we were like a couple of animals the first time last night."

"We can't get together much, our jobs are so demanding," explained Katherine, "but there has to be a way."

"I could come to your newspaper and we could have sex in the closet," laughed Leroy, "Or we could have sex in the back seat of the Police car while Ashley drives us around."

Katherine giggled, "Be serious."

"How about we both try to get our vacation time together and go to my home. We can visit my folks, do some sightseeing and visit Mike and Linda Love on their ranch. Mike trains horses for the movies and he is good at it."

Katherine said, "Sounds like fun if we can pull it off."

Leroy replied, "We can try. I got to go or I'll be late for work."

He went home and took a shower, shave, and changed clothes. He just made it to work on time for briefing. Ashley stared at Leroy, "You look like hell."

"I didn't get much sleep last night. I hope you will take pity on me and drive today."

Ashley laughed, "And what does Katherine look like today?"

"I didn't say I spent the night at her apartment."

"You didn't have to. You have that pussy whipped look. My husband has that look every now and then when we make love all night."

"I feel like I have jet lag, but I haven't been on an airplane."

"At least you don't have the problem Katherine has. She is probably sore from too much lovemaking."

"I never thought of that. She was sore last night after we made love the first time. I guess we should have stopped after the first time."

"Stud, just how many times did you two make love last night?"

"Would you believe, we lost count."

"You do realize you have other nights?"

Sergeant O'Malley took the stand and started the briefing. Leroy tried to keep his mind on the briefing, but a certain little woman kept running through his head. He finally figured out what it was. Katherine had said, "I love you," while they were making love. He wandered if she said in the heat of sex or did she really mean it? He thought, was he in love with her? He had never been in love before.

Ashley broke his chain of thought, "Come on lover, time to earn our paycheck."

"What did O'Malley give you in there?"

"You may or may not like it, "she teases.

"Is it that bad?"

"No, we have an easy day. We have funeral escort and we are the lead car. It usually takes almost all day."

"Well, sounds like fun. When do we go to the funeral home?"

"We can go get coffee first." They stopped at a coffee shop on the way. When they got to the funeral, Ashley parked in front of the funeral lead car. She knew the routine because she had been here several times before. She said, "Now we find the funeral director and find out our route to the cemetery."

Ashley found the funeral director and got directions. Leroy waited patiently in the car. She said, "Now we park cars for the service and after the service is over, we help line up the cars. This is going to be a big funeral. He was a big shot in one of the companies here in Dallas."

They parked cars for an hour. The lot was full and cars were parked up and down the street. The service began so they had time to take a break and have some lunch. Ashley said, "It will be a long service, at least an hour and a half, so we have plenty of time to eat." "They found a McDonald's and had fast food.

The service lasted two hours. As the pallbearers brought the body out to the hearse, three more Police cars pulled in and parked. Ashley explained, "We lead, two cars will leap frog to block intersections and the other one will tailgate."

When the funeral director gave Ashley the signal to go she started the engine and slowly pulled out in the lead with the hearse behind them, followed by five family cars. The two Police cars raced on ahead. Ashley said, "Hand me the mike." She called the two Police cars and gave them the route to follow.

"Where are we going?" asked Leroy.

"We are going to a large cemetery in Colleyville. That will be about an hour drive with this large line of cars." They took I-30 through Dallas, turned right on 360 toward the airport, left on Glade Road until they hit 26, then right on 26 until they came to the cemetery.

Two Police cars left when they went through the last intersection and the other one on the end left when the last car was in the cemetery. Ashley called, "Thanks for your help."

"You're welcome," they called back. "Take care of Leroy. He looked like hell at briefing."

"He had a good reason," but she didn't tell them what it was. We'll stay here until the service is over and direct traffic on highway 26 until all the cars are out of the cemetery. The service lasted an hour. By the time they directed all the cars out of the cemetery, it wasn't long until their shift was over. "We have a car stalled in the middle of the street, the eight hundred block of Ranger. Please direct traffic until the tow truck can get there."

"Car seven responding and we are on our way."

By the time they reached the stalled car, someone had plowed into his rear end. Ashley called for another tow truck. Both parties were arguing over who was to blame. Leroy directed traffic while Ashley took both parties away from harm's way to hear their story.

Ashley said, "Normally the person who hits the person in the rear is to blame, but under the circumstances, I don't know." They both had State Farm Insurance. Ashley said, "I'm not going to give either one of you a ticket. File with your insurance company and they can figure it out. Either way, they will have to pay."

The tow trucks arrived. Ashley and Leroy directed traffic around them until they had both cars gone. Leroy asked, "Can we go home now?"

"Yes and Leroy you still look like hell."

Leroy thought of three things, food, shower and a bed. They got back to the station, late as usual. They filed their reports and went home.

Leroy stopped for food at the grocery store deli. Marie stared at Leroy, "You look like hell."

He replied, "Don't I know it."

"I could give you some castor oil, it cures everything."

Leroy made a face, "No thank you, I had soon die, as take castor oil. Mom made me take it when I was little. I hate castor oil."

He pulled into the parking in front of his apartment. Walking up to his door, Ann came out of her apartment. She smiled at Leroy. "Long time no see. What have you been up to?"

"Just work," he replied.

She giggled, "All work and no play makes for a dull life." Ann smiled at Leroy again. He thought, something was up, she was too friendly. Leroy asked, "How are you and your biker boyfriend doing?"

"He is out of town on a trip with his biker friends."

I thought you went with him most of the time?"

"I only go on weekend trips. I have a job and car payments. How would you like to mow the lawn while he's gone?"

"No thanks, I'm seeing someone." Also he didn't have a death wish. The biker was one big biker and Leroy wanted to stay clear of him.

Ann giggled, "I won't tell if you won't, they will never know. I like doing it with you. You are so big and it feels so good." She ran her tongue slowly around her lips. His body wanted her and his fly gave him away.

"I've got to go." Leroy made a fast exit. He didn't want that big biker after him. When he got inside, he called Katherine. He asked, "How was your day?"

"You don't want to know. I went to sleep at my desk. I was so sore. I blushed every time someone made a joke about last night. Some of my girlfriends wanted to know if we were going steady, if not, they wanted your phone number. It was some day."

"What did you tell them about us?"

"I told them you were taken and that shut them up. What about your day?"

"I was out of it to, but I had an easier day. We were on funeral escort and it lasted almost all day. We had to work one accident, but it wasn't a bad one. We worked it after our shift. By the way, did you think about what I said about taking off at the same time?"

"Ok, I'll put in for it tomorrow, but it takes time before they approve it."

"I miss you," Leroy said. "I could get used to you being here when I get off work, eating together and nights in my bed." He had an erection just talking to Katherine.

She giggled, "Are we going to have phone sex?"

"No, I want the real thing, but I know how tired we both are, so we'll wait until another time, like this weekend if we both are off."

"Sorry, it's my turn to work at the newspaper this weekend."

Leroy groaned, "We both work too hard. See you later," and he hung up. He played back in his mind what Ann had said, all work and no play makes a dull life. He thought she was right. He ached to hold Katherine in his arms and make love to her, like they did last night. He just couldn't get enough loving from Katherine, the more they made love, the more he wanted to do it again. He would have to settle for a cold shower tonight.

After Katherine hung up, her body was hot and she could picture Leroy above her, just before he slammed into her body. She knew she was wet just talking to him.

CHAPTER THREE

The next morning Leroy and Ann walked out their doors at the same time.

Ann said, "Looks like we both go to work at the same time now. Too bad we don't work in the same place, we could car pool. I got a new job at JC Penney's."

Leroy said, "That's great. I see you got a new sports car."

'Yes, I love it, but the payments and insurance kills me. You will have to take a ride with me sometimes, but right now I got to run or I'll be late for work."

Leroy said firmly, "Be sure to lock you're your doors. There is a lot of theft going on right now."

"Thanks for the warning, I'll see you later."

Ashley met Leroy at briefing, "You look like you might live today."

He replied, "I learned my lesson the hard way, never again."

"Never is a very long time. If you two are together and she is hot for your body, it will happen again. It has happen with Jim and me."

Sergeant O'Malley took the stand for the briefing. It was a standard briefing, but when it was over he told Leroy the Captain wanted to see them.

"What did we do wrong now?" asked Leroy.

Ashley laughed, "Maybe he wants to tell us how good we have been staying out of trouble."

"Yeah and pigs fly."

Captain Curry met them at the door, "Come into the office." They sat down and waited for the ax to fall. Captain Curry smiled, "It's not what you think, you haven't done something I don't know about, or have you?"

"No sir," they said together.

"Good, then I have a special assignment for you. The governor is coming to Dallas tomorrow and will leave Sunday. You will be beside him everywhere he goes for his protection while he is in Dallas."

"Body guard duty, are you sure you want us?" asked Leroy. "You know how trouble follows us."

"The Governor asked for you. He has seen the newspaper with you in it. He wants you to dress western all the way, Colt 45 and all. He is dressing western himself.

Leroy said, "It could be fun."

"Do you have a complete western outfit?"

"Yes sir, I do."

"Ashley, do you have a complete outfit?"

"What I don't have, I will come up with it."

"Good, you will meet his plane at seven tomorrow morning at DFW Airport. You will escort him wherever he wants to go and when he is out of his car you will be at his side."

Ashley asked, "Who will we take orders from sir?"

"His personal assistant will tell you what to do, just follow her orders."

"Is that all sir?" asked Leroy.

"Yes, except for one thing, you two can take the day off. You will put in a full day on Saturday and part of Sunday. Now get out of here."

Ashley said, "Thank you sir. We won't let you down."

"Just try not to kill anyone."

Ashley asked, "What can we do with our day off?"

"I'm going to surprise someone."

"Let me guess, a cute little newspaper woman."

"I'm going to the newspaper and take her to lunch if she can get off. Would you like to go with us? It could be fun."

"No, I don't want to be a third wheel, but thanks anyway. I should go home and clean house. I never have time to clean and my house stays a mess."

"I'll see you bright and early at six." Leroy went home to change clothes. He wanted out of uniform before he went to the newspaper. He put on a white shirt and dress pants. He was thinking about Katherine and smiled.

Leroy arrived at the newspaper as people were leaving for lunch. Katherine was still at her desk working on a story. She didn't see Leroy come in so he took advantage and watched her work. Standing there watching her made his heart beat faster. She was wearing a short dress and high heels. He knew she was trying to look taller. Leroy had a funny feeling in his chest. Was this love he was feeling for her? He still didn't know what love was or what kind of effect it would have on a person. He just knew every time he was with her, he wasn't normal.

Her body became hot. Katherine glanced around the room to figure out why. She saw Leroy and knew why she was hot. He always had that effect on her.

She got up slowly from her desk with a big smile on her face. She was so glad to see him. Leroy couldn't find his voice so he opened his arms. Katherine went into them, slid her arms around his neck and turned her face up for a kiss.

He covered her mouth with his. She opened to him and shyly touched her tongue to his. He deepened the kiss and pulled her tighter, her breasts were flat against his chest, her nipples hard and she couldn't get close enough. Katherine could feel his arousal on her belly. When they finally came up for air, people laughed and clapped. They thought they were by themselves.

They broke apart as several people bunched around them. Katherine was embarrassed, her face bright red, but she didn't care. She only had eyes for Leroy. She introduced everyone to Leroy. They stared at him. Finally a woman said, "You are the one she is always writing about."

Leroy wanted to get away to take Katherine to lunch. He said, "We had better get going if you are going to get lunch."

Katherine said, "Sorry but we have to go. I want Leroy to myself for lunch." Leroy put her hand in his and headed for the door.

As they went out the door, her boss came out to see what was going on. "Who was that Katherine was with?"

One of the girls said, "That was Leroy Cooper, sometimes called Dirty Harry."

"Well I'll be a monkey's uncle. I would like to meet him."

Leroy took Katherine to lunch. He wanted to take her to a nice place for lunch.

Leroy took her to a Steak and Ale for lunch. They didn't talk much. They just wanted to stare at each other and touch. After they placed their order, Katherine asked, "How did you manage to get off so early?"

"I have to work all day Saturday and part of Sunday. Ashley and I are bodyguards for the Governor and party. We are to dress western because the Governor will be dressing western."

"That should be fun and a lot better than being on patrol."

"Yes, except for the nuts that will protest something. That will put a lot of stress on us to keep the Governor safe."

Katherine said, "I will be covering the Governor's visit, so I will see you and get to take your picture again."

"It will probably be a boring day. He will be giving speeches and doing fundraisers."

"With you there, it won't be boring. A lot of people will want to see and talk to you. The Governor will probably have to field questions about you."

"I sure hope not."

Their order arrived. Leroy had his favorite meal of steak, baked potato and a salad. Katherine had a large chicken salad. They were seated in a booth with high backs which made it a little private, but not near as private as Leroy would have liked it to be. His tortured eyes gazed into hers, "When are we going on a date again? I want to be with you more."

"I don't know, but I will be looking forward to it." Katherine slid her shoe off and ran her foot up and down his leg. She giggled as she saw the shock on his face.

After they had finished lunch, they sat staring at each other and holding hands across the table. "I love you," she said softly.

He heard her this time and his heart did a flip, she did love him. Leroy declared, "I love you too."

The couple across from them heard them and the lady said, "Oh how sweet, a couple of lovebirds."

Katherine slipped her shoe back on, time to go back to work. When they got back to the newspaper, Leroy dropped her at the front door. He didn't want to answer any more questions from her fellow workers. He gave her a quick kiss and was gone. She watched until his car turned the corner. She missed him already. She never knew being in love could feel so good.

Leroy decided since he had the rest of the day off, it would be a good time to wash and wax his car. After he got home and started on it, he wasn't sure it was a good idea after all. His car was filthy. It took the rest of the day to do the job. After he finished and started in his apartment, he met Ann on her way to work. Ann gave him a big smile.

"I get off at ten tonight and the grass still needs mowing bad." Ann liked to tease him. She knew he had someone and wouldn't cheat on her. He was a one woman man. She, on the other hand liked men and not just one.

Leroy ate an early dinner. He laid out his western outfit for tomorrow.

He polished his boots until you could see yourself in them. He went to bed early and dreamed about Katherine. He could see the desire in her eyes, feel the heat from her body, she lowered himself between her legs, she would open to him, she would take all of him slowly and then he would start to move. She would moan as he slammed into her body. She would spasm after spasm and he would finally give her a final thrust. With his hands on her buttocks holding her tight against him he would climax with his seed going deep into her body.

Leroy woke up with a wet dream. He thought teenagers were the only ones who did it. He had to get up and take a cold shower. Morning came early. Leroy was up, dressed, shaved and on his way to work. He stopped at the deli for breakfast. Marie stared at Leroy, "Is this the new uniform at the Police station?"

He replied, "No, I'm a bodyguard for the Governor while he is here in Dallas. He will be giving speeches and doing fundraisers." He then explained how he got stuck with the job.

Leroy met Ashley in the parking lot at the Police station. "Are we ready for a fun day?" he asked.

"Yeah right, let's do it."

Leroy got in the driver seat and they headed out to the airport. When they arrived, they were told the Governor would be coming by private jet and where the jet would be. They went to a private strip where the smaller planes parked. The Governor's personal assistant was coming down the ramp as they got out of the Police car.

She looked at Leroy and Ashley, "Wow, you two look great. You look like you just stepped out of the old west. We won't be formal today, first names only. I'm Shirley and you must be Leroy and Ashley."

"Yes ma'am," replied Ashley.

"What are our duties?" asked Leroy.

"Simple, every time he is out of his limousine you will be with him. When we break for lunch, dinner, or breakfast, you will be at his table. If he goes to the bathroom, Leroy you will go with him. At night you two will have a room next to him with a door between you. You will take turns sleeping, while one of you is awake and dressed in case he needs you. The rest of the time you stay close to him, in case of trouble. Do you have any questions?"

Ashley and Leroy looked at each other. Ashley replied, "No ma'am we got it."

The Governor and his staff came down the ramp. Shirley said, "Well, it's show time." Leroy and Ashley took up their post on either side of the ramp at the bottom. The Governor was dressed western, boots, hat and clothes. He wanted to have a relaxed attitude among his staff and the many different places he would attend.

The Governor stood with Ashley on his left side and Leroy on his right side and answered questions by the press. Katherine was among the press asking questions and taking pictures. She smiled at Leroy. He was handsome in his western clothes. Ashley had on her split western skirt, blouse, hat, boots and gunfighter gun low on her hip to match Leroy. They made a fine picture of the old west. After twenty minutes, the press was told that was all for now. "Shirley, you did a great job picking my bodyguards. They look like the old west. I love it."

Shirley said, "You do know who this Policeman is, don't you?"

"No, should I know him?"

"Leroy is called Dirty Harry by some here in Dallas."

"Now I remember him. He killed three men in a bank robbery."

"Yes and he killed two robbers at a grocery store. The public thinks he uses too much force on his duties. I don't think so, myself."

"Sir, with them along, you can feel safe. He will stand before you and take a bullet if it comes to that." I have a place reserved for breakfast and then you have a speech at the World Trade Center." As soon as the Governor and staff were in their limousine, Leroy and Ashley got in their car and took the lead.

When they reached the restaurant, they took their post next to the limousine as the Governor and his staff unloaded. Leroy took the lead in front of the Governor and Ashley to his side. The table was ready and a waiter was standing by to take their orders.

Leroy sat on the side with the Governor to take care of any trouble head on, while Ashley sat on the other side to watch their back. The Governor said, "You two really know how to make a person feel safe from harm."

Ashley said, "Thank you sir."

Breakfast was served and the staff went over the first stop at the World Trade Center.

Arriving at the World Trade Center, Leroy and Ashley took their post. Leroy took the lead as they went inside. The Governor took the podium with Leroy on the right and Ashley on the left.

The Governor started his speech. There were some demonstrators in the crowd, but they seem to be peaceful. Leroy and Ashley watched for any sign of trouble. The speech lasted an hour.

At the end of the speech, a man stepped out in front of the crowd. Leroy saw he had a shotgun at his side. He stepped in front of the Governor and walked slowly toward the man. Ashley stepped in front of the Governor and behind Leroy. The man would have to go through both of them to get to the Governor.

As Leroy approached the man he said, "Give me the shotgun. You don't want to die today."

The man stared at Leroy, "I know who you are, they call you Dirty Harry and you kill people."

"Only if I have to, now give me the shotgun butt first."

The man stared at Leroy a long time and finally turned the shotgun around and handed it to him. Leroy broke the shotgun down, removed the shells, closed the breach and stepped up close to the man. Leroy whispered to the man. We can end this or you are in big trouble."

"How do I do that?"

He handed the shotgun back to the man, "Take the shotgun and give to the Governor and tell him it is a gift."

Leroy walked side by side with the man until they faced the Governor. Ashley stepped back to her position. The man said, "Governor, sir, I would like to give you this shotgun on behalf of the Local M410." The Governor stepped forward and took the shotgun. He thanked the man. The man went back into the crowd.

Leroy returned to his position, but his body became hot and he knew it wasn't from the trouble with the demonstrator. He searched the crowd until he found Katherine with her camera. She smiled at him and he thought he would burn up. She always had that effect on him when she was close by. Ashley looked at Leroy and grinned, knowing the effect Katherine was having on him.

With the speech finished, it was time to be on the road again. The next stop was the hotel across the highway from the World Trade Center. It was a fundraiser for the party. The cost was one hundred dollars per plate. Leroy and Ashley were glad they didn't have to pay. They had reserve seats. Leroy sat on the side with the Governor and Ashley sat on the other side of the table.

A man across the table from the Governor said, "I see you have the Policeman known as Dirty Harry with you. Some of us think he uses too much force in his duties. What do you think about it?"

The Governor hesitated for a short time. "Since I don't live in Dallas and don't know the whole story, I would like for Policeman Cooper to tell his side of the story."

Leroy looked the man in the eye. "It's a case of me or him. I never shot anyone that wasn't shooting at me. You will ask why I killed them. These kinds of men are like a wounded bear, they keep coming until you kill them or they kill you. Sir if someone was shooting at you or your family, what would you do?" The man was confused, he didn't like killing, but he would defend himself and his family.

The Governor said, "After hearing Leroy's side of the story, I go with him. In cases like those, it is a time for killing. By doing what he did, he saved the lives of good people. Leroy liked the way the Governor defended him. He had his vote in the next election.

That afternoon they made several stops for speeches and fundraisers. When they loaded into their limousine, Shirley came over and gave them directions to where they would eat dinner. She said, "We have one more function before the night is over. We are going to a big ball for drinks and some dancing. Ashley, are you married?"

"Ye ma'am, I am."

"The Governor said you could invite him to the ball. Leroy, I don't think you are married, but do you have someone you would like to invite?"

"Yes I do, but I don't know if it would be ok, she is a reporter."

Shirley said, "That should prove interesting, invite her to come."

Ashley caught Jim at home fixing his dinner and told him where to join them. Leroy caught Katherine still at the newspaper. She couldn't believe she was going to the ball.

Reporters were only allowed outside the building. Katherine rushed home to change. What to wear, oh what to wear. She changed dresses several times trying to make up her mind. Katherine finally found the dress she wanted, a red silk short cocktail dress to show off her legs and red heels to match. She took a shower and a lot of time with her hair and makeup. She wanted Leroy to have eyes for her only. She dropped a small camera in her purse, never leave home without it. You never know when a story will pop up.

Leroy led the Governor's party into the ballroom. A large table had been set up for them. Leroy sat on the Governor's side and Ashley sat across the table from them. There were reserve seats for Jim and Katherine.

When Katherine arrived, her car was parked for her. At the door, the doorman checked the list for her name. Inside a young man escorted her to her table where he pulled out a chair for her.

Leroy smiled, "You look beautiful tonight."

"Thank you. I didn't know what to wear. I have never been to a ball before." The place was huge, with a dance floor in the middle and tables all around the dance floor. Lights were flashing down on the dance floor. A country western band was at the front of the dance floor. They were tuning up to get started with the music. Leroy was glad to see a western band. He glanced at Katherine, "My kind of music." She liked country music also.

The Governor was asked to start with the first dance. He looked at Leroy and asked permission to dance with Katherine, since his wife wasn't with him. The Governor led her out on the dance floor for a slow number. Katherine felt like the bell of the ball.

Katherine returned to the table with Leroy watching her all the time. He said, "You looked like a princess out there. I only wish I had been dancing with you."

Jim finally arrived and was escorted to the table. Ashley smiled at him, "You finally arrived." She was happy to have her man beside her. Drinks were served, fruit punch and a little junk food to eat on, peanuts, popcorn and crackers. They had a big dinner so everyone wasn't hungry.

Shirley whispered to Ashley, "You can dance as long as one of you is at the table at all times." Ashley relayed the news to Leroy. Ashley and Jim got up on the next song and danced to a fast two step. They were good together.

Leroy asked, "Do you dance?"

Katherine replied, "Not too good. I'm still learning, but I like to try."

"Good, on the next slow dance we will give it a try."

Katherine and Leroy danced the next slow dance and did fair. They enjoyed holding each other close. They were over heated like a car radiator by the time the dance ended. When they were seated, Katherine placed her hand on his inner thigh. Leroy had an instant hard on. Katherine smiled at him as she laid her hand on it and caressed him.

He squirmed in his seat and had a tortured look on his face like he was in pain. Katherine squeezed his organ and it started throbbing. She removed her hand and giggled, "Sorry

I got carried away." Leroy was so worked up he could make love to her on the floor, table, closet, or anywhere he could.

Ashley and Jim took turns with Leroy and Katherine the rest of the night dancing. They had a fun time. The night turned into a night out for them, but when it was over, Jim and Katherine left together. Ashley and Leroy had to stay.

When the Governor was in his room, Leroy and Ashley went into their room next door. Ashley said, "You take the first shift and I will take the last shift."

"Ok by me," replied Leroy.

Ashley picked up her overnight bag and went into the bathroom. She took a shower, removed her makeup, brushed her teeth and put on her nightgown. When she came out, Leroy was watching the news on television. Ashley said, "Wake me in four hours and I will relieve you."

"Ok, enjoy your short sleep."

"What was on the news?"

Leroy replied, "Bad news as always. The same bunch robbed another bank and shot another person. They got away again."

Ashley said, "They are a smart bunch. They must plan the robbery down to the minute."

"Yes but sooner or later they will make a mistake and get caught. I hope you and I are there when they do."

Four hours later, Leroy woke Ashley to relieve him. He took his overnight bag and went to the bathroom. He went ahead and shaved. He would be that much ahead in the morning. He took a shower and put on pajamas. When he came out Ashley laughed at him, "Lover where did you get the hearts?"

"If you must know, my mother gave them to me and it is the only pair I own. I usually sleep in the nude."

Ashley giggled, "If you got the guts, go for it. I have seen naked men before and it wouldn't shock me." Leroy thought about it, but better not, what if something went down? He could see himself running down the hall in the nude with his Colt 45 in his hand. Ashley saw the smile on his face. "What?" she asked.

"Nothing honey, I was daydreaming."

The next morning at eight they were on the move again. They had breakfast at the hotel and left for the airport. Shirley said, "Well, they are all on the airplane and your job is finished. You two did a great job and if we come again I would like to ask for you again, if that is ok with you?"

Ashley replied, "We would enjoy doing it again."

"The Governor was well pleased since we usually have at least four officers where we go. The way you were dressed most people didn't even know he had bodyguards."

Ashley and Leroy watched the plane take off, then got in their car and headed back to the Police station. Ashley asked, "What are we going to do with the rest of the day off?"

"Go home and sleep."

"Sounds like a good idea. I think I will to, if Jim will let me."

At the briefing next day, they caught ribbing from the other Policemen, some people will do anything to get to go to a ball. That was supposed to be bodyguard duty. "Leroy, who was the body you were guarding? She was fine looking."

"Ok break it up," Sergeant O'Malley took the podium. "I guess all of you know we had another bank robbery by the same bunch yesterday. Keep an eye out for anyone near a bank that looks like they are casing the bank. The bunch is smart. They know what they are doing when they hit a bank. They are in and out before anyone has a chance to sound the alarm. If they do, they will kill the one who sounds the alarm. They don't care if they kill someone because they have killed already. That makes them very dangerous men. As Leroy said, it is kill or be killed."

"Don't worry about using too much force, hesitation can get you killed. I know it will be hard for a lot of you who has never killed anyone before. It may help to talk to the men who has killed before. Are there any questions? Ok, you can hit the road."

Ashley pulled out into traffic, "That was fun last night. I like to dance. How would you and Katherine like to go to Billy Bob's dancing one night?"

"Sounds like fun, I have never been there. Where is it located?"

"It's in Fort Worth at the stockyards. It's about an hour drive from here. They also have bull riding sometimes."

A car went speeding by them, "Time to go to work," said Ashley.

Leroy joked, "Do we have to?" Ashley turned on the overhead lights. The driver saw them and found a place to pull over. Leroy gave the man a ticket without any problem. The man was going eighteen miles over the posted speed limit. An old couple ran a red light and Ashley took them. They argued before they finally signed the ticket. It was a slow morning. "Time for lunch," said Leroy. "Where do you want to eat?"

"Fast food, chicken I guess. Ok with you?" Ashley said, "I think there is a Kentucky Fried Chicken about two blocks down the street."

"That's ok with me. I'm tired of hamburgers and fries."

Chicken was good for a change, with mashed potatoes, gray, corn, and apple pie for desert. The only thing Leroy didn't like was they had had Pepsi. He wanted a Coke. "Poor baby, want me to run to a grocery store and get you a Coke?"

"Very funny," Leroy replied. It was time to go back to work. They had a slow afternoon. It was boring just riding up and down streets. Leroy asked, "Did you ever think about being a detective?"

"Yes, but it is so hard to ever make detective. I don't know if I have what it takes to be a detective. You have to be real smart, but it would be nice not to wear a uniform."

Leroy said, "My mother wants me to go back to college. I was going to be a lawyer, but now I don't know what I want to do with my life. I dropped out when the money ran out and I had to get a job. I don't want to be a cop all my life. I want a wife and family someday, but being a cop isn't good for a family."

"I know what you are saying. Jim would like me to work someplace else. He worries about me all the time."

"Quitting time, another day and another dollar," said Leroy.

"Where did you learn that saying?"

"That's what my dad always said. He had a saying fir everything. Another one he used all the time was when things didn't do the way he wanted, he would say, such is life. He told jokes all the time and he was full of life. I'll tell you one I always liked. Dad said it was a true story, but I am doubtful, you never knew if he was pulling your leg. Do you want to hear it?"

"Sure, I need a good laugh after a boring day."

"Ok, this lady was working at the shipyard during World War II in Houston. She was only woman working with a bunch of men. She picked up a five gallon paint bucket to move it. This big guy told her she had to have hair on her chest to move heavy things and she told him she had hair on her chest, He told her she did not and she said did to. So he said for her to prove it. She dropped her pants and panties and said, see I have hair on my chest. He said it wasn't her chest. She said yes it is, before I got married it was my hope chest, after I got married it was my husband's tool chest and after he got killed in the war, it became a community chest. That's the end of the story."

"I needed that. Now I can go home and tell Jim he has a tool Chest," giggled Ashley. "See you tomorrow." They got in their cars and headed for home. Leroy wanted something to do. He didn't want to stay home tonight. When he got home he called Rex Johnson. He asked, "Do you want to go out tonight?"

Rex replied, "Yes I'm horny, maybe we can find some women."

"Rex I'm seeing someone."

"No problem, you can watch me work the women and you might learn something."

"Where do you want to go?"

"There's a bar on the way downtown, just where it becomes wet, called the Watering Hole. Do you know where it is located?"

"No, but I'll find it. I'll meet you in an hour at the bar."

Leroy showered, shaved, put on new jeans and a shirt. He decided to wear his cowboy boots and hat. He didn't carry his badge or his weapon. He didn't want people to know he was a Policeman, sometimes it caused trouble and he just wanted to blend in tonight.

When Leroy found the bar, it didn't look like much. When he went inside he saw two big bouncers. His thought was to leave, but Rex was already at the bar. "Come on over." He didn't like it, but he went over to the bar. Rex was looking over the women as they came in. "Nothing but hogs so far, but it will get better. I picked up a good looking woman in her about a month ago. Boy was she a tiger in bed. She rode me until I thought I would die."

"Rex when are you going to quit playing the field and settle down with one woman?"

"Never, it's always more fun to play the field."

Leroy ordered a Coors Lite and took a long drink. He had a bad feeling about tonight. He should have stayed home. Nothing came in the door that Rex liked. "Well, it's time to go get the ear of corn and the string I left in my truck. It's time to troll for hogs."

"That's it, I'm leaving. I can't afford to get in trouble."

Rex laughed, "Got you."

Two good looking women came in the front door. They would look better at closing time, as the song goes, but it had been awhile since Rex had made out, so they must look good to him. They had on short miniskirts, a very low neckline and too much makeup for Leroy

Rex said, "Watch me work, give me tem minutes and then come on over."

"No thanks, you're on your own."

"Party-pooper, what happen to the old Leroy?"

I guess I'm getting old. I need a wife and kids to come home to." Now where did that come from? Rex stared at him like he was crazy.

"Watch and learn," Rex said, as he walked off toward the end of the bar. Leroy drank his beer and was content to watch Rex. He hadn't changed a bit since high school. A fair looking red head came over and asked Leroy to dance. Why not, he might as well relax and enjoy the night.

They had a band playing a slow two step and the small dance floor had sawdust on it. Leroy took her in his arms and moved around the floor. "My name is Carol, what's yours?"

"Leroy Cooper." She moved in closer to him.

"I haven't seen you here before."

"It's my first time." Carol moved even closer, so they were belt buckle to belt buckle. He could smell her female scent and roses. He could see desire and passion in her eyes. Leroy knew he had a hot one on his hands. He would like to give her to Rex. The music changed to a slow number and she melted on his body. Her full breasts and nipples were flat against his chest. His erection peaked and dug into her belly. She curled around him like a snake, rubbing her belly against his erection. Leroy knew if this dance didn't end soon he would have a climax on the dance floor. "You are so big and it feels good against my belly, but I would like it in me."

A fight broke out behind them. Leroy turned to see two men holding Rex, while a third man slammed his fists into him. Leroy broke away from Carol and ran to the bar. He jerked the one around and decked him. The other two men dropped Rex to the floor and charged him. He decked the first one but, the second one nailed him. Everything went black and he was out for the count.

Leroy came to in the back alley and glanced around for Rex. He was a few feet away. "I'm sorry about the fight. You know how dumb I am at times. The big guy that decked you was her boyfriend. I should have left when he told me to, but stupid me I told him she was my girl for tonight and you know the rest."

"What did the guy hit me with?"

"He hit you with his fist."

"Wow, lights out and only one punch. I'm glad he wasn't mad at me, he would have killed me." Leroy looked around, "Where is my hat?" The bartender opened the back door and sailed his hat at him, Leroy caught it. "Thanks for giving my hat back."

"Just stay away from my bar. Find you another sandbox to play in. I run a nice quiet place and I want to keep it that way."

"I guess he told us," said Rex. "I guess I'm going to have to change my ways."

"How many times has this happen to you since you came to Dallas?"

"I don't remember."

"How many times has it happen?" Leroy persisted.

"Would you believe only three times counting tonight?"

Leroy groaned, "I should have known. You haven't changed a bit since you were in high school. You need to grow up."

"Do you want to go to another bar?"

"No, I have had enough fun for one night."

"Do you want to get something to eat or just some coffee."

"No, I'm going home. I'm sore all over."

"Rex said, "You have changed, before you would have laughed this off and we would be on our way to another bar."

"I guess I'm getting old. Let's get out of here before those three come out to work us over again."

On his way home Leroy thought what used to be fun wasn't fun anymore. When did it all change? He and Rex were the same age, so why had he changed? A young woman floated in front of his eyes, Katherine. His body became hot thinking about her. She had changed his life so much. He wasn't the hell raiser he used to be.

He was asleep as soon as his head hit the pillow. Waking up the next morning was pure torture, his whole body hurt, but he finally got up. He showered and started to shave, that was when he saw his big black eye. This was not going to be a good day. It was a cloudy day and looked like rain.

Leroy sat down beside Ashley in the briefing room. He had on sunglasses. She asked, "Why the dark sunglasses? There's not any sun out today or in here." He didn't want to tell her he had a black eye, but he knew she wouldn't back off. "If you must know I have a black eye. I ran into a door."

"Yeah right, if I believe that one you will tell me another. Now come clean."

"Ok, this guy twice my size gave it to me when I was helping a friend of mine. They were three on one, so I had to help him. This big guy put out my lights and I woke up in the back alley."

Ashley giggled, "So you had fun last night."

"If I had fun last night, why do I feel so bad today?"

Ashley was having fun teasing him, "Poor baby, do you want me to kiss it and make it better?"

"No thinks, I think I will just die."

"Ok knock off the noise, it's time for a briefing," said O'Malley. "Today we have construction on Garner, Corporal Lewis. You and Leroy will keep the traffic moving and help the crew for the highway department any way you can. Are there questions? Then move out."

Leroy said, "Well another boring day. We get to work traffic in a construction area."

Ashley accused, "With you around something is bound to happen. You have that kind of luck."

It was murder working the traffic. It was always backed up with heavy equipment moving back and forth across the road. They took turns playing traffic cop. They got a break when the crew stopped for lunch and they went to the Dairy Queen for lunch.

"How is your love life with Katherine?"

"It sucks, she works late all the time and when she's off I end up working. We both need some time off together."

""To make a little love and get down tonight," giggled Ashley.

"Have your little joke. I hope Jim has to work late tonight."

"Well if he has to work late, I'll give him something for working overtime. I'll be in bed naked when he comes in."

"Ok you win. It's time to give the taxpayer a full day's work."

For the next three hours they worked traffic. Leroy was directing traffic and thought only one more hour before they could leave.

Ashley yelled, "We got to go now." Leroy jumped in the car and put on his seat belt. Ashley was burning rubber, turning on the overhead lights and had the siren wailing. "What's going on?"

"There was a drive by shooting just two blocks over and I'm trying to cut him off. Another unit went to the house that they shot into. A little girl was hit inside the house. "How bad was it?"

"They don't know yet."

"When we get to the inner section, watch out for a red Ford Mustang. It should be coming up on our right."

Ashley pulled into the inner section and blocked the oncoming lane. Leroy said, "Here he comes, about a half block from here." They got out with their weapons drawn using the car for protection, while they waited for the Mustang. The driver saw them and slid around, heading back the way he had come from. They jumped back in their car and gave chase. Leroy called for backup and gave street names and number. "The driver is a good driver, stay on him."

Ashley replied, "I'm trying, but he has the pedal to the metal and he is driving a Mustang."

"Just try to stay with him."

"Car seven, car twelve, we have the road blocked. Car eleven is helping me to block the road." The Mustang driver didn't even slow down when he saw the road block. He jumped the curb, ran across a lawn, through a six foot fence, through another lawn and back on the road again. Ashley followed the Mustang through yards and back on the road. The other two Police gave chase.

"It's time to shut this guy down." Leroy reached in the back for his Colt 45. "Get close as you can to him." Ashley drove the Police car in close. Someone in back seat of the Mustang kicked out the back glass and fired on them, some of the bullets hitting the Police car windshield. Leroy called, "Shots fired and I am returning fire."

The Policeman in the car behind them said, "Leroy is going to do it again. If I was in that car with him shooting at me, I would stop. "I'll give them a couple of warning shots." Leroy's first shot took off the driver rear view mirror. The second shot took off the right rear view mirror and the third shot went through the back window taking out the inside rear view mirror. That got the point across. The driver looked over at the other guy in the front seat. "Do you know who that is shooting at us?"

The man in the back seat started to fir again. "No and I don't care. I'll get them this time."

The driver started slowing down. "Don't be a fool. Drop your gun so he can see you or he will kill you on his next shot. That is Dirty Harry behind us and I don't want to die today." The driver pulled over to the curb. Ashley pulled in behind them. Car twelve pulled in front of the Mustang and car eleven pulled beside the Mustang boxing them in.

The Policemen got out of their cars on the opposite side and used them for protection. Leroy said, "Everybody out of the car with your hands in the air." Leroy kept his Colt 45 at the ready.

Three large black men slowly got out of the car with their hands in the air. The driver said, "See, I told you it was Dirty Harry." The guy from the back seat looked at the big Colt 45 and decided they had done the right thing by stopping. The Police read them their rights, searched them, put their hands behind them and handcuffed them. They loaded the prisoners into car eleven and took them to the police station. They would be booked for the drive by shooting, attempted murder, resisting arrest and murder if the little girl was to die.

"See I told you today wouldn't be boring, not with your luck," Ashley explained. Trouble always follows you like a little black cloud."

"Well I'm just glad today is over. The detectives can sort out what the drive by shooting was all about." It was time to go to the Police station and fill out reports.

Ashley asked, "Sergeant O'Malley, how is the little girl doing"

"The last word I had looks like she will pull through."

"Do you know what started the drive by shooting?"

"They think it was a love triangle. An ex-husband did the shooting. He was mad at his ex-wife. She was at her new boyfriend's house and the ex-husband shot his daughter as they drove by trying to hit his ex-wife or her boyfriend."

"How is the eye?" asked Ashley.

"Not too good, time to go home and put a steak on it. It is still real black."

Ashley teased Leroy, "Are you going to a bar tonight?"

"Not no, but hell no, I learned my lesson last night. I'm going home, see you tomorrow."

Leroy called Katherine when he got home, but she wasn't home yet. He decided to go out for fast food and drive around for nothing better to do. He ate at Long John Silvers. He had the combination platter and a Pepsi.

With a full belly, he was ready to go home. The cashier watched him the whole time he was eating. She was looking him over like a primer piece of meat. He looked her over and decided she would be fine, but another face crossed his eyes, Katherine. Leroy could never look at another girl without thinking about Katherine. Something had to give. He needed some loving.

Leroy decided to drive around the neighborhood before going back to his apartment. He had a lot on his mind, that being his relationship with Katherine. He wanted more time with her, but the only way he could do it was to move in together and he didn't think she would buy that. They could get married, but he didn't think she was ready for that. He could see other women on the side, like Ann, who was always trying to get him in her bed. He laughed, he could mow the grass. No, he would feel guilty for cheating on her, so that was out. He was a one woman man.

It was dark so Leroy decided to go home. Driving by a house without any lights on, he saw a flicker of light beside the house and stopped. He reached in the back seat for his Colt 45 and got out of the car. He walked around to the side of the house for a better look.

Standing beside the house was a man with a mask on his face, a cape like Zorro and tennis shoes. He had the cape wide open to show off his body which was naked. Leroy couldn't believe his eyes. He was looking at a stupid exhibitionist holding a flashlight on his naked body.

Leroy stepped out, "Police, hold it right there."

The man turned and ran through the bushes. Leroy grinned, that had to have hurt. The lights in an upstairs window came on and an old lady stuck her head out. "What are you doing? Leave him alone."

"Ma'am I am a Police officer. That was a flasher in your yard."

"I'm not stupid, I know that, but you ran off a naked man. I haven't seen a naked man since my husband died ten years ago and you just ran him off. He didn't have much to show, but it was better than nothing. Go arrest some bad guys and leave him alone. If I'm lucky he might come back."

"Ma'am he may come back and rape you."

"It won't be rape. I'll just lay back and enjoy it. Now will you please go?"

Leroy left mumbling to himself. What a nut case and she liked the flasher. Le laughed, the flasher did look funny in his costume and maybe it was some old guy trying to impress her. This had been a fun night after all.

He thought about Katherine. What if he stood outside her window and flashed her, what would she do? Call the cops or stand there and watch him? What costume would he look good in? He laughed, he was on a roll. He knew what she would do, call the cops.

One month later

School started back and so did the headache of traffic in school zones and drug dealers selling drugs to kids. They sold them to younger kids each year. Leroy hated drug dealers and would like to catch one, so he could break every bone in his body.

At briefing, Ashley and Leroy knew what it would be mostly about, school starting back and all the problems. The rest of the briefing was standard items. When the briefing was over, Sergeant O'Malley addressed Ashley and Leroy, "I want you to patrol all the schools in the area looking for drug dealers. I hope you catch a scumbag selling drugs to kids. I hope he falls down and hurts himself on the way here."

Ashley pulled out into traffic and headed for the high school. They circled the school several times, but didn't see any drugs being sold. They left to make the rounds at the rest of the schools. After checking all the schools, they came up with nothing. After class took up at the schools, they went for coffee.

They decided to have breakfast, so they went to Wanda's Hen House. A cute little blond waitress wearing a short black skirt and a low cut white blouse came to take their order. She kept her eyes on Leroy while they ordered. After she left, Ashley said, "That girl has eyes for you. Are you and Katherine still seeing one another?"

"Yes, only in a blue moon because she works so much."

"Too bad, you don't have much of a love life do you?"

"Try none at all."

"Tell you what," Ashley said, "To make life more interesting I bet the little blonde when she brings our order bends over and gives you a good look at her hooters. Loser buys breakfast."

Leroy thought that was a sucker bet, but he said, "Ok, but she has to bend over so I can see all of them."

"No problem, I'm sure she will do just that." Ashley liked to study people and how they respond to different situations. She was sure she had a safe bet.

Their waitress brought their orders. She was beside Ashley when she set her plate down. She should have gone around the table to give Leroy his plate, but she slowly bent way over the table and set his plate in front of him. She had a nice set of hooters and Leroy saw all of them. Ashley had to put her hand over her mouth to keep from giggling. When the waitress turned to leave, she dropped her ticket pad on the floor. She bent over and gave Leroy a good view all the way to her panties, which were red. When she left she turned and smiled at Leroy.

Ashley was about to bust a gut to keep from laughing. Leroy glared at her, "So you win." Ashley couldn't hold back any longer. She started to laugh and couldn't stop.

"Ok, just you wait because payback is hell. I'll get you big time, just you wait and see."

The waitress came with the ticket and Leroy reached for it. She smiled at Leroy, "Thank you and you all come back to see us." Leroy left her a three dollar tip and went to the register to pay. On the back of the ticket was a telephone number.

When they got in the Police car and Ashley pulled out into traffic, She said, "I'll bet the blonde put her telephone number on the back of the ticket."

"How did you guess?"

"You could tell she was hot for your body and that would be the next step. Did you take it down?"

"No, Katherine's face popped up in front of my eyes and I couldn't do it."

"Boy, you sure have it bad."

"Well I got something to tell you. It will make your day." He told her about the flasher and the little old lady. They had a good laugh about it. Leroy had to ask, "What do you think Katherine would do if I dressed up in a costume and flashed her?"

"Simple, she wouldn't look. She would call the cops."

"That's what I thought, but it would be fun to do it."

""If you got the guts then go for it. I'll bail you out of jail."

"No thanks, I think I'll pass."

Schools were starting to let out so they covered all of them. The high school let out last. They cruised up close to the school parking. Ashley said, "Do you see what I see?"

"Yes I do. The guy looks like in his late twenty's just passed some small items to the girl in black pants and black shirt. She had chains hanging down her pants and her face was made up with black lipstick. Ashley said, "I'll cut him off."

She ran the Police car in behind the parked car and blocked him from running. The man ran off to left and the girl ran off to the right. They jumped out of the car. Leroy went after the man while Ashley went after the girl.

The man went across the street and down the alley with Leroy hot on his heels. He climbed a fence and ran across another street. Leroy was still right behind him, but he was tiring fast. If the guy would pull a gun then he could stop him. This guy was in good shape and Leroy was beginning to lose ground. He thought the guy was going to get away.

The man ran through a yard, looking back at Leroy, he tripped over a toy left in the yard by a child and went down hard. Leroy landed on top of the man before he could get up. His knee hit the man in the back and took all the fight out of him.

Leroy put the cuffs on him, pulled him up to his feet and searched him. He found a knife, a pocket full of money and lots of different kinds of drugs. He knew what grass was. There were bags of white powder and some pills. Leroy read him his rights.

Ashley chased the girl into the school, up and down halls and into the girl's bathroom. She was trying to get rid of the drugs. She had got rid of all but two bags of white powder which was probably cocaine. Ashley handcuffed the girl, searched her, and read her rights. The girl was a hell cat and Ashley had her hands full taking her back to the Police car. She put her in back and called in. She was going to ask for backup but she saw Leroy coming down the street.

Leroy put the man in the car. Ashley drove back to the Police station. "Not a bad day's work," said Leroy. They took them in to book them.

While they were booking them, Captain Curry walked by, "Well, well, well, look what we got here. We've been trying to catch this punk for a long time."

Ashley said, "Leroy chased him down and caught him."

"Good job both of you. It seems like you two are always in the middle of what is going down. Go catch me another punk to make a pair."

Leroy replied, "We'll try sir."

As the Captain walked off he was mumbling, he brought the punk in alive, too bad, he hated drug dealers as much as Leroy.

The drug bust turned out to be a big one. The powder turned out to be cocaine with a street value of twenty thousand dollars. The grass and pills had a street value of five thousand dollars and he had six thousand dollars cash on him. The car which now belonged to the Police to be sold at auction was worth fifteen thousand dollars. It turned out to be a forty six thousand dollar bust.

"This was a good day," said Leroy. "We took a lot of drugs off the street and caught the scumbag selling them."

The next three months were routine and Leroy was getting bored from lack of action, but Ashley liked it. Leroy said, "Katherine got off for Thanksgiving and I did to. We are going to my home and a ranch that belongs to a friend. I went to high school with him. If we can get through the rest of the day,

I'll be off starting tomorrow and won't be back until Sunday evening."

"Where are you going to spend Thanksgiving Day.?"

"We will spend Wednesday night at my home, have Thanksgiving there and stay Thursday night at my home. We will go to the ranch on Friday. We will stay there until Sunday.

"I think I told you about Mike training horses for the movies. He is real good with horses. I think he is what people call a horse whisperer. He talks to horses and they seem to know what he says. They do what he wants them to do."

"Sounds like it would be fun to watch him work."

"He had this one horse, the last day all my friends were there together, he was trying to get to play dead, but the horse didn't want to miss anything going on. He would play dead and then raise his head to see what was going on. We thought Mike would have to shoot him to make him play dead. We were telling about where we were going, when his wife Linda, out of the blue, told Mike she was going to have a baby. Mike fainted and fell over backward and would you believe that dumb horse fell over playing dead. A minute later he raised his head to see what was going on."

"You sure ran with a wild bunch."

"Yes I did, but it looks like all of us turned out okay. I'm a cop, Punky is a Navy pilot, Mike has his ranch, Rex is here in Dallas at Texas Instruments and Gary is the only one still trying to figure out what he wants to do with his life. I don't know where he is right now. Well, that sums up my past. We came close to going to jail, but we didn't."

Ashley said, "It's time to go back to the station and you can enjoy your time off."

"Who will be your partner the next few days?"

"Nobody, I don't want anyone."

"I know you did it a long time before I got here, but you be careful while I'm gone."

"I will, you and Katherine have a good time."

Early the next morning, Leroy knocked on Katherine's door. She heard the pounding in her head, no it was the door. She had got to bed late and couldn't go to sleep. Her mind was on Leroy and their going off together. They had waited so long to have time together. She tiptoed to the door, "Who is it?"

"The big bad wolf let me in or I'll huff and puff and blow your house down."

Katherine giggled as she opened the door. "Better come in before one of my neighbors shoots you." As soon as he was inside, Katherine stood on tiptoe and put her arms around his neck, waiting for a kiss. Leroy kissed her like a man starving for water. With his hands on her waist, he could feel her heat on his belly.

He put his hands on her buttocks, slowly lowered her to the floor, her nightgown sliding up around her waist, her belly sliding over his big hard erection. She slept in a short nightgown and nothing else. Her bare bottom felt good on his hands, nice and soft like a baby's butt.

They pulled apart. Katherine took his hand and led him toward the bedroom. She raised her arms for him to pull her nightgown over her head. She stood before him naked as she reached for the buttons on his shirt. "Let me do that."

She pushed his hands away. "No I want to undress you, taking my time and then have my way with you. I want us to make slow love and make it last."

Leroy pulled her to him and slowly kissed her, then set her back. "Go for it. "I'm your slave, sex slave that is." She giggled and started pulling his clothes off. When he stood before her naked with a big hard on, she said, "Is that for me?"

"Yes and anyway you want it."

"I want you to lie down on your back. I want to be in charge." Leroy lay down on his back with his flagpole standing straight up. She looked at his flagpole and groaned, "It seems to get bigger every time we make love."

"I hope so," replied Leroy.

Katherine straddled his hips. She took his erection in her hand and stroked it, then slowly lowered herself down until Leroy was fully sheathed. She sat still giving her time to adjust to his size. She wiggled her buttocks and slowly started to move up and down. Leroy asked, "Want some help?" as he arched his back to go deeper in her hot passion.

"No I want to do it. It feels so good when I go down and take all of it." Katherine started to go faster and moaned each time she went down as she took all of it. She rotated her hips each time she went down.

Katherine threw her head back and rode him hard. Her inner muscles squeezed him until he thought he would faint. It was pure torture and then he felt spasm after spasm. She knew

Leroy was about ready to come. He was throbbing and she tightened her muscles more and more. Leroy cried her name as he slammed into her softness and shot his seed deep into her hot passion.

Katherine sat still and watched Leroy as he reached up and touched a nipple. It felt so good. She leaned toward him so he could take it in his mouth. She moaned as the sensation gave her body pure pleasure. She laid her head on his chest to rest. Her rest didn't last long before Leroy rolled over with him on top. He was still inside her and she could feel him becoming hard again. It made her body tingle with imagining what his intention was. She put her arms around Leroy's back, grabbed his buttocks, arching her back and pulling on his buttocks. She pulled him deep into her body.

Leroy pushed and pounded her, pleasuring her body until she thought she would die from it. She climaxed first, his throbbing erection deep inside her driving her crazy. Katherine moaned, "I love you,"

Leroy followed her with his climax. He slowly pulled out and lay beside her. "I love you more." They cuddled together and went to sleep. They were exhausted but very content. It was noon before they finally woke up. They showered together and made sandwiches for lunch. They were content to just be with each other. Katherine said, "Do you want to stay home and make love the whole time?"

"I would like to but, I promised Mom we would be down and I told Mike to look for us, so we better get on the road." They loaded the Thunderbird and hit the road.

On the way out of town Leroy saw a rental car lot and pulled into it. Katherine asked, "What do you think you are doing?"

"How would you like to go home in style?"

"What are you talking about?"

"See that big van with pictures painted on the side, do you know what it is?"

"I think they call them goodtime vans."

"Right on, let's go look at it."

"You got to be kidding."

Leroy got out and Katherine followed.

As they drove down the road, Katherine turned around and looked at the inside of the van. It had curtains on the windows, soft black fur on the walls, floor and overhead. A bed took up most of the floor with a mirror above the bed, a small bar and table took up the rest of the space. There were pillows to sit on at the small table. It had an icebox under the bar. She couldn't believe Leroy had rented the van for the trip.

"What will your parents say when we drive up in this?"

"Well, the bad boy is back," He grinned. "They will think it is normal. If I don't do something crazy, they wouldn't believe I was their son."

"Were you really that bad when you were growing up?"

"I'm afraid so. Please don't believe everything Mom may tell you."

Katherine thought this was going to be a fun trip. She would find out all the bad things Leroy did while growing up.

They stopped in Athens and got food, drinks, and ice to stock their ice box. They headed on down the road. Just outside of Boonville, the County Sheriff pulled him over. The Sheriff walked up to the van, "Let me see your driver's license. Well I'll be a monkey's uncle, is that you Leroy?"

"Yes sir, I came home to give you a bad time. It has probably been too quiet around here since us bad boys left."

The Sheriff started laughing, "I've been keeping up with you in Dallas and you have a name for yourself, Dirty Harry, I believe."

"Yes, but I don't like it. I get teased all the time."

"Well, I won't call you that while you are home. Who is the pretty lady with you? Doesn't she know she is traveling in bad company?" teased the Sheriff.

"This is Katherine Stewart. She is a reporter for a Dallas paper. This is the man who kept me out of jail."

"You are the one who writes about Leroy all the time."

"Guilty as charged. Leroy sells a lot of papers. His partner is a woman, would you believe that?"

"I read about her also. Ashley, I believe is her name."

"She is the best," said Leroy. "She covers my back and I know I can always count on her.

"I won't keep you two any longer. It was good to see you and keep up the good work."

"Take care Sheriff."

"Before I go, could I ask one stupid question?"

"Sure thing, what do you want to know?"

"Why are you driving the van?"

Leroy laughed, "Why, we are here for a good time so we needed a good time van."

"Same old Leroy," said the Sheriff as he drove off.

Leroy showed Katherine the movie theatre he worked at while he was in high school. It was an old theatre, but it had been a job. There weren't many jobs to be had in a small town. He drove around the square with a courthouse in the middle and side streets leading off each corner of the square. Leroy said, "We used to do stupid things when we were in high school."

"Like what?"

"The Police station is on the second floor of the courthouse. We used to set off firecrackers on the corner of the square and drive like hell before the Police caught us. One time Punky made a u- turn in front of a Police car, then tried to outrun him, but we got caught."

"What happened?"

"They took Punky to night court and made him pay a fine."

"You guys were so bad."

Well, that's water under the bridge, look at us now."

"The Dairy Queen is on your left where we used to hang out and try to make out with the girls."

"Did you make out?"

"Sometimes, there's the Drive –in Theatre on your right. Have you ever been to one?"

"No, but it looks like fun."

"It's a good place to make out and lots of girls lose their cherry in the Drive- in Theatre."

"How would you know, did you get a few yourself?"

Should he lie or tell the truth? After a few moments of hesitation, Leroy confessed, "Well maybe one or two."

Katherine teased, "And maybe a few more."

"Maybe one or two more," murmured Leroy

Leroy's home was on the edge of town still inside the city limits. It was time to change the subject. He turned into the driveway. ""This is home."

It was an average size brick home with three bedrooms, two bathrooms and large trees in front and back. Mrs. Cooper saw them pull in and knew by the van that it was the same boy that had left home. Never a dull moment when Leroy was around, plus the friends he ran with and got in trouble with. As Leroy and Katherine got out of the van, his Mother ran out to meet them. Leroy opened his arms and his Mother ran into them. She hugged him, "What's the matter, you get hungry and come home for some food?"

"Yes, you know I could never cook."

She stepped back and looked at Katherine, "And who is this beautiful young woman. She is so small, did you rob the cradle?"

"No Mom, she is only one year younger than me. This is Katherine Stewart. She is a reporter for a Dallas paper. Katherine, this is my mother I think, I haven't done a DNA test yet to be sure."

Katherine giggled, "Are you two always like this?"

"All the time," replied Mrs. Cooper.

"Where is Dad?" asked Leroy.

"He is still at work but should be home shortly. Get your bags and come on in." Mrs. Cooper showed them to their bedrooms. Leroy had his old room and Katherine got the guest bedroom. There was a bathroom between the two bedrooms, with a door from each bedroom, so they could share the bathroom. "You two come on into the kitchen when you are done unpacking."

Mrs. Cooper had dinner on the table, his Dad walked in as they came onto the kitchen. She said, "Our hungry kid is home to sponge off of us, She winked at Katherine. Katherine almost giggled, this was one crazy family. They never let up.

His Dad came over and gave Leroy a hug. He defended his son, "You know Policemen don't make much and it is a high cost of living in Dallas, so maybe we can put him up and feed him for a few days."

"Thanks Dad." Leroy grinned as he looked at his Mother and Katherine. His Dad looked at Leroy and then at Katherine, "What's going on, this is the first time you have ever brought a girl home with you?"

Katherine looked at Leroy, "We are just friends."

Mr. Cooper said, "Yeah right and bulls fly. I see the way you look at each other. She looks at you the way your Mother looked at me and you look at her the way I did your Mother before we were married. I see love in both your eyes. You may say no but the heart doesn't lie."

They didn't know what to say. They just stared at each other. Did it show that much so everyone knew it? She was in love with Leroy but she hadn't known until now, for sure that he was in love with her. She wanted to scream, "Leroy loves me."

Mrs. Cooper said, "Honey sit down and quit teasing the kids. You two sit on that side of the table." Katherine sat down and looked at the kitchen. It was antique with an old wood burning stove, an old table and chairs, old wallpaper, old dishes, old pots and pans. Everything was old, even the pictures on the walls. It was like stepping back in time. The refrigerator was in the back storage room so everything in the kitchen would be old.

Mrs. Cooper said, "Nothing cooks better than an old wood stove." She cooked roast beef, potatoes, and carrots. She had made a green salad, a cherry pie with ice cream for dessert. Leroy and Katherine filled their plates and ate like they were starved.

Mrs. Cooper smiled at the kids.

After dinner Katherine helped Mrs. Cooper clean and wash the dishes. Then she asked what she had been dying to ask, all about Leroy and his growing up. Mrs. Cooper didn't hold anything back. She told how Leroy got in trouble and how he got out of it. She told all that she knew about his love life. He went with so many girls it was hard to keep up with the one he was seeing.

Katherine was happy she was the only girl he was going with and she was the only girl he had ever brought home. She became hot all over just thinking of Leroy. Mrs. Cooper said, "You are in love with my son. I can tell just by looking at you."

"How can you tell?"

"Your face glows every time you look at him or when his name is mentioned."

"I love him so much it scares me all the time, him being a Policeman. He always seems to be where the trouble is. I don't know how long I can take it, him being a Policeman and always in harm's way. He knows I don't like it, but he doesn't know how bad it is on me."

"Don't give up on him. Maybe he will go back to college and become a lawyer."

"If he lives that long," Katherine said without thinking. Mrs. Cooper gasped. "I'm sorry I say things sometimes without thinking."

The men were in the den watching football and catching up on all that had happened after Leroy left home. Mr. Cooper said, "Mike has done real well with his ranch. He runs cattle and horses. He trains horses for anyone and is good at it. Rex you know is in Dallas. Punky is in the Navy and is on the U.S.S. Bennington out on a West Pack Cruise."

"Do you know where Gary is?"

"Nobody seems to know where he went. His parents don't know where he is and they are worried about him."

"Dad, you know how Gary is. He was probably the wildness of all our hell raisers. No telling what he is doing."

"Well, I sure am proud of you."

"Thanks Dad, I'll try not to be a pain in the butt anymore."

Mrs. Cooper came in, "Time for bed. You kids are probably tired from your trip" Katherine went on to her room.

"We are tired from our jobs and came home for rest and relaxation."

"Just be sure that's all you do in my house, if you know what I mean."

"Yes ma'am, I'll be good in your house. I think I'll go to bed, goodnight Mom and Dad."

"Goodnight Son."

When all was quiet and everyone was in bed, Leroy went through the bathroom into Katherine's bedroom. She was not asleep. She was waiting on him to come to her.

Leroy whispered, "Come with me."

"Where are we going?"

"You'll see, now be quiet. We don't want to wake Mom and Dad." He took her hand and led her to the back door of the house then out to the van. Leroy slowly opened the door and lifted her inside. Katherine giggled, "Now I know why you wanted the van."

"Mamma didn't raise, no fool."

They got in the middle of the bed. Katherine raised her arms so Leroy could remove her nightgown. He lay on his back and she removed his shorts. She straddled him and reached down to guide his erection into her hot folds. Katherine said, "We can take our time and enjoy making love tonight." And they did make love several times, late into the night hours.

Finally exhausted and content, they went back into the house to their own rooms. Leroy mumbled, Mom, I was good in the house, but you didn't say anything about outside the house.

Mrs. Cooper was up early and started cooking Thanksgiving, while everyone else slept in. She fixed coffee and waited to see what everyone wanted for breakfast. Katherine was the first to arrive. All she wanted was coffee and toast.

Katherine looked happy and content. Mrs. Cooper knew that look. Leroy had made love to her, but he had promised to be good, she smiled and remembered the van. That little son-of-a-gun had put one over on her.

Mr. Cooper and Leroy came in next. They had bacon, eggs, toast and coffee. Leroy looked at his Mom. She smiled at him and he knew she knew what they did last night, but she wouldn't say anything to embarrass them. His Mom and Dad had been pretty wild in their day.

Katherine helped Mrs. Cooper with the cooking and setting the table. She liked Mrs. Cooper and the way they all had fun together. One day she wanted her own home and children. She looked into the den and Leroy was staring at her and she became hot all over. He always had that effect on her and she wandered if it would always be like that.

Mrs. Cooper looked at her and said, "Yes, it will always be that way if you love each other enough." Katherine looked at her and couldn't believe she could read her mind. "Honey, it's in your eyes."

Mr. Cooper and Leroy watched football while the women finished cooking. When it came time to eat, they sat around the table and looked at all the food. Mrs. Cooper had cooked a turkey, dressing, corn on the cob and green peas. She fixed a green salad and a fruit salad. For dessert there was cake, pie, and ice cream. There was enough food to feed an army. Katherine had never seen that much food on a table.

Mr. Cooper said grace, "Ok, help yourself before Leroy eats it all up." And eat he did, Katherine couldn't believe how he put two big plates of food away and cake, pie with ice cream.

Leroy grinned at her, "Mom said I come home for food, how right she is. After finishing eating and cleaning up, Leroy asked her to go sightseeing.

There wasn't much to see in a small town, so they went out to the lake and watched the sun go down. "We used to swim in the lake naked."

"Did any girls swim with you guys?"

"Sometimes there would be some brave enough to swim on a dare."

"You were such a bad boy, your Mother told me about a lot of trouble you got into."

"Don't believe everything she tells you. I was a good boy part of the time."

"Yeah right," she giggled, "When you were asleep and not dreaming bad dreams."

They went back to Leroy's house and watched television until time to go to bed. Leroy told her how he would like to become a detective so he could get off the street. He liked the challenge of the work. It would something different all the time, not the same old grind every day. After everyone went to bed and it got quiet, Leroy eased into Katherine's room. He kissed her and they decided to get a good night's sleep. She was sore from too much sex. The next morning everyone slept in late except Mrs. Cooper who always got up early. She made coffee and waited for everyone to get up. She didn't have long to wait. Katherine was again the next to get up. She had coffee and toast. Mr. Cooper and Leroy finally came in and wanted a full breakfast, which Mrs. Cooper fixed for them.

They had enjoyed their visit with the Cooper's and told them so. Mrs. Cooper really liked Katherine and hoped things would work out with Leroy and her. Leroy and Katherine packed up to leave, but he wanted her to see his room and everything he had collected over the years. He showed her a picture of him and his buddies, who was always in trouble. She wanted to see the pictures of his old girlfriends, but he was smart and got rid of all of them before he left home.

"Sorry," he said. They loaded up and said bye to his parents. They stopped at the Dairy Queen and had lunch. It hadn't changed much since he left. The help was new and he didn't know anyone. They had burgers and fries with a shake for lunch. They had a new jukebox, so he dropped some money in.

Leroy played some country western songs. He daydreamed as the country songs played. He dreamed about the times he spent here.

Katherine said, "Hello, hello, earth to Leroy, over."

He said, "What is it?"

"You have been out of it for about ten minutes."

"Sorry, I was daydreaming about times gone by."

They left the Dairy Queen and headed out to Mike's ranch which was a little ways from town. Leroy turned off the road under a sign that stated Double L Ranch and stopped. "What are you stopping for?" asked Katherine.

"I'm waiting for our escort to the house." Two beautiful horses came running to meet them as they drove over the cattle guard. They were both pure white. Leroy started toward the house with a horse on each side. When they reached the house, he got out and both horses came to him. Katherine stayed in the van. Leroy said, "Come on out, they won't hurt you. They know me." Slowly she got out and came over to Leroy. The horses looked her over while she looked them over. Leroy put his arm around one horse, "This is Thunder." He put his other arm around the other horse, "and Lighting. They are the pride of the ranch." Katherine finally got up enough nerve to pet them. This was something new to her. It was so cool.

Mike came over from the barn, "You two leave the guests alone." Lighting and Thunder walked off. "They can be a pain in the rear at times."

Katherine said, "They sure mind good."

Mike said, "It takes training and you can get them to do anything you want."

Mike stared at the van, "Is that what I think it is?"

"Yes it is, come take a look," said Leroy. He opened the door and Mike looked in.

"Wow, I didn't think they made good time vans anymore."

"I don't think they do, this is an old model."

"Tell you what, Mike said, "You and her stay in the house, Linda I will sleep in the van tonight."

Leroy grinned, "She is Katherine and this is Mike."

"Linda will be home shortly. She went off shopping."

They watched as a pickup came through the gate, the two horses went to escort her to the house. Linda got out and got their little girl out of the car seat. Mike introduced everyone. Linda said, "This is a first for Leroy. You are the first girl he has ever brought home to meet his parents. What's going on?"

Katherine said, "We are just friends." This was the second time someone thought it was odd Leroy bringing someone home with him. It made her happy, that it was her he had brought home. She got a warm feeling, maybe they would make it.

Mike said, "Linda come with me, I want you to see something." He opened the van door and she stared at the back of the van. The little girl pointed to the mirror on the ceiling, "What's that for, Daddy?"

Mike's mind went blank, "Cindy your Mother will tell you." If looks could kill, Mike would be dead. Linda stared at him while trying to come up with an answer. Katherine laughed, "Men are so dumb. Women need a mirror to put makeup on."

Cindy asked, "But how can she put makeup on and see the mirror. Why is it up there?" Linda looked at Katherine for an answer. Katherine was ready for the question. She explained, "There wasn't any place else to put the mirror, so they had to put it there. It makes it real nice. You can lie in bed and put your makeup on."

"Momma she is so smart. Would you like to come to my room and see my dolls? I have a whole lot of them."

""That would be fun," said Katherine.

Linda looked at her daughter, "Let our company get moved in and then Katherine can come see your room."

Cindy went over and grabbed a suitcase, "Ok, I'll help." It was too heavy. As she was pulling it out of the van, she dropped it. It flew open, spilling Katherine's panties, bras, and nightgowns all over the place. "Oops, I'm sorry. I didn't mean to do it." Cindy started to cry.

Katherine said, "That's alright honey, accidents happen." She hugged her and she stopped crying. Katherine glanced around to find, Leroy and Mike were picking up her panties. She blushed, Linda rolled her eyes, "Give me those and you two get the rest of the luggage."

Mike held up a bra and handed it to Linda. He glanced at Leroy, "Size 34c."

"I think so," he replied. Katherine's face was burning now. Linda was ready to kill both of them.

Cindy giggled, "I don't wear one of them things. Mom says I am too young yet, I don't need one right now."

Linda said, "Don't be embarrassed. You just wait. You haven't seen anything yet, wait until Rex shows up. He is another one of the bad boys. If he had been here he would have put the bra to his chest and made a remark."

Katherine mumbled, "I can't wait."

Linda showed Katherine to her room. Mike showed Leroy to his room. They had separate bedrooms because of Cindy. They didn't want her asking why the company was sleeping together.

The house was all western. It wasn't a show place but, you could tell it was lived in. Linda wanted company to feel at home when they came to visit. The only room that was different was the kitchen, with modern appliances. The table and chairs were western as were the pictures on the walls. She had a hand pump at the sink for water which came from an underground spring and the water was always cold. The outside was a sight to see, cattle grazing, horses everywhere in different corrals and different breeds of horses.

There was a large cedar deck out back off the kitchen. Mike had fired up a huge grill while he was waiting on them. Leroy looked at the table covered with food. "Are you feeding an army?"

"Oh, I forgot to tell you we have a group of high school kids we sponsor. They square dance and we have a clogging group also. We have them over on Friday to dance and eat. They country western dance and have a good time. They stay out of trouble or we don't let them in the group."

"They aren't like the hell raiser we were in high school," accused Leroy.

"Right on, we could never have joined a group like these kids." Mike put steak and baked potatoes on for the adults, as they took longer to cook. He would put the hot dogs, fries, and hamburgers on later. Mike said, "You will enjoy the group. They are fun to watch. They are good dancers and have won several dance contests."

Linda made a green salad, brought out drinks and turned on the stereo record player, with easy listing music to play while they ate. The kids started to arrive, so Mike put on the hot dogs, hamburgers and fries.

Rex arrived with Joy, an old classmate, wearing short shorts and a white shirt tied at the waist showing a lot of skin at the top. Linda whispered to Katherine, "That's Rex and Joy. She always has to put on a show and Rex is just as bad about showing off."

The boys all stared at Joy as she walked by. When they reached the table, Linda introduced Katherine to them. Rex said, "I know her. Joy, this is the reporter for the Dallas paper. She writes about Leroy all the time."

Katherine said, "Leroy is always where the trouble starts. Sometimes I look to see if a little black cloud is over him."

Rex said, "He was in trouble a lot when he was growing up, but the rest of us were there with him."

Mike came over to the table with the steaks and baked potatoes, while Linda set up drinks and salads. Mike sat down and everyone dug into their food. Mike, Rex and Leroy caught up on old times, while the girls talked girl talk. Linda and Joy wanted to know where Katherine met Leroy. She told them about the bank robbery, but she left out her kissing him. Joy said, "I believe you left something out, the most important part where you were kissing Leroy."

Katherine blushed, "It must have slipped my mind and how did you know?"

"Rex told me and I believe Leroy told him, a newspaper woman kissed him at the robbery so that would be you."

"And what else did he tell Rex?"

"That you were a fox and he wanted to get to know you." She had never been called a fox, but it must mean a good thing because he wanted to see her again.

Mike said, "It's time to get the show on the road."

Mike stepped up next to the record player and turned down the music. He picked up a microphone. "We have guests with us tonight, Leroy Cooper, a Policeman from Dallas, Katherine Stewart a newspaper reporter from Dallas, Rex Johnson an electronics engineer at Texas Instruments in Dallas and last but not least Joy whom you already know."

One of the boys asked, "Is Leroy the one they call Dirty Harry?"

"Yes I'm afraid so, he doesn't like to be called that, so be nice."

"Wow," was all the kid could say. All the kids stared at Leroy. He had people stare at him all the time so it didn't bother him.

Mike explained to the kids that he wanted them to put on a show for the guests. He put on square dance music first and the kids paired off. Mike called the square dance as the boys whirled the girls around the floor. Katherine asked, "Where did Mike learn to call a square dance?"

Linda replied, "His Mother and Father had square dances at their home when Mike was small and his Father called square dances, so he just picked it up from them."

After the square dancers finished, the clogging was next and they put on a good show. Mike was proud of his group and it showed on his face. Linda told Katherine, Mike was an old country boy growing up, from a poor dirt farmer family, but I fell in love with him. My Mother had a fit. She wanted me to marry a rich man, but she finally came around and loves him now. She watched how happy Mike had made me."

Katherine said, "It looks like you got it all."

"We started small but we have it all now."

When the clogging was finished, Mike put on some rock and roll for the kids to dance to. They blew the place away. Joy asked Rex to dance and they put on a show. "I'll wait until Mike puts on some country western music. I like to two-step," Katherine said.

After a while, Mike changed the music to country. Katherine and Leroy got up to dance followed by Linda and Mike. Rex and Joy sat out and rested. The rock and roll had done a number on them. Mike shut down the party at ten o'clock. The kids left the old people and went home. Leroy said, "I think I'm getting old." He was tired from dancing. Mike went inside and brought out the beer.

Rex said, "That's more like it," as he downed half a bottle. Linda, Joy and Katherine cleaned up after the party while the guys talked.

A short time later Rex and Joy left, Leroy and Mike smiled at each other, knowing what would happen next. Joy was a hot one, who couldn't get enough sex. When you went out with her, you would always get some before you took her home.

Linda had put Cindy to bed early. Leroy and Katherine glanced at each other with lust and love in their eyes. Linda said, "Time to call it a night." They got up to go inside. Linda whispered to Katherine, "The side door will be unlocked." Katherine blushed red. "Don't be embarrassed, there's nothing wrong with making love with someone you love. After being married several years, Mike and I still make love several times a week and it's just as good, or maybe better than when we were going together."

Going upstairs, Katherine told Leroy about the side door being unlocked. Leroy laughed, "Mike told me the same thing." After it got quiet, Katherine met Leroy at the side door. She had on a shirt and Leroy had on shorts. He took her hand and led her to the van. He opened the door and put his hand on her bare bottom helping her into the van.

Katherine pulled her shirt off and lay down with her buttocks in the air. Leroy pulled off his shorts. She tilted her head back, shyly she said, "I want you to ride me," and she wiggled her buttocks at him. He touched the tip of his erection into her folds. She moaned, "Now give it to me." Leroy grabbed her hips and slammed into her. He rode her hard until she climaxed and he was right behind her.

It had been a long day, so he curled his body around her spoon fashion. They talked for about any and everything. "Have you ever ridden a horse?"

"Only a couple of times and I didn't ride too well."

"Mike is taking us riding tomorrow, so you get a chance to practice riding again."

"Oh lucky me, I can hardly wait."

"It won't be that bad. Mike will put you on a horse you can handle." They dosed off to sleep.

About two o'clock in the morning something bumped into the van. Leroy sat up. "Now what did that?" He opened the door, Lighting and Thunder were there. They turned toward the barn, took a couple of steps, stopped and looked back at him. "You want me to follow you?" They took a couple of steps and looked back again. "Katherine, go to the house and get Mike. Something is wrong and I don't know what."

She protested, "I only have a shirt and it's too short."

He reached in the glove box and got his 38 pistol. "I only have my shorts, now go."

Leroy followed the horses to the barn. He eased inside the open door and switched on the lights. A young boy of about twelve years old was trying to break into a storage room. He started to run, but Leroy was blocking the only way out. "What's your name boy?"

"Bobby Coon, sir."

Mike came running into the barn. "Bobby, what are you doing here?"

Bobby looked at Mike and Leroy. "My Dad broke his leg at the saw mill. We don't have any food or money and I was trying to find something we could eat." Mike walked over and put his arms around the boy as he started to cry.

Mike said, "It's not so bad, it can be fixed, come up to the house with me." As they walked by Leroy, mike glanced at Leroy, "Nice outfit, but not as good as Katherine's." Leroy followed them in his shorts and a 38 pistol in his hand. He had caught the bad guy. The guys at the Police station would get a good laugh if they found out.

Linda and Katherine were in the kitchen they walked in. Leroy went over to stand by Katherine. She was still only wearing a shirt. Linda giggled, "I like your outfits." They glared at her.

Mike said, "Linda, get a box." He pulled food out of the refrigerator. He put steaks, a whole ham, apples, oranges, bread, butter, milk, and can goods in the box. He picked up the box, "Come on son, I'll take you home."

Mike took Bobby home in his pickup. When they got there, "Mr. Love, I don't know what to say?"

"I have been where you are and I know what it's like to go hungry."

"I don't know how to thank you?"

"Tell you what, how would you like a job in the evenings after school?"

"Boy would I?"

"Then be at the ranch after school and I will have a job for you, the same one I had in high school.

"Thank you, thank you sir."

Mike handed him twenty dollars, "In advance on your first pay check." Bobby had tears in his eyes. Bobby took the box and waved as he went into the house.

Leroy and Katherine put on some clothes and came back to the kitchen. Linda put on the coffee pot while they waited for Mike to return. Linda said, "The Coons are dirt farmers that live about a mile down the road. When the crops are in, Mr. Coon works at the saw mill to keep food on the table. Mike has been there and he knows what it is like to be hungry. His Dad was a dirt farmer." Mike walked in just as the coffee pot finished making coffee. Linda said, "Coffee anyone?" She poured coffee for everyone and they sat down to talk.

Mike said, "I hired Bobby to help out around here. He can have the big barn to clean and sweep up. I'll teach him to feed the horses and how to care for them. He will be doing the same thing I did when I worked for Linda's Father."

Linda said, "I'm proud of you, no wonder I fell in love with you."

Katherine was getting a lesson in how kind people could be. She was thinking of writing an article on kindness to people. It would be different from her usual reporting. Linda said, "Time to hit the sack. Mike I have something for you." She winked at Katherine as she led Mike away. Leroy and Katherine went to their rooms. It was only a couple of hours till daybreak.

The next morning they slept in. Around nine o'clock Cindy jumped in bed with Mike and Linda. "Time to get up, I'm hungry," Cindy was always hungry, how could she eat so much and stay skinny?

Linda got up, went to the kitchen, put on coffee, and started breakfast. Katherine drifted in and headed for the coffee pot. Linda giggled, "You're not a morning person, are you?"

"I'm okay after I have my first cup of coffee."

"Mike said we would go riding today. Are you up to it?"

"I don't know, but I'm willing to try. Your ranch is so pretty and I want to see all of it."

Linda said, "We could make it like a trail drive and camp out tonight. Mike dammed up a creek and built a small lake on the back of the property. It has trees and is a great place to camp."

Mike and Leroy came dragging in for breakfast. As they ate Linda explained what she and Katherine had been discussing. They were all for it. After breakfast Linda and Katherine packed food and drinks for the trip while Mike and Leroy settled the horses, then loaded the supplies on a pack horse. They were ready to go.

Mike gave Leroy and Katherine cowboy hats to keep the sun off their faces, but it would cool of at night with winter not too far off. Mike rode Thunder, Linda rode Lightning, Leroy and Katherine rode two quarter horses while Cindy rode behind Mike. She would have her horse in a couple of years. They started out beside a spring fed creek with a waterfall and then cut across the level part of the ranch.

The ranch was like a split level home, low, medium, and high. They climbed to the high country where they could see all over the ranch and beyond. Katherine stated as she gazed over the ranch. "It's beautiful from up here."

Linda replied with pride, "Mike and I loved it the first time we saw it."

They started down through the trees and out into open again where cattle were grazing. A large white-faced bull came over to great them. Mike got down off his horse and went to meet the bull. Katherine watched as Mike went over to the bull, "Is it safe what he is doing?"

"Sure, every animal on the ranch loves Mike. Sometimes I get jealous of them. He spends so much time with them." Mike put his arm around the bull's neck and talked low to him. The bull ate it up. "See what I mean," explained Linda.

Mike sent the bull on his way and mounted Thunder. He turned another direction and led out with Leroy bringing up the rear. He was leading the pack animal. They came to a lake about one o'clock. They rode around until Mike found a good place to camp.

Leroy and Mike unsaddled the horses, unloaded the pack horse and turned them loose to graze. Leroy asked, "Won't they wonder off?"

"If they do, Thunder and Lighting will bring them back when we get ready to leave." The girls set up two small tents, got rocks to go around the campfire and wood for the campfire.

Breaking out some fishing gear Mike said, "Let's go catch supper, there's bass and catfish in the lake, some are large." They went down to the lake to fish with Cindy right behind them.

"Daddy, I want to fish."

Mike had brought a small pole for her, "Ok honey, I got a pole for you."

The three of them baited up and put their hooks in the water. They were using some left over blood bait and hotdogs for bait. Mike pulled in the first fish, about a four pound catfish. Mike pulled in another fish, about a five pound catfish. They didn't get any more bites for a long time.

They got lazy and relaxed. All at once, Cindy's pole bent down to the water and took off dragging her toward the water. Mike screamed, "Cindy let go of the pole." She had her fish and hung on for dear life. Leroy grabbed her legs as she was pulled under water. He pulled her back to land. She was still holding on to her pole. Leroy sat down with his arms holding her around the waist.

Cindy coughed, shook her hair out of her eyes and pulled on her pole. Mike ran over to help. Leroy said, "Let her land him. She is doing okay." The fish fought the line until he finally tired out and Leroy slowly inched back holding Cindy until she pulled the fish onto the bank. She still had a death grip on her fishing pole

Mike said, "Honey, you can let go of the pole. The fish is on the bank." He reached down to remove the hook. Leroy and Cindy looked at the other fish. "Daddy my fish is bigger than yours."

"Yeah, beginner's luck," her Dad muttered. Leroy laughed at him. "What are you laughing at, you haven't caught a fish."

They went backing to fishing. All three caught more fish, but not as big as the one Cindy caught. They carried their fish back to camp. Mike told Cindy, "You clean what you catch." He looked around and Cindy was dragging her fish back toward the water. "What are you doing?"

"I'm throwing them back. I don't want to clean fish."

Leroy and Mike laughed, "Bring them back, Daddy will clean them." They carried the fish back to camp. Leroy and Mike cleaned the fish while Linda cooked them. She also made hushpuppies and fries. Mike and Leroy set up a folding table, folding chairs and lit a lantern to set on the table. "All the comforts of home," said Mike. The girls brought the food and heaped it on the table. There was fish, fish, and more fish. Mike explained, "When we are on the trail we live mostly off the land. That's the fun of it."

Katherine wasn't so sure about the live off the land bit. She glanced at Leroy and he was watching her. "So I'm a city girl."

Leroy laughed, "Wait until you need to go to the bathroom or take a bath."

She hadn't thought of that. "Where do we use the bathroom?"

Leroy grinned and pointed to the bushes.

"And where do we wash up?"

He pointed to the lake "But think of all the fun you are having," he teased.

"I loved the ride today, but my buttocks feel like you spanked me and they are sore."

"You want me to rub them, kiss them and make it better," teased Leroy.

Linda walked over with a roll of tissue. "Ok girls, time to use the ladies room and get ready for bed." She walked off with Katherine and Cindy following her.

"Watch out for snakes," warned Mike. Katherine jumped around looking the ground over.

Linda warned, "Shut up Mike."

They came back and Cindy explained, "We only have two tents, so girls sleep in one tent and boys in the other." It was starting to get cold. Crawling into the tent, Cindy asked, "Mom, are you and Katherine coming to bed?" Katherine grinned at Leroy and he knew what she was thinking, no loving tonight and payback for teasing her. Leroy was not a happy camper. Mike and Leroy made a trip to the bushes.

The next morning was cold, so they stayed in their tents until the sun came up. Mike was up first so he made a fire and put on coffee. The rest of them dragged out when they smelled the coffee. "What's for breakfast?" asked Leroy.

Cindy replied, "You know the rule, we live off the land so we have fish for breakfast."

Katherine made a face, "No way."

Mike laughed, "Since this was not a trail drive, I cheated. How about we have eggs, bacon, potatoes, fish and biscuits?"

"Now that's more like it," responded Leroy. Mike broke out the pots, pans and food while Linda started to cook. Cindy set the table.

Leroy took Katherine by the hand. "Come on let's wash up."

"Where are we going?"

"Just get your toothbrush and follow me." He led her down to the lake and filled as pan with water. He washed his face and hands. That was a wakeup call. The water was ice cold. He brushed his teeth. "Now it's your turn."

She touched the water, "You got to be kidding. No way, I'll just stay dirty."

"Come on chicken, it will wake you up." Finally she dabbed in the water, but just enough to get clean.

When they went back to camp, Linda giggled, "Leroy put one over on you. I have a pan of hot water on the fire." Katherine turned and glared at Leroy who had a silly grin on his face. If looks could kill, he would be dead.

Mike whistled for the horses. Lighting and Thunder rounded up the other horses. Katherine watched as the horses came into camp. Mike loaded the pack horse while Leroy settled the horses. Linda put out the fire while Katherine picked up the trash and put it in a bag. They mounted the horses and headed back to the barn. Cindy rode with Mike.

When they came in sight of the barn, Cindy said," Let's race to the barn and the last one there is a rotten egg."

"Ok honey. Is everyone up for a race?" Katherine wasn't but she wouldn't admit it, so she pulled her horse up even with the other horses. Leroy let go of the pack horse.

Cindy counted down, "One for the money, two for the show, three to get ready and four to go." Lightening took the lead, Thunder close behind carrying double, both quarter horses close on his tail. Katherine couldn't believe she was riding a horse so fast and such a smooth ride. She thought she would be left in the dust and here she was only two horse lengths behind the leader. Quarter horses are known for speed on short distances. She didn't know that.

Linda said, "I won. Mike you can cook lunch."

He argued, "But Thunder was carrying double and I'm heavy." Leroy and Katherine laughed at the exchange between them. Katherine wondered if she and Leroy would have as much fun when they were married. Now where did that come from?

Cindy giggled, "Daddy you are a spoiled sport, take it like a man. I'll help you cook.

Mike unloaded the pack horse while Leroy unsaddled the horses and fed them. They finished up and went inside where Linda had built a fire in the fireplace. It was cool outside and the fire felt good. They sat around and talked until it was time for Mike to cook.

Mike fried a chicken, made mashed potatoes, corn, and a salad. Cindy set the table and made tea to drink. She made cookies for desert. Katherine said to Linda, "Cindy sure is a big help to be so small."

"She is six going on sixteen." They both laughed as they watched her work. "She helps Mike a lot in the barn and with the horses. She wants to ride in the rodeo and compete in barrel racing. She also wants to do trick riding."

Katherine mused, "Like mother, like daughter, you being a good horsewoman yourself."

Cindy yelled, "Come and get it or we'll throw it out to the chickens."

"Cindy Love, where are your manners?"

"Oh Mom, I was just funning. I wouldn't throw it out until I ate," giggled Cindy.

"What am I going to do with that child?"

Katherine asked, "Are you going to have another child?"

"Now where did you hear that?"

"I thought Leroy said something about it."

"Well you can set him straight. I may have another child one of these days, but not right now."

They sat down and had a large lunch. They were full by the time Cindy served the cookies. Leroy said, "It's been fun here on the ranch, but tomorrow we have to go back to the old grind. Katherine and I put in long and odd hours, so we don't get to see each other very often."

That afternoon they packed up and started home. Katherine sighed, "Such a loving family, I wish we ---, "her voice choked up. They stopped at a rest stop about halfway home. Leroy stopped at the rental and loaded their baggage into the car. They looked at the van for the last time. It had been a fun trip.

It was dark when they parked at Katherine's apartment. They unloaded her baggage. She didn't want the day to end. "Let's order pizza."

"Sounds good to me, I'll order. What kind do you like?"

"I like pepperoni."

"Pepperoni it is." Leroy ordered a large pepperoni with double cheese, cinnamon sticks and an order of wings of fire.

Katherine changed clothes while Leroy was ordering dinner. She put on a short nightgown and nothing else under it. She wanted to get his attention. She came in the living room and sat down on the couch. Leroy was in a chair across from her. Their eyes locked on each other and Leroy glanced at her legs as she spread them, so he got his eyes full.

"See something you like," teased Katherine."

"Yes, why didn't you do that before I ordered pizza?"

"I wanted to pay you back for all the teasing you have done to me the last couple of days." Leroy's pants became tight and he wanted her now. She got up and went over to him. She could see he wanted her and she smiled.

The doorbell sounded and they jumped like two kids caught making love by her parents. Leroy went to the door and got their order. He paid and tipped the young man. "You still want pizza?" he asked.

She grinned, "Yes I'm hungry."

They made short work of the food and then their eyes locked. Katherine took his hand and led him to the bedroom. "I'm so hot and I want you in me now." She didn't have to tell him a second time, he was hard and ready. She raised her arms above her head and he removed her nightgown.

Katherine reached for Leroy's buckle, unzipped his pants, pulled them down along with his shorts. A large organ sprang up in her face. She looked up shyly at Leroy as she touched him and then started to stroke him. He threw his head back and arched into her hand while his body trembled.

She liked the power she had over him and wanted to do more. Shyly she touched the head of his erection with her tongue and felt Leroy tense. She curled her tongue around him and took as much as she could in her mouth and sucked on it. Leroy became brain dead, couldn't think, couldn't hear, couldn't see, his body clamoring for release.

He took her by her arms and pulled her up. "I can't take it any longer." He laid her back on the bed and slid between her legs, as she spread her legs wide opening for him. I want you inside me now." He poised above her, their eyes locked as he thrust into her giving her sensuous pleasure. He lowered his head and took a nipple in his mouth. She whimpered as she ran her fingers through his hair and pulled his head closer. She thought she would die if she didn't get release soon.

Leroy felt her tighten around him and her body throbbed. Katherine climaxed and arched against him. He was close behind her. He fell forward crushing her breasts between them. They were wet with sweat but, she still clung to him, putting her hands on his buttocks and pulling him deep inside her while arching her back. She had another climax. Katherine screamed his name as she went over the edge. Leroy finally pulled out and lay down beside her. They turned over facing each other, kissed and cuddled, then went off to sleep.

The next morning was a hassle. Leroy got up early and went home while Katherine tried to get it together for the day. They both didn't want to go to work, but you got to pay your bills or go to the poor house.

Katherine walked into her office to the sly glances of the girls she worked with. Finally some of them walked into her office. "Well, how was your weekend?" She told them everything how she made love with Leroy. Then it was back to work as usual. There had been another bank robbery over the weekend by the same five robbers. It was a small branch off the main bank. They made a clean getaway. They always used the same plan, in and out in about three minutes, drive a few blocks and have another car waiting. The car they used for the robbery was stolen.

Leroy met Ashley in the briefing room. She told him about the robbery. They will make a mistake on of these times and get caught."

"I hope it is soon before someone else gets killed."

"Tell me about your weekend." He told her everything except making love to Katherine. She knew he would do that if they were alone. "I can't believe you rented a good time van."

"Well we did and it was fun."

"Did you get to make love in the van?"

"Ashley that is something you don't ask."

"Why not, don't partners tell one another everything?"

He told her how they sneaked out of the house at night to make love in the van.

"Now that's more like it and yes, Jim and I made love over the weekend."

Sergeant O'Malley took the podium, "Ok, we have a lot to cover. As you know we had another robbery over the weekend and they got away. We don't have any leads, so ask around the area where we found the stolen car. Maybe someone saw them when they changed cars. We need help from the public. We have several cars reported stolen over the weekend. I have a list that you can pick up one on the way out. Leroy, Ashley, Frank, and Bill put on shorts and a t-shirt. All of you report to the training room for self-defense classes. Dismissed, go to work."

"Just what I needed," grumbled Leroy, "I haven't done this since the police academy. This is going to hurt."

Ashley said, "Don't worry I'll be easy on you."

They gathered around the instructor, "Well guys and gals are we ready for some fun?" They knew it wasn't going to be fun, more like hard knocks. "I'm going to show you some moves using each one of you to assist me. Who wants to go first?" Leroy thought he might as well get it over with. He stepped up. The instructor showed them the move and then told Leroy to attack as he gave him a knife. He went after the instructor, but found himself on the floor staring at the ceiling.

The instructor showed the other three moves and then did a number on them. "Ok, I'm going to pair you off to practice your moves. Leroy will work against Frank and Ashley against Bill." Leroy thought this is going to hurt, it did. Leroy won only one fall. He hurt all over. Ashley was good as she won all of her falls. She had been in self-defense classes for the last five years and it showed. The instructor said, "Very good Ashley, see you all again soon."

Leroy and Ashley showered and dressed to go on patrol. "I hurt all over," complained Leroy as he eased into the car.

"Poor baby, maybe we will have an easy day." Leroy was never that lucky. They gave a few tickets and it looked like it was going to be an easy day. About an hour before their shift was over, they spotted two men trying to break into a new Ford Mustang.

"Do we have to? Maybe it's their car."

"Get ready for a bust." She pulled in front of the Mustang just as they got the driver door open. Leroy and Ashley jumped out of the car.

"Hold it right there," warned Ashley. They turned and saw the Police, then took off running, one to the right and one to the left. "Oh no, not a foot race," moaned Leroy as he took off after the one on the right.

Ashley took off after the other one. Ashley chased him a couple of blocks before he turned down an alley. That was his mistake. He ran into an eight foot fence. He turned with a tool he was using to break in the car. He raised it to hit Ashley and that was his second mistake. She didn't draw her weapon. She stood her ground and waited for him to make the first move. He charged her with the tool over his head and the next moment he was on his back looking up at Ashley. She twisted his arm and turned him over with a knee in his back. Then she handcuffed him. She pulled him up and slammed him head first into the wall. She spread his legs, searched him and read him his rights. She turned him around and headed toward the Police car. He tried to struggle but Ashley slammed her fist in his side and that stopped that.

Meanwhile Leroy was having a hard time catching his man. They had run several blocks and Leroy had not gained on him at all. If he would turn around with a gun, he would have an excuse to draw his weapon, but he just kept running. He was increasing his lead on Leroy and he thought he was going to lose him, but as he ran down an alley, a car was making a turn and he ran out of the alley slamming into the car. Leroy caught the man while he was face down, handcuffed him and read him his rights. He stood him up against the car and searched him. He was clean, "I'm going to get you bitch."

Leroy slammed a fist into his side. "That's no way to talk to a lady." He glanced over at the lady. Katherine said, "Hi, fancy meeting you here."

"What are you doing here?"

"I was on my way back to the newspaper. What's going down?"

"This one and another one Ashley is chasing was trying to steal a car. We caught them in the act and I hope they are part of the ones doing all the car thefts."

Katherine followed Leroy back to the police car where Ashley had put her suspect in the back seat of the car. Katherine got out of her car, took pictures and got her story. As Leroy opened the car door to put his man in the car, his guy yelled at Katherine, "I'll get you for this."

Leroy quoted grimly, "You touch a hair on her head and you will deal with me, have a gun in your when you do."

"And just who are you pig?"

"Some people call me Dirty Harry. Now remember to have that gun in your hand when you face me or are you a back shooter?"

The man turned white when he heard the name. All the crooks had heard the name and seen him in the newspaper.

Ashley drove as they headed toward the Police station. "I don't like Katherine being involved with the bust. I think he meant what he said about getting Katherine."

"Maybe he is just a small time crook with a big mouth."

"I hope you are right, but I meant what I said. I love Katherine and he had better stay away from her."

They booked the men in to jail and went to fill out their reports. Captain Curry came in while they were working on their reports to tell them a job well done. He asked, "Do you think they are part of the car theft ring?"

"I don't know, but we should find out shortly." They had made their phone call and a big city lawyer was already there to bail them out. They were facing a fist full of charges and a big bond.

"They will be out by tomorrow," said Captain Curry. "We won't even get a chance to interrogate them before they are out." Leroy finished the report, signed it and passed it over to Ashley to sign.

"Well, was it worth it?" asked Leroy. "We put them in jail and before the ink is dry on the paper, they are out the front door."

"You're right, there is something wrong with the legal system, but how can we fix it?" Leroy and Ashley turned in their report and left to go home.

Leroy stopped at the grocery store to get some groceries. He was getting low on food. He wanted to check on Marie and John, so far they hadn't had any more trouble. News got around what happened to the last ones who tried to rob the store.

As Leroy pulled in front of his apartment and parked, he met Ann and her biker boyfriend coming out of her apartment. She had on shorts, a t-shirt with the bottom cut off showing her belly, and a new tattoo on her left leg. Her hair was red and green, a piece of art, but she still looked hot enough to light a guy's fire, with nice firm breasts, curves in all the right places and lips that begged to be kissed. The biker was a lucky man to have Ann.

"Haven't seen you much lately," said Ann. "I usually see you in the morning on the way to work."

"I went home for Thanksgiving and took an extra day."

"Teddy Bear got a job at a bike shot, so he won't be going on very many trips anymore. The bike shop is big, sells a lot of bikes and they repair what they sell. Plus anyone else that wants a bike fixed."

"I like fixing bikes and being home with Ann," said the biker boyfriend.

Leroy knew why he liked being home with Ann. She blushed when he looked at her. She knew what Leroy was thinking. Leroy wished him luck in his new job. They shook hands and Leroy turned to go in his apartment. When Leroy entered his apartment his answering machine was blinking. He had a bunch of calls on the machine.

Leroy fixed a ham and cheese sandwich, chips and beer to drink. He sat down to eat and answer his phone calls. The first one was from his mother which he called and they talked for a long time. She was still on the kick of him going back to college to be a lawyer. Maybe it wasn't a bad idea if he got married and had kids. Now where did that thought come from?

His next call was from Rex wanting to know when he wanted to go out again, forget that, only if they went out to eat. The next call was from Mike thanking him and Katherine for coming to see them, which they enjoyed their company very much. The last call was from Katherine. She was out of town on assignment and wouldn't be back for a couple of days.

He finished his dinner and decided to take a shower and go to bed early. Well he could at least dream about Katherine. He hated it when they didn't get to see each for long periods of time. Someday he was going to fix that, maybe go back to college and become a lawyer. It was something he thought about more and more. Just maybe his mother was right to want him to go back to college, but first he had to save the money to go back and on his small paycheck it was going to take some time.

He met Ashley in briefing next day and she could tell something was wrong. "What's wrong with you?"

"Nothing a good pay raise wouldn't fix," he replied. "I think I want to go back to college and it takes a lot of money."

"You could get a part time job or maybe a grant."

"I just might do that."

As they were leaving they met the two punks they put in Jail yesterday leaving the station. "Well, if it isn't the two pigs that put us in jail yesterday."

Ashley caught Leroy by the shirt, "Let it go. We'll see them again, once a thief, always a thief."

As they were on their way out, Sergeant O'Malley spotted them, "Leroy, report to the self- defense class for more training. You need some more sessions to bring you up to par."

"Well just what I needed to start the day," grumbled Leroy.

"Poor baby, think how bad you will be when they finish with you."

"If I live through it, I had rather use my weapon than this self- defense. I'm good with it."

"Yes, but sometimes you can't draw your weapon like yesterday."

"You have made your point, but I still don't want to go. What if they put me with a girl and she beats me? I'll be embarrassed to show my face. They call me Dirty Harry and I get beat by a girl. That would be too much.

"I'll pick you up in a couple of hours." Ashley would cruise the schools for a couple of hours looking for drug dealers while Leroy got his butt kicked.

When Ashley picked Leroy up a couple of hours later, he looked like a whipped puppy. "Did you get your butt kicked by a girl?"

"Yes, how did you know?"

"They have to do better to make them look as good as men."

"I hope I don't get that girl again, she tried to break my neck."

Ashley pulled out into traffic and started to patrol. They gave a few tickets, but all and all the day was slow and easy. "Don't say it warned Ashley."

"Say what?"

"Every time you say we are going to have an easy day something happens. We still have an hour to go on our shift."

Five minutes later car10 called for backup. They were after two men trying to steal a car. "Are you thinking what I'm thinking?" asked Leroy.

"No it couldn't be the same two that got out this morning." When they arrived at the crime scene, none other than the same ones caught yesterday were there. Leroy got out and strapped on his Colt 45. "All of you stand down, this scumbag is all mine." One was on the other side of the car, while big mouth was standing in front of the car with a woman as a human shield. "I'll cut her if you come any closer."

Leroy stopped, "That's alright, I think I'm close enough, last chance to give up."

"Forget it you fat pig."

"I thought so. Ma'am did you read about the woman in the bank robbery?" She nodded her head. "Spread your legs." As she spread her legs Leroy pulled his Colt 45 and fired. She had on a dress. The bullet passed about two inches below her buttocks striking the man in his right leg too close to his balls. The impact took him back and he fell to the ground screaming. He dropped the knife.

Leroy said, "Call an ambulance, I think he needs to go to the hospital." He dropped his Colt 45 back into his holster. "Are you alright Ma'am?"

She ran over hugged him and kissed him. The two police took over and Ashley came over to tease Leroy, "You have caught the bad guys and kissed the girl, can we go home now." The lady left in her car while car 10 took the two suspects to the hospital.

Ashley drove pulling the car into traffic and headed back to the Police station. "You know something? That lady will never get rid of that dress with the hole just two inches below her buttocks. That will be a show and tell to her kids and grandchildren, how you put a bullet between her legs and took out the bad guy."

"I have a confession to make I couldn't see the bad guy's legs when I took the shot. What if he had his legs spread?"

"No problem, then you would have shot his balls off." Leroy looked at Ashley and laughed. "I never thought of that, provided they were large and hung down low."

They arrived back at the Police station and Captain Curry was waiting for them. "Good job again. I think we will be able to hold them long enough to interrogate them this time. The dispatcher already told the story how you took the guy out. They are at the hospital getting him patched up. The bullet went through the flesh and didn't hit anything, so we should have him back here and booked shortly."

Captain Curry scratched his head. "The two of you amaze me the things you get into and get out of. You always come out on top."

Ashley laughed, "It is never boring riding with Leroy. Trouble follows him around like a little black cloud."

"Well you two watch your back. You have a lot of enemies in the short time you have been here."

"We will sir," replied Leroy.

They did their report and filed it. Leroy asked, "Do you think somebody may put out a hit on us?"

"Yes, it has been done several times over the years."

"Maybe you should change partners. I don't want to be the one that gets you hurt. If I do Jim will kill me."

"No way, you are stuck with me. I like being your partner, besides I'm the only one who wants to be your partner. Everyone says you take too many chances. They call you a maverick because you don't go by the rules.

"I have never liked the rules. My rule is rules are made to be broken."

"I had always gone by the rules until I became your partner. Now I don't care when we break the rules because some of them is stupid anyway."

"Let's go home," said Leroy.

The next day Leroy had to go to self – defense training again. "How did you do this time?" asked Ashley when he got in the car.

"I won two out of the five falls today."

"That's better, but do you want me to teach you how to kick ass?"

"That would be good, but when would you have time to teach me?"

"How about we stay thirty minutes in the evening and work out?"

"Sounds good but what about Jim?"

"No problem, we never get home at the same time."

They went to high school to give lectures on car safety and drugs all day. Leroy stayed in the background and handed Ashley things as she talked. He ran the slide projector and movie projector for her. Ashley was good since she had been doing it for a long time and a lot of the kids knew her so it was easy for her to get through to them.

Back at the station they went into the training room. "I'll change and meet you in a few minutes," said Leroy.

"No don't change, we are going to work out like we are in the street and attacked by scumbags."

"You are breaking the rules," he argued. "And if we get caught we are in trouble."

"Ashley laughed, "Since when did you worry about rules?"

They took the bullets out of their weapons for safety. Ashley instructed him, "We are going to do what we do on the street. Pull your weapon to shoot me or attack me. I don't want to know what you are doing."

This is going to hurt he thought as he pulled his weapon. She stepped sideways knocking his arm away from her one hand, grabbing the barrel and twisting out of one hand, holding the barrel while twisting the gun out of his hand with the other.

"It has to be quick, the first move deflects the gun, so it fired by me and second move you twist the gun this way to break his fingers, but I didn't go that far with you."

"Thanks, it would be hard to explain my broken fingers at briefing tomorrow."

"I'm sure you will come up with something. Ok try it again." They did several more times before Ashley was satisfied he was good at it.

"Ok let's move on."

They faced each other again. "Ok try something," she said. Leroy attacked her and hit the floor hard. Captain Curry was on his way home when he heard the noise in the training room. He walked in while Leroy was still on the floor. They turned and stared at him. Ashley said, "Leroy fell down."

Captain Curry sighed, "I don't want to know what is going on." He turned around, left then and went on home.

After he was gone, Leroy and Ashley laughed out loud. "Did you see his face? He knew we were doing something wrong, but he didn't want to catch us," giggled Ashley. "Like I said there's never a dull moment when I'm with you."

Ashley showed him what to do when attacked with a knife, front assault or rear assault. After thirty minutes he was doing well and he thought he could take her. Laying on his back starring at her, he thought maybe next time.

The next day he had to go to self – defense training again. Afterwards as he got in the car, he was grinning ear to ear, "I won five falls out of five today. Thanks for the instructions."

"A little more training and you will be able to take on anybody. Now it's time to earn our paycheck," grinned Ashley as she pulled out into traffic.

CHAPTER FOUR

Two weeks until Christmas:

Leroy met Ashley in briefing. He asked, "Are you ready for Christmas?"

"No, I haven't even started yet and I hate last minute shopping."

"I'm not spending much this year since I decided to go back to college."

Ashley said, "Someday I want to do something else with my life, I just don't know what, but I don't want to be a Policewoman all my life."

Sergeant O'Malley took the podium, "Short and sweet today, all crime is up as always close to Christmas. Shoplifting as usual is number one so stay on the lookout for them. Hit the road."

Leroy drove out into traffic. They got a call before they got a block away from the station. An eighteen- wheeler was turned over blocking the road. Leroy said, "It's going to be one of those days." Ashley told the dispatcher they were en route to the scene. The driver was out of the truck, but traffic was a mess. Ashley called for two big wreckers while Leroy directed traffic around the truck. He knew it would take a long time to clear this wreckage.

Meanwhile a bank robbery was going down in downtown Dallas. Ashley came over and told Leroy what was going on. The first wrecker arrived and Ashley directed him in place to pull the truck back over. The second wrecker pulled in and got in place. It would take two wreckers to turn the eight-wheeler back over. When they were ready they started to pull the truck back over.

The eighteen-wheeler was easy to turn back over with two big wreckers. A city street truck pulled up with four men to clean up the mess. One wrecker hooked on to the truck and towed it away. As soon as the street was clean, Leroy stepped out of the way and let traffic flow normal. It was almost noon before they finished with the accident. Leroy pulled back out into traffic, "Did they catch the bank robbers?"

"No, they are still in the bank and have hostages. They killed the girl that set off the alarm. They are sending in a negotiator now to find out if they can end this without more bloodshed."

They pulled into McDonald's for lunch. They watched as the standoff continued on television while they ate lunch. "That was a bad move sending a negotiator into the bank. He is at their mercy without a weapon. I wouldn't step foot in that bank without my Colt 45."

"But maybe he can talk them into giving up." argued Ashley.

"This kind, the only thing they understand is kill or be killed. They will never give up."

They got back in their car and pulled out into traffic. Ashley said, "I'm glad I'm not calling the shots on this one.

"Who is calling the shots?"

"The Police Chief himself."

"Oh my God, they just killed the negotiator," Ashley said grimly. "They didn't like him. They are going to kill a hostage in one hour if they don't get what they want. Leroy asked, "What do they want?"

"They want the money, five female hostages to keep them company, a car to take them to the airport and a plane to fly them out of the country."

"The Chief will never go for that. It would be like sending the hostages to their death."

"But what can he do?"

Leroy replied, "It's a catch twenty two, someone is going to die. If they storm the bank, hostages will get killed in the cross fire."

"What would you do?" asked Ashley.

Leroy thought about it so long she thought he wasn't going to answer. "I would strap on my Colt 45 and go in to negotiate."

"You are crazy?"

"Maybe I am sometimes, but I don't see any other way."

"They would kill you."

Leroy glanced at her, "They probably would."

"And you would still do it." "Yes"

The Police Chief knew he was between a rock and a hard place. He didn't know what to do. Then he thought about the Newspaper, Harry, Harry, Harry, that's it. He called Captain Curry. "Bill I got a big problem and I need help. For the first time in my life I don't know what to do."

"Chief you do have a big problem, but how can I help?"

"Tell me about the man you call Dirty Harry."

"You mean Leroy Cooper."

"Yes, that's his name."

"Leroy breaks all the rules. He makes his own and you don't ever want to face him with that Colt 45 in his hand, because he doesn't miss. He is a maverick and does it his way, but he gets the job done. His partner Ashley and Leroy make a crazy pair."

The Chief thought about it for a minute. "Bill it sounds like just what I need. Send them to me at the bank."

"Are you sure?"

"I'm sure. Get them here as soon as possible."

Captain Curry called Leroy and Ashley, "The Chief wants you two at the bank now."

Leroy turned on the lights and siren. "I told you it was going to be one of those days."

"Ashley asked, "What do you think the Chief wants?"

"You know what he wants. He has run out of options, he will want me to go in. That's what he wants me to do."

"Then I'm going in with you."

"No you're not you're not up to killing people like I wasn't up to self-defense."

Ashley was scared to death, she wasn't going to let Leroy go in alone, but he just didn't know it.

Leroy pulled up in front of the bank. They got out of the car and Leroy strapped on his Colt 45. They left their hats in the car. They walked over to the Chief. "Any change?" asked Leroy.

The Chief looked grimly at Leroy and Ashley, They killed a hostage. They were to wait an hour like they said they would, but they didn't."

"They are like mad dogs, kill or be killed, replied Leroy.

"Now we will have to storm the bank."

"No sir, give me fifteen minutes to negotiate."

"They won't negotiate. They killed our negotiator."

Leroy put his hand on his Colt 45, "You haven't seen me negotiate.

"Are you sure you want to do this?"

"It's the only way."

As Leroy turned to go in the bank, Katherine blocked his path. "You aren't going in there because I love you. There has to be another way."

Leroy pulled her into his arms and kissed her hard. "I love you to, but this is the only way to do this, I'm sorry."

Leroy turned from her and started into the bank. He glanced back to see her covered with other reporters wanting to know about her and Leroy. Katherine was crying her eyes out. Ashley slipped her bulletproof vest on under her coat and followed Leroy. At the front door they stopped.

Leroy told her, "You kill anyone that comes out that door with a gun in his hand. Do not hesitate or they will kill you."

Jim, Ashley's husband was in his office watching the scene on television. "Oh my God, that's my wife at the door of the bank." He jumped up and ran for the door.

Leroy turned to go in the bank. He walked into the bank like he owned the place and came face to face with five gunmen. The leader asked, "What do you think you are doing?" They stood around lazy. Only one man wasn't much of a threat.

"I'm here to negotiate," said Leroy.

They laughed, "I guess they finally know we mean business."

"No, I'm here to tell you how it is going down. We can do it the easy way or the hard way."

The leader laughed again, "You got balls, but we are five to one."

"No, but I will kill three of you on the way down and big mouth, you are the first one I will kill." "Who are you?"

"Some people call me Dirty Harry because I'm like the one in the movies."

"That made the leader nervous because he knew the name from the newspapers. Ashley eased up beside Leroy, "Make that five to two."

"Leroy glanced at Ashley, "Now."

They both slapped leather at the same time catching the robbers by surprise. Ashley hit the man on the left in the chest and he went down. Leroy hit the leader right between the eyes.

He was dead before he hit the floor. Ashley hit her second man in the chest, but he fired the same time with an automatic weapon hitting her in the chest and her left leg. They both went down. Leroy had taken out his second man with a shot to the chest. He glanced at Ashley as she went down. The last man fired and hit Leroy in the left shoulder, spinning him around. He kept firing and killed the last man. Leroy passed out from shock.

People came running out the front of the bank. A man came up and told the Chief everyone was down in there, but he didn't know how many was dead. The Police stormed the bank alone with the paramedics. Jim came running up just in time to catch Katherine as she fainted. A paramedic ran over and gave Katherine smelling salts. She came to and stared at Jim.

"Are they dead?"

"I don't know?"

The paramedics found all the robbers dead and turned their full attention on Ashley. She was not breathing. They pulled her coat off and seen the bullet in her bulletproof vest. They pulled the vest off and opened her shirt. A paramedic slapped her in the chest and she started breathing.

"Ok this one is going to be alright. She had the wind knocked out of her, but the vest saved her life. "How is the other one?"

The other paramedic said, "He took a hit to the shoulder, but the bullet went on through without hitting anything. He is in shock, but he should come around soon. How is the girl's leg?"

"It is just a flesh wound. She is going to be alright. She will have a black and blue chest where the bullet hit her vest, but it will fade."

They put her on a stretcher and carried her out to the ambulance. They put Leroy on a stretcher and followed. They had been bringing body bags out. Jim and Katherine were going crazy. When they came out with the first stretcher, Jim and Katherine rushed over to the ambulance.

Ashley smiled at Jim, "We killed all the bad guys. Leroy kisses all the girls. Do I get a kiss from the guys?"

Jim was so mad he didn't know if he wanted to kiss her or kill her. He pulled her into his arms and kissed her.

"Ashley, don't you scare me like that ever again."

Ashley said, "I couldn't let my partner face them alone. He is good, but I knew he couldn't take five of them by himself."

They came out with the second stretcher and Katherine turned her attention to Leroy. He was still unconscious. She started to cry. The paramedic told Katherine that Leroy would be all right. He was just in shock. She broke down and Jim came over to confront her.

"Come on, let's go to the hospital and wait." The ambulance took off and they followed.

When the ambulance arrived at the hospital, they took both of them to emergency to be patched up. They finished with Ashley first. As she was being moved to a room, she said, "You will put both of us in the same room, we are partners and where he goes I go with him.

Leroy finally came to and opened his eyes. "Where is Ashley, is she dead?"

Doctor Jones said, "She is alright, but we have to patch you up."

When they were finished with Leroy, the orderly was told to take him to Ashley's room. As He entered, Ashley said, "What took you so long?"

"You are a maverick and I told you to wait outside."

"What, and let you have all the fun. I got to kiss the guy," she giggled, "And you haven't been kissed yet."

The Doctor came to the waiting room and said they could have visitors, family members only. Katherine told the nurse, "I'm his wife," she lied and went to his room. When Katherine and Jim entered the room, Ashley and Leroy were laughing, but turned their attention to them.

Jim stared at Ashley, "You two don't look sick to me and what's so funny?"

Ashley giggled, "I got my kiss, but Leroy didn't get kissed."

"What is with this kissing?" asked Jim.

"Ask Katherine, she knows all about it."

Katherine blushed and looked at Leroy. He held one arm open and Katherine ran to the bed. She lay down beside Leroy and kissed him.

"I think is against hospital rules," stated Jim.

"Leroy and I never follow rules because we make them up as we go along," laughed Ashley.

They had a good laugh.

The door opened and Captain Curry entered followed by the Police Chief. Captain Curry laughed, "Didn't I tell you these two never follow rules. I'll bet Leroy told Ashley to stay outside the bank, am I right?"

Ashley explained, "Yes sir he did, but I couldn't let him have all the fun."

Katherine eased out of bed and sat in the chair next to Leroy. The Chief said to Katherine, "I see how you get your story first hand." She stared at the Chief, "Oh no, I didn't turn in a story on the biggest story in Dallas. I will probably get fired. I forgot to turn one in. I was so worried about Leroy."

"Don't worry about it, we'll fix it," said Leroy.

The Chief told Leroy and Ashley how much the city of Dallas owes them, plus the lives they saved.

The Chief said, "You will get metals, but that doesn't seem like much for what you have done. Is there anything you want besides my job?"

Leroy glanced at Ashley, "There is something I want."

The Chief replied, "Name it and it's yours."

Leroy stared at the Chief and Captain Curry. "I would like to be a Detective and work all types of cases."

"No problem, you got it."

"And Ashley will be a Detective as my partner."

The Chief laughed, "I knew that was coming, she goes where you go. Where do you want to work out of?"

"Leroy and Ashley looked at Captain Curry, "Out of the same Police station, if it's ok with Captain Curry."

Captain Curry laughed, "And I thought I was getting rid of you two."

The Chief said, "Well now it is official. You will report back to Bill when you get out of the hospital. Come on Bill time to leave and let them get back to what they were doing when we walked in."

As soon as they were gone Leroy and Ashley let out a yell. They tried the names on for size. "They are crazy, "said Jim, as a nurse walked in. They were told to be quiet, that this was a hospital not a playground.

Leroy handed Katherine the phone, "Call your boss at the newspaper. I'll be right here to fix your problem." She trusted him to do just that.

"Katherine, where have you been? The biggest story to hit Dallas in years and we had nothing. "I'm sorry, but I'm at the hospital. I can fix everything with the inside scoop on the shoot out and another thing that happened after the shoot out here at the hospital.

"You can do all of that?"

"Yes, I'm sitting beside the man of the hour. And by now I'm sure you know that he is my boyfriend from the other reporters. Ashley and her husband are our best friends. I'll get you play by play how it went down in the bank and the Police Chief just left here. He promoted Leroy and Ashley to Detective. I'll have you the story before press time."

"Is everything fixed?"

"My boss is beside himself," laughed Katherine, "He can't believe he is getting the story. We will be the only newspaper to carry the story."

Katherine crawled back in bed with Leroy to cuddle with him. She kissed him again and ran her tongue deep into his mouth. "I love you," she sighed.

A nurse opened the door, "I'm sure you do, but you will have to do it later because visiting hours are over."

Katherine slowly got out of bed, she wanted to stay, but she had a story to write. Jim and Katherine left as the nurse stayed to be sure they were gone.

Two days later they were released from the hospital, Leroy with his arm in a sling and Ashley with a slight limp, Leroy and Katherine went home with Ashley and Jim. They wanted to celebrate just being alive and being promoted to Detective. They ordered take- out and beer.

Ashley said, "To us, may we never try that stunt again because life is too short."

"Here, here," replied Jim.

CHAPTER FIVE

Katherine looked at Leroy, "I'm sleepy so can we go home now?"

Ashley glanced at Jim and smiled, they knew why Katherine wanted to go home and it wasn't to sleep. Leroy and Ashley had the next day off. Katherine took off from the newspaper to spend some time with Leroy. They could do without her for one day. Leroy was more important to her than the newspaper.

Katherine pulled in and parked. She helped Leroy out of the car. His shoulder was still hurting him some. She opened the front door and pulled him in. "We finally got some time to ourselves," purred Katherine.

"I'm sleepy," teased Leroy.

"Do you think they bought it?"

"No they knew exactly why we came home."

"Then let's not waste time," she whispered as she led him into the bedroom. Katherine slowly removed Leroy from his clothes, trying not to hurt his shoulder. He lay down on the bed as Katherine removed her clothes and stood naked before him. She got in bed and straddled him.

"Be careful with me," teased Leroy.

She slowly raised her buttocks to give him room for his big erection to enter her softness. He was so big and her so small that she was amazed how she sheathed all of him. She started to move up and down while Leroy groaned at the pleasure she was giving him. She was slippery and that made it easy to pick up the pace. Katherine knew she was stretched to the limit, but she didn't care since it felt so good.

"Slow down honey, we got all night."

"We can slow down next time. I need it fast the first time because I'm burning up."

Leroy thought she would kill him with pleasure. She was so hot he thought they would burst into flames. She was bouncing up and down as her breasts bounced with her. Leroy grabbed a nipple with each hand and squeezed them. It made her go faster and faster. The evocative sensation drove her crazy and she exploded, her juices running down his shaft. Katherine collapsed on his chest. She squeezed his throbbing shaft and he came deep in her softness. Finally she rolled off and lay on her back exhausted and contented. Katherine had never felt so good. She turned over and Leroy snuggled up to her spoon fashion. They went to sleep.

The next morning Leroy woke up first with a big erection which he eased into her hot folds. He pushed slowly until she had it all. He lay still enjoying the pleasure of her hot passion. Finally she woke up to what she thought was dream, but realized it was real and felt so good. "I want to lie here all day and enjoy the pleasure you are giving me so don't move, just lay still."

"I can lay passive until you start to squeeze and then it's over."

Leroy thought he had control of his body, but his erection starting throbbing and he knew quiet time was over.

Katherine giggled, "You lied, I thought you said you could control your body."

"Sorry I thought I could, but you are so hot."

Leroy grabbed her hips and slammed deep and hard with a surge of satisfaction. He pulled her buttocks up in the air so he could go deeper. She moaned and cried his name as spasm after spasm racked her body. Leroy couldn't hold back any longer, with his final thrust he came and held her until she squeezed him dry.

"What are we going to do today?" asked Katherine.

"I thought I would take you Christmas shopping and then we could eat out."

"Sounds good to me, but we need to take a shower." They took a shower together and dressed.

The stores we full to the brim with shoppers. They went to a coffee shop for coffee and a donut to hold them until lunch. They didn't buy much, it was just fun being together.

Leroy took Katherine to a Steak and Ale for lunch. They entered into a hall with a podium. They elected a nonsmoking area. They passed a salad bar as they were seated in a divided off section. The whole restaurant was dived off to make it more private. Leroy ordered a New York strip and a baked potato. Katherine had shrimp and fries. They both went to the salad bar. They each had ale to drink. They took their time eating since they had all day.

Leroy had left his sling in the car and his shoulder was starting to hurt. He put his hand in his shirt and used it as a sling on the way out to the car. "I guess I took the sling off too soon."

They went to get Leroy's car so he could take it home. It had been in the Police parking lot since the day he was shot. Katherine followed him back to his apartment. They lounged around until after dark. They had made love a couple more times. They sat on the couch and cuddled. Leroy said, "Why don't we move in together?"

That was not what Katherine wanted to hear. She knew he loved her, but she wanted more. "Why didn't he ask her to marry him?"

She teased, "Move in together and mess up a good thing, I don't think so."

Leroy knew the sound of her voice, he had hurt her. She wouldn't be a live in girlfriend. He loved her so why didn't he ask her to marry him? He didn't think he was ready to take that step yet, but how could he explain that to her.

Katherine said, ""I got to go, I have to get up early tomorrow," she lied.

Leroy walked her to her car and kissed her. When she drove off, he could tell she was hurting, but what had he done, he loved her? Too late to cry over spilt milk. He would have to fix it later.

They wouldn't get to see one another for a long time with the hours they worked. Leroy would have to think of a way to mend fences, but he didn't sleep well that night. Katherine went home crying, she thought he would ask her to marry him. Well she would just have to play the game and let things play out. She was in love with so what else could she do? Why did love have to hurt so much? Ashley waited in the parking lot for Leroy. When he arrived she met him at his car. "I didn't want to go in by myself."

Ashley had on a skirt and blouse. Leroy had on dress pants and a dress shirt. They didn't have to wear a uniform anymore and felt out of place. They didn't have their weapons on and felt naked. Leroy said, "Let's do it."

They walked in the front door and were met by a round of applause. Captain Curry came over to welcome them back to the Police station. He said, "Follow me."

He led them over to an office. On the door was painted Detective Lewis and Detective Cooper. There were two desks, chairs, filing cabinets and a large black board to plot their cases on. It gives me great pleasure to give these to you." He handed them their new badges. "And something else a Detective should have," as he handed them each an ankle holster and a small pistol. Captain glanced at Ashley, "I guess you won't be wearing yours today."

Ashley laughed, "I'll find a way to carry it." They could carry their weapons any way they wanted to.

"There is a stack of files on the cabinet. Take your choice and when you finish those cases there are plenty more. Meet Detectives Joe Boswell, Doug Masters in homicide, Chris Wade, Megan Harris in drugs and prostitution." All the Detectives had filled into the office to greet them.

Captain Curry said, "All of you will be working together some time or another." Detective Lewis knew everybody and Leroy knew them by their faces. "I'll leave and let you get to work."

Leroy said, "This is our battle room and anyone can use anything here. We share information on a case. Lewis and I don't go by the rules as you probably know by now. They call Lewis and I mavericks, but we get the job done. Going by the rules is up to you."

The Detectives looked at each other. They weren't used to working with people like Leroy and Ashley. "One rule and it will not be broken. You will always cover your partner's back. If it weren't for Ashley I would be dead because I could never have taken five gunmen. She came in and made it five to two. She took out two while I took out three."

"I was scared to death, but I couldn't let Leroy take on all five men," said Ashley.

"You got balls," said Masters, "Sorry Lewis bad choice of words." Everyone laughed.

Ashley replied, "No problem, wait until you have been around Cooper, he will grow on you and he always protects his partner. Nobody wants to be his partner because they are afraid he will get them killed."

"But how do you step in when you know you might die?"

"Someone has to do it," explained Leroy.

"Now we know why they call you Dirty Harry."

All the Detectives left to work on their cases. Ashley spread all the cases out on her desk. "Well Detective Cooper, which case do you want to work on first?"

"Let's pick an easy one to start with."

Leroy picked up a folder on a missing little girl of six years old. He scanned the file and smiled, "We'll take this one today. It should be easy."

"How can you tell?"

"Call it a gut feeling."

"What do we use for wheels?" asked Ashley. Their car had been picked up at the bank after they were taken to the hospital.

As they left the office, Captain Curry pitched a set of keys to Leroy. "I forgot to give you your keys. They are for the unmarked car out front. Are you on your way out on your first case?"

"Yes sir, we're going looking for a lost little girl."

"Good luck, sometimes those are the hardest cases."

They found a brand new Crown Victoria in front of the station. "Wow that can't be our car," said Ashley, but it was their car.

Leroy took the first turn driving. "Where to?" she asked.

"To the Home Savings and Loan, that is where the Mother works." Leroy pulled into the parking lot, "You do the talking and I'll join in."

Mrs. Barnes worked in the loan department. She was sick with worry about her little girl Mary Ann.

Ashley said, "I need to ask you a few questions." They sat across from Mrs. Barnes. I need to know the addresses of your ex-husband, his parents, grandparents and friends, also telephone numbers. Leroy took notes while Ashley asked the questions.

"Can you find my little girl?"

"We hope so," replied Leroy. "Has anyone called about a ransom?"

"No not so far."

"That could be good news or bad news. Good news if it was a relative or friend and bad news if it was a child predator or a pervert."

"How old is the little girl?"

"She is six years old."

"Where did you last see her?"

"The school bus driver said he dropped her off in front of the house, but she never came in the house. I heard the bus stop and drive off, but after a few minutes when she didn't come in the house I went to check on her and she was gone."

"How many days has she been missing?"

"Four days."

Leroy said, May I ask you a couple of personnel Questions?"

"If it will help find my little girl, yes ask away."

"Why did you leave your husband?"

"What kind of question is that and how can it help find my little girl?"

'You never know, but then again it could give us a lead."

"I let him for cheating on me. He got drunk at a party and I found him in bed with my best friend."

"How drunk was he?"

"I don't know."

"You know sometimes when a person is drunk they do some crazy things."

"Where you having troubles at the time?"

'Yes maybe a little."

"When was the last time you had sex?"

"You are crazy. I don't have to answer that."

"That could explain why he looked for love someplace else. Do you still love your husband?"

"Yes," and she started to cry.

Leroy looked at Ashley, "I think we have enough."

They stood up and started to leave. Leroy went and hugged the woman. "How would you like to come with us and look for your little girl?"

"I can do that, but isn't it against the rules to go with you?"

Ashley laughed, "We never go by any rules."

Mrs. Barnes talked to her boss and got the rest of the day off. She couldn't believe she was with them looking for her little girl. Leroy said, "You drive, I want to make some phone calls with this new car phone."

"Where to?" asked Ashley.

"Let's go to Denton." On the way to Denton, Leroy called her ex-husband, his parents, his grandmother, and some close friends. He didn't tell them they were on their way to Denton. He wanted to get their reaction to the little girl missing.

Leroy asked, "Do you have a picture of your little girl?"

Mrs. Barnes fished around in her purse for a picture and gave it to Leroy.

"We're going to grandmother's house," and he gave her the address.

"Why are we going to grandmother's house?"

"Call it that gut feeling."

Ashley pulled up in front of a small two-story brick house with a white picket fence, several mall trees and flowerbeds full of red roses. Leroy instructed, "You talk to grandmother while I have a look see. Keep her turned away from the door."

Mrs. Barnes couldn't believe what they were going to do, no search warrant or anything. "Yes I know you don't follow rules."

'You stay in the car for now," instructed Leroy.

Ashley got out of the car and walked upon a large porch where she rang the doorbell. A gray haired lady came to the door and wanted to know what she wanted. Ashley told her who she was and she was looking for a little girl. The lady came out on the porch and followed Ashley over to some chairs. Ashley took the chair facing the door and the lady took the chair facing Ashley. She noticed the grandmother was very nervous, so she took her time asking questions.

Leroy eased out of the car and made a run for the door. He eased the door open and went inside. The living room had nice warm furniture. It had the homey lived in look. Leroy saw a doll in one corner and smiled. He was getting warm. He slowly walked up the stairs. He heard someone talking, glancing in the room a little girl was talking to her doll. He pulled out the picture and looked at it. Bingo, he had found the little girl. Leroy walked in and sat down on the floor next to the little girl. "Your Mamma is downstairs and she wants to see you very much."

"Oh goody, is Daddy there to?"

"Not yet, but I have a feeling he will be here soon."

They got to their feet and Leroy led her down the stairs out onto the porch. A car pulled up and a man got out and rushed over. The little girl ran to him and he took her in his arms. Ashley came down and confronted the man. "You have your daughter without the Mother's permission." Tears sprang into his eyes, "I just wanted some time with her. I love her so much. I was going to bring her back to her Mother."

The Grandmother said, "I told you not to take her, it was wrong."

"I just wanted to see her and hold her."

The little girl said, "It's alright Grandma, I love Mommy and Daddy. I want to be with both of them."

Mrs. Barnes stepped out of the car and walked toward them. She had seen enough and there was only one thing to do. "Would you like to see your Daughter all the time?"

"Yes, I would do anything you want."

"It's very simple, come home."

"Do you want me to come home?"

"Yes, I need you and our Daughter needs you."

Mrs. Barnes came over, kissed Leroy on the cheek and hugged him, "Thank you."

Leroy smiled at Ashley, "I think this case is closed."

"Would you like a ride back to Dallas?" asked Ashley.

"No thank you, I will ride back with my Husband and Daughter."

Ashley teased, "You got your kiss, now can we go home?" Ashley drove as they headed back to Dallas. "Why were you so sure the Grandmother was hiding the little girl?"

"When I made the phone calls everyone seemed normal, but when I talked to the Grandmother she was nervous and didn't give direct answers like she was hiding something or didn't want to lie."

"You didn't believe she was in danger or you wouldn't have asked Mrs. Barnes to ride along with us."

"No, but I could have been wrong. It was just a gut feeling." Back at the Police station they wrote up their report and turned it in along with the file marked case closed. Captain Curry took the report and smiled at them. "You didn't let any grass grow under your feet."

"That case was fun and we got a family back together," explained Ashley.

CHAPTER SIX

"I hate to bust your bubble, but we had a girl missing and car theft reported today." He handed Ashley the report, "That goes with the file you have already."

"Let me see that picture," said Leroy, "I know that girl. She is my next door neighbor." He read the report and saw that her biker boyfriend reported her and her car missing. Leroy glanced at Captain Curry, "Don't even think the biker harmed her. He is just a big teddy bear."

Captain Curry said, "I want you to start on this file tomorrow. I know it won't be easy, but we got to find out where the cars and girls are going. They are either chopping the cars up for parts or taking them out of the country, but what are they doing with the girls?"

Leroy said, 'I got a bad jut feeling we are going to find a lot of bodies."

"Well you two get a good night's sleep and start fresh in the morning."

As Leroy and Ashley walked to their cars, He said, "I think we have a hard row to hoe."

"We're not going to like this one," replied Ashley.

As Leroy drove to his apartment he couldn't get Ann off his mind, He was afraid she was dead already. He was mad and wanted to get his hands on the one that hurt her. She was a little crazy, but she was good people and never hurt anyone. Why couldn't they just take the car and go?"

Leroy didn't sleep much that night. He swore he would catch the ones that hurt her and make them pay. He would become Dirty Harry on this case and do whatever it took to get the scumbags. Ashley met Leroy in their office the next day. He looked as mean as a pit bull. Boy what an attitude.

"I can see this is going to be one of those days," said Ashley.

"Probably so, but I have been working on a battle plan for this operation. First of all I don't think the cars are being taken out of the country because they have never caught one being shipped."

"Maybe they have a good system to get them out of the country."

"Maybe, but they should have caught at least one. I'm going to put a list on the board and we will check out each item for a lead."

"How do you want to start?"

"First we can't work all the cases at one time so let's take the last five missing cars and women. We will try to see if anything ties them together. I'll put the list on the board and we can start contacting the person who called in the missing report. Would you write the names and car on the board? You write better than I do."

"I think you are just lazy," she teased. Ashley put the list on the board. Kelly Ellis –Mercury, Brittney Brooks – Ford Crown Victoria, Tammy Lewis – Plymouth, Sharron Wilson – Cadillac and Ann Mitchell – Thunder Bird.

Leroy had notes to describe each car and id number. He had a picture of each missing woman. "Now comes the hard part, they live all over Dallas, you can drive since you know Dallas better than I do."

The first one on the list was Kelly Ellis. She lived in a nice area in Mesquite. She lived at home with her Mother and Father. They reported her missing. The house was a large brick home with a nice manicured lawn. "You ask the questions while I take notes," instructed Leroy.

Mrs. Ellis answered the door and asked them in. She started to cry when Ashley told her why they were there. Ashley explained they were on the case and wanted to start from the beginning. She asked the standard questions, what was she wearing, was she with someone, did she have a boyfriend, was she in college, how long had she been missing? Did she know where she went that day?

Ashley said, "I guess that will be all for now, but if you remember anything please give us a call."

They got almost to their car when Mrs. Ellis called them back. "I remember Kelly had tickets to the Renaissance south of Dallas, but I don't know if she used them."

Leroy wrote in his notebook. "Thank you Mrs. Ellis, we'll be in touch." He gave Ashley the address for Brittany Brooks. It was in Dallas. Ashley pulled into a circle drive of a large mansion that looked big enough for a King.

"Dream on catfish," teased Leroy.

A butler met them at the door and showed them in. The living room was big enough to fit the Dallas Cowboy football team in and have space left over. Ashley stared at the furniture as the butler led them into the study. It had shelves and shelves of books. Mr. Brooks stood up from behind a large oak desk. "How may I help you?"

Ashley said, "We would like to ask you some questions about your missing Daughter."

Mr. Brooks looked at them with a sad look and motioned for them to sit down in the big over stuffed leather chairs. "I told the Police everything I know."

"We are new on the case and would like to go over it again if you don't mind."

"I'll do anything to help find my Brittany."

Mrs. Brooks came in as Ashley started to ask the standard questions. Britney was in her second year of college and had a boyfriend. "Could he be involved with her missing?" asked Mrs. Brooks.

Leroy asked, "Is he a nice boy?"

"Yes, Britney loves him," confirmed Mrs. Brooks.

Leroy said, "I don't think he had anything to do with her missing. I think it was her car. I think it was a car hijacking." He didn't want to tell them what he thought happen to their Daughter, but he knew they would ask. Mrs. Brooks started to cry. "What happen to Brittany? What did they do with her?"

"That's what we are trying to find out," Ashley answered grimly.

"One last question," asked Leroy, "Where did she go on the day she went missing?"

Mrs. Brooks thought for some time before she answered, "I think she was going to the Renaissance, but I'm not sure where it is located."

Ashley looked at Leroy and he stared back. "Thank you for your time and call us if you remember anything else," insisted Ashley.

Ashley pulled out into traffic, "Well what do you think, do we have a lead or not?"

"Maybe, let's wait until we check the other three, but right now I'm hungry. There's a McDonald's up ahead on your right."

They ate lunch and got back to work. Leroy gave Ashley the address for Tammy Lewis. She was a young married woman. Ashley asked, "Do you think her husband will be home?"

"I'll give him a call."

Mr. Lewis picked up on the second ring. Leroy asked if he would be home and he said he was home for lunch. He said he would wait for them. Ashley parked in front of an apartment with their number on the door. It was located in Dallas. Leroy rang the doorbell and Mr. Lewis opened the door for them to come in. Ashley explained they were new on the case and wanted to start over. She started the standard questions. Then asked how long they had been married. They had been married only six months.

"The Police, when I reported Tammy missing acted like I had something to do with her missing."

Leroy said, "Well we don't, I think your car was the cause, I think it was a car high jacking."

"Then what happen to Tammy?"

"I don't know, but we are trying to find out."

He looked at Leroy, "You think she is dead."

"Don't give up hope. One last question, where did Tammy go the day she went missing?"

"She was having a girl's day out. Tammy and the girls from the office were going to the Renaissance."

Leroy glanced at Ashley, "That should be all for now, but give us a call anytime." Ashley pulled out into traffic. ""That's three out of three so far. It looks like the cars are stolen in the Renaissance parking lot."

"Uh-hum could be, but someone should have seen them breaking into the cars unless they have the keys from the girls. It would be easy to steal the car and not get caught."

Ashley quoted grimly, "But how would they get rid of the girls?"

"That my dear Watson is the sixty four thousand dollar question." We can get a search warrant.

Ashley explained, "We could never get a warrant because there are too many businesses in the Renaissance. You have to know which one to pick for a warrant unless we can prove there are bodies everywhere, which we can't. You and I will come and spend a day there and look the place over, but right now let's finish what we started."

Leroy gave Ashley the address for Shannon Wilson. She lived in Grand Prairie, in a rich neighborhood. They parked in the driveway and walked up to the front door. Mrs. Wilson was working in a flowerbed and called to them. They went over where she was working. Ashley told her they were new on the case and would she answer some questions. Ashley asked her the same questions she asked everyone else.

Shannon was going to college and living at home. She had a boyfriend also, didn't they all have one? Mrs. Wilson was nervous and upset. She didn't ask what they thought happen to her daughter so they didn't give an opinion.

"One last question, do you know where Shannon went the day she went missing?" asked Leroy.

"Yes, she went to the Renaissance with a girlfriend and they both haven't been found. She wanted to go to the Renaissance so bad that was all she talked about."

Ashley said, "That will be all for now, but call us if you remember anything." Ashley pulled out into traffic, "That's four out of four and one to go."

"You know where I live, Ann Mitchel was my next door neighbor. I'll call and see if Teddy Bear is there." He answered on the third ring and Leroy told him they were on their way there. "I wouldn't call him Teddy Bear to his face," giggled Ashley.

"No I don't think I will because he is one large dude."

Ashley pulled up in front of Leroy's apartment and the big biker was waiting for them on the sidewalk. Leroy shook his hand and told him how sorry they were. "I know the answers to most the questions we were going to ask you so it won't take long. Did Ann get a new car?"

"Yes she just got it, a new Ford Thunderbird."

"I got one more question and I bet I know the answer. Where did Ann go that day she went missing?"

"She went to the Renaissance with one of the biker girls, but she came home with her biker boyfriend. She said Ann was still there when they left to come home."

Leroy said, "I think you can take it so I'm going to tell you what I think happen to Ann. I think someone abducted her and stole her car."

"But what happen to Ann?"

"I don't know, but we are working on it."

"The Police, when I filed a report acted like I had something to do with her missing."

"Don't worry about it, I got you covered."

"Leroy if you need any help of any kind just call and I will be there. There are a bunch of bikers if you need something done. We are there for you."

"Thanks, I'll keep that in mind."

Ashley pulled back out into traffic, "That's five out of five, what do you think now?"

"I think all the cars are being stolen from the Renaissance parking lot. They are stealing new cars, but what are they doing with the girls?"

Ashley said, "I don't want to think about it."

They went back to the police station. After getting two cups of coffee they went to their office to brainstorm. Ashley took Leroy's notes and added them to their blackboard. Number one, we know the cars are stolen at the Renaissance, two the cars are all new and three they were all girls driving the cars. "Do you think they are selling the cars?"

"Yes, but I don't know how. They would have to have a title."

"What if they had a phony title?"

"Ashley, you may be on to something."

"She said, "If they had a title they could sell them from any car lot."

"I like the way you think, keep going."

"If they had someone where you get license plates to make a phony title, you could sell the car anywhere."

"I got an idea, but it would take a lot of manpower and we don't have it."

They thought about it for some time. Ashley asked, "Why can't we use the bikers?"

Leroy laughed, "You know the Captain would never go for that."

"So who's going to tell him? We could have it done before he finds out."

They never went by the rules so why start now. Leroy called Ann's boyfriend. He said they would help so he told them to meet him in the parking lot in the morning. "Ashley we need to make several lists of the cars. I want to hand them out to the bikers. Tomorrow we start a search of the used car lots in the Dallas area. I know it may take a few days. There are a lot of used car lots, but if we find out that they are selling them off the used car lots, it will be worth our time."

"I will make the lists."

"We will have to go by description because they will have changed the Id number."

Ashley complained, "This has been a long day so let's call it quits and start new tomorrow."

Leroy went home, stopping at the grocery store deli for some take- out food. John and Marie were both working. They were happy to see him since he hadn't come by in a long time.

He was tired when he finally sat down for dinner. He checked his answering machine. Mike had called so he called back. Mike and Linda were happy to hear he had made Detective. They wanted to know when he was coming home again. Christmas was only three days off. He told them about the case he was working on and wouldn't be home for Christmas.

Leroy had a call from his Mother. She wanted to know about Christmas and she was not happy when he told her he wouldn't be home for Christmas. He hadn't talked to Katherine in several days so he gave her a call. She wasn't home yet and he knew she was still put out with him. She had been cool when they talked last and he just wanted to hear her voice. He missed her very much. Was this love? Where did that come from? He left a message to call when she could.

He went to bed, but couldn't sleep. He kept thinking about the case. It wasn't going to be easy to solve and the longer it took, he was afraid more girls would die.

Finally he went to sleep dreaming about Katherine.

The next morning in the Police parking lot, bikes were lined up in the back of the lot. Leroy didn't know how many bikers would show up to help. There were twenty-eight bikes in the lot. Leroy thanked them for coming and gave them each a list of the missing cars. He sent them out in pairs, each pair covering a different area. If they found a car that matched one on the list they were to get the name of the car lot and an ID number off the car.

Leroy said, "If anyone gives you any trouble call me, my number is on the sheet I gave you."

Captain Curry drove into the parking lot as a stream of bikes left the lot. What were Leroy and Ashley up to now? He got out of his car as they pulled out into traffic, he didn't want to know. What- ever they were doing it wasn't by the book. He would bet his last dollar on it.

Ashley was driving, "Where to?"

"We will stay around the Garland area. The others can call if they have anything."

Ashley and Leroy went from car lot to car lot without finding anything. The bikers did the same.

"It's like looking for a needle in a haystack," complained Ashley.

"Yes, but it's all we have to right now so we keep looking."

After two days it looked like they had struck out. Leroy said, "We should finish up tomorrow. We got to get lucky. We need a break."

The next day they were at it again. About two, one of the bikers called Leroy. He was at a used car lot in Plano. He thought he might have found two of the cars on the list. Ashley turned their car around and headed for Plano.

Ashley pulled into the used car lot next to the biker. The owner was giving the biker a fit. He wanted to know what was going on. The biker told him to take it up with Detective Cooper. Leroy showed the owner his badge and told him they needed to check a couple of his cars that they might be stolen. Leroy checked the cars and one car was the Thunderbird. The other one was the Cadillac. He got the ID numbers off the cars. "Sir I need to see the titles for the cars."

"Do you have a warrant?"

"No, but if these are the cars we are looking for the girls that owned them may already be dead. We don't have time to mess around."

"Follow me and I will get the titles for you."

He pulled the titles out of a file cabinet and handed them to Leroy. He glanced at the place the title was issued. "I bought them at two different times. The guy said he went around to auctions, bought cars and then sold them. I didn't think anything about it since it is done all the time. Car dealers can't go to auctions."

"Would you make me copies of the titles?"

The car dealer made copies for Leroy. "Could you describe the man that sold you the cars?" Leroy wrote it down as the dealer gave it to him. "Thank you for your help and we will let you know if the cars turn out to be stolen. Don't sell them until we give you the ok."

Leroy pulled out into traffic as the biker left them behind. Ashley said, "He is speeding."

"So what?" laughed Leroy, "Thanks to the biker, we have our first lead."

"Do you know what today is?" she asked.

"Yes it's Christmas Eve. Let's go back to the station and wrap it up until after Christmas Day."

Back at the Police Station, they added notes to the blackboard. Leroy scanned the titles to the two cars both were issued in Dallas by the same cashier at the tag office.

Leroy said, "After Christmas we need to check some of other cars and see if we come up with phony titles, but right now let's get out of here. In the parking lot, Leroy asked, "Would you do me a favor. I would like for you to go with me to get Katherine a Christmas gift?"

"Ok come on, we'll take my car. Where are we going?"

"Zale's should do it."

Ashley pulled in and parked beside Zale's. When they entered, she asked, "What did you have in mind?"

"I want something in the ring section."

Ashley jumped up and down, "Are you going to do what I think you are?"

"Yes, I'm going to ask her to marry me. She is mad at me right now. Do you think I should wait awhile before I pop the question?"

"No, I think tonight would be the perfect time to ask her to marry you."

"But she is still mad at me, I hurt her bad."

"She'll get over it."

Zale's was a large store with everything in jewelry that a girl could want. They made their way over to the counter with the wedding rings. Leroy stared at them, "Now you know why I wanted you to come with me. There are too many to choose from. I don't know what she would like."

"No problem, let's look at them and I think I can decide what she would like."

"I sure hope you can."

"Katherine is a working girl and will want to wear her rings all the time. Look at my rings, not too big and not too small. I wear my rings all the time." They looked until they found a set with about the same size stones as Ashley's rings. "I think she would like that set."

A young lady came over, "May I help you sir?"

"Yes may we look at that set?"

Leroy and Ashley looked the set of rings over and decided they were the ones.

"We'll take the set and would you wrap it as a Christmas gift. Put it in a large box and then a small box inside the large box."

She wrapped the rings and Leroy paid for them. When they were outside he said, "Well I'm broke until payday."

"It will worth it. I would like to see the look on her face when you give them to her."

"Am I doing the right thing? I know she loves me and I love her, but I am a cop. I know how hard it will be on her. What if I get killed right after we get married, then what?"

Ashley quoted, "It's better to loved and lost than never loved at all. Jim and I take it a day at a time."

"Thanks Ashley for being here and helping me. I know you want to be home with Jim"

"What's a partner for? We share a lot, good and bad."

"Let's get out of here," Leroy said.

Back at the parking lot, Ashley dropped him off and headed for home. Leroy went to his apartment and changed into jeans and a t-shirt. He called Katherine, but she wasn't home yet. He was hungry so he decided to eat and then go over to Katherine's. He checked his ankle holster and weapon that he was going to take with him tonight. Leroy stopped at McDonald's and ate so much he should have stock in the company. He decided to eat and kill time. He left his coat and cap in the car. Leroy ordered a hamburger, fries, and a coke. After getting his order he was eating when three young men came in and ordered. They started to use sexual remarks to the cashier. She tried to avoid any trouble with the young men, but they kept on.

Not tonight thought Leroy, he had a long day and was tired. The cashier was embarrassed, turning red as she looked down at the counter. A young man walked up beside her and told them to knock it off. He was shift Manager, but they just laughed at him.

That was enough. Leroy wouldn't listen to any more cracks. He got up and walked up behind the three men. "That will be enough, get your order and move on," Leroy said reasonably.

They turned on Leroy, "This is none of your business, get lost if you know what is good for you."

"I guess I'm making it my business so we can do this the easy way or the hard way."

The one in the middle pulled a knife, ""I'll take care of this punk."

He lunged at Leroy and Leroy used his self- defense training. He sidestepped, caught his arm twisting the knife from him and slammed him to the floor. "Anybody else want to play? I didn't think so, pick your friend up and get out of here now."

As they left Leroy broke the blade on the knife and tossed it in the garbage can. The cashier and Manager stared at him. "Thanks for your help. Who are you?"

"My name is Detective Cooper."

"Why didn't you put them in jail?"

"I'm on my way to my girlfriend's apartment and didn't want to do the paperwork. Maybe they learned a lesson tonight and won't do it again."

Leroy finished his food and left. Katherine still wasn't home yet. He put on his Dallas Cowboy coat and cap. It was starting to get cold. He was as nervous as a cat on a hot tin roof. He had rather face another bad guy than do what he was about to do. He had never asked a girl to marry him before.

He didn't know if she was still mad at him. Ashley had said she would get over being mad. He sure hoped she was right.

Katherine pulled in and parked in front of her apartment. She got out and walked slowly toward him. Leroy tried to read the expression on her face, but it was too dark to see her face. She wanted to be mad at him, but she was so glad to see him her defenses melted away. She opened her arms and Leroy went into them. He kissed her hard and knew he was home.

"I love you," he whispered.

She heard him and thought Leroy had changed. Just maybe they had a future together. She had decided she would take what she could get. She wanted to be with Leroy anyway he would have her. She loved him and love was blind. While she unlocked the door he got her Christmas gift from the car. When they were inside she went into his arms.

Katherine couldn't get enough of him. It had been so long since they been together. Tonight Leroy hoped to change all of that. "I have missed you so much," confessed Leroy.

Leroy had set the gift on the table. Katherine was hot and wanted to take Leroy to bed.

"We need to talk," he said and sat down at the table. She sat across from him. She didn't know what to expect since they usually made love before anything else. He handed her the gift. "I want you to open this now."

Katherine said, "Let me get your gift. I haven't wrapped it yet."

"No it can wait, this can't."

She stared at him as she tore the paper from the gift. He stared back with so much love in his eyes that it brought tears to her eyes. She took the small box out of the big box. "What's going on?"

"Just keep going."

She opened the small box and took out the ring box. A lump formed in her throat and she lost her breath. Could it be what she thought it was? She slowly opened the ring box and cried out.

"Yes I do."

Katherine grabbed Leroy across the table and he thought she would choke him to death. "I do, I do," she kept saying over and over.

Leroy could see the love in her eyes. It made him the happiest man in the world and he thought back to what Ashley told him. He didn't care if he only had a week, a month, or a year it would be worth it.

"I love the rings."

"Ashley helped me pick them out."

"Well she knew exactly what I would like."

Leroy came around the table and dropped down on his knee. "I want to do this right. Katherine Stewart will you marry me? I know I'm a cop and not much of a catch, but I will love you until the day I die."

"Oh, yes, yes, yes."

She threw herself at him. Leroy slipped her engagement ring on her finger. She was so happy she could scream.

"What made you change your mind about marriage?"

"I was afraid to get married and then get killed on the job. Ashley changed my mind. She told me it was better to love and lost than never loved at all. She was right."

Katherine said, "You talk too much, come with me and show me how much you love me."

She took his hand and led him to her bedroom. Leroy slowly undressed her, kissing her body as each part was exposed to him. Her body was trembling in anticipation of what was to come. She stood before him naked and reached for Leroy to undress him. When he was naked she went into his arms. His erection pushed onto her belly and she knew how much he wanted her.

Katherine pushed him back on the bed and straddled him. She was a wanton woman tonight and wanted to be in charge. Leroy didn't care as long as they made love. She smiled at him, taking his erection in her hand and guided him into her hot passion. She took all of him and picked up a fast rhythm. They would go slow next time. She was burning up and wanted him to put out the fire as only he could do.

It didn't take long for both of them to reach a climax and they finished together. Katherine said, "I'm hungry from all the exercise. Let's get dressed and go out to a good dinner."

"I'm sorry, but I'm broke until my next paycheck."

CHAPTER SEVEN

"Don't worry I got some money, for tonight you can be a kept man. I'm going to keep you forever."

"Does that mean I can quit working and you'll take care of me?" teased Leroy.

"No, it means we put all our money together so I have more to spend."

Just as they were ready to leave the phone rang. She would let it ring, but it might be important. She picked up on the third ring. Ashley wanted to know if Leroy had popped the question.

"Yes and thanks for the help picking out my rings, I love them."

"Did you make him beg?"

"No, I was too happy to think. I couldn't believe he was asking me to marry him. I was in deep shock.

"I'm happy for you two and I want to invite you over for Christmas dinner. We won't eat until about two to give you two a little time to be together."

"We'll be there and do you want me to bring anything?"

'No, just be here, see you tomorrow."

They went out to Steak and Ale since they both liked the place. The waiter set them in a nice quiet corner. They both ordered a steak, baked potato all the way and got a salad off the salad bar. They had ale to drink. The waiter brought a hot loaf of bread to go with the meal.

"You better eat good to get your energy built up because I don't plan on letting you sleep much tonight," giggled Katherine. "Please go easy on me," groaned Leroy.

"Not tonight, tonight we make memories to last a lifetime."

Katherine was so happy she couldn't sit still. The waiter brought their food and they dug in. "Are we going to move in together," asked Leroy.

"Yes we are, you can move in with me. My apartment is larger than your apartment."

"Ok, we can move my things over tomorrow when we leave Ashley's. I don't have much to move."

They ordered cherry pie and ice cream for, desert. They sat staring at each other like a couple of teenagers. "When do you want to tie the knot?" teased Leroy.

She thought about it. Since they would be living together they didn't have to be in a hurry and it would give them a chance to see if they could make it together.

"How about we get married on Saint Valentine Day?"

"Sounds good to me, I'll have a chance to break the news to Mom, Dad and all my friends. Do you want a large church wedding?"

"No, we can have just a small church wedding with family and a few friends."

"That works for me."

They finished their desert. Ashley paid the waiter and tipped him. "Let's get out of here."

They were back at Katherine's apartment in nothing flat. They were naked in a few minutes and she put on soft music before they hit the sack. Katherine lay back and spread her legs inviting further intimacies which Leroy took her upon.

He moved between her legs and touched her hot folds with his erection. Katherine arched her back taking part of his erection in her hot body. "I want all of you in me now." Leroy slammed into her and she let out a little cry. "Did I hurt you?"

"It only hurts until I stretch to take that big tool. I love it and it feels so good."

Leroy picked up a slow rhythm making it last as long as he could. They took their time giving pleasure to each other. Katherine wanted it to last all night. Leroy held out as long as he could before his shaft started throbbing. She knew he was about to come so she squeezed his shaft and picked up the pace. They climaxed together. Leroy rolled over with her on top, her breasts flat on his chest, her hard nipples digging into his chest and her mouth covering his. They were contented to lay connected forever. They finally went to sleep with her still on top.

About three in the morning Leroy woke up, his shaft had got hard and wanted some attention. He lay still until he had a full erection. Katherine squeezed his shaft while she was still sleeping. He couldn't take it any longer so he arched his back giving her all of his erection. She woke up, that had got her attention. She kissed Leroy and started to move.

Katherine was hot and slippery so it didn't take long until she had a climax. Leroy slammed into her, lifting her off the bed, grabbing her buttocks, he came deep into her quivering body. She rolled off exhausted and content. Katherine snuggled close to Leroy and went to sleep. Leroy stroked her hair and drifted off to sleep. They didn't get up until ten o'clock Christmas morning. Katherine didn't put up a tree since she was by herself, but she dreamed about kids and a tree.

Staring at Leroy, she could picture a little boy looking like him. She thought her heart would burst with love for the man beside her. She watched him until he finally opened his eyes and stared at her. She smiled at him, "Good morning sleepy head."

"You wore me out last night, you wanton woman, I needed my sleep to get my strength back."

"Good because I need you in me one more time before we get up."

Much later Leroy got up and went to fix breakfast while Katherine showered. They took a couple of hours to get it together as they teased at each other. They were in love and people do silly things when they are in love. After eating peaches and ice cream off of Katherine's stomach they decided it was time to go over to Ashley's house.

They laughed and giggled all the way to Ashley's. They were excided just being together. Ashley opened the door for them. She saw the glow on Katherine's face and knew that she was one happy girl. They went into the kitchen for coffee. Jim joined them shortly, smiling at Leroy. "Well you chased her until she caught you. How does it feel to be caught in a woman's trap?"

All eyes turned on Leroy, "It feels great."

The guys went into the den to watch television while the women fixed Christmas dinner. Jim and Leroy discussed his and Ashley's new jobs. Jim liked it because they had more time together. They didn't have to punch a clock like they did when they were Police. If they were in the middle of something they would work late and when it was slack they would take off early. The main reason was they probably wouldn't have to face bad guys with guns as much.

Jim was doing real great at Enron. He had just got another big pay raise, but the one thing he didn't like was he would have to travel sometimes. Jim said, "I take it you and Ashley are having trouble with the case you are working on now."

"Yes we are making progress, but it is slow and that is worrying me. I'm afraid we are going to find a lot of bodies. Every time we have a car theft we have a girl missing. I think they are stealing the car and doing away with the girl."

"I'm sure you and Ashley will break the case sooner or later. You need a break."

Ashley called them to dinner. She had cooked a turkey, dressing, yams, corn-on-the-cob, rolls, and a fruit salad. They had tea to drink. Jim blessed the food and they dug in. Ashley had cooked enough for an army.

They had fresh apple pie and ice cream as desert. It was a fun day. Katherine couldn't keep her eyes off of Leroy. Ashley watched her.

"I think I know what you like for desert," giggled Ashley.

Katherine knew she had been caught daydreaming about Leroy. They both laughed, they were good friends or more like sisters. They liked each other very much and talked to one another about anything. The guys were in the den watching television while the girls cleaned up. They got a chance to talk more girl talk. Katherine asked, "What's it like to wake up every morning with Jim beside you?"

"It's like heaven on earth, I don't know what I would do without him, he is my rock, he has my heart and my whole world revolves around him."

"Wow, you make it sound wonderful."

"Wait until you and Leroy, have lived together awhile, you will feel cold when he leaves the house, it's like part of you is missing and when he walks in you will become warm all over again. It's like your two bodies become one and when he is gone half of you are missing. I hope you and Leroy will be as happy as Jim and I are."

When they finished cleaning up they went into the den to get the men to play cards. The women won and the guys said they were cheating.

They left Ashley and Jim at ten o'clock, tomorrow would be a long workday for all of them. They stopped by Leroy's apartment and picked up his gear. He didn't have much so it didn't take long to load.

By the time they got home it was midnight. They cuddled together and went to sleep. They were tired and wouldn't make love tonight since from now on they would be together every night.

The next day they didn't want to get up, but they had jobs to do. Leroy made breakfast while Katherine showered and got ready for work. They ate a quick breakfast and Katherine cleaned up while Leroy showered and got ready for work. They took a long minute to kiss before they left for work.

Katherine was walking on a cloud when she walked into her office. The other girls watched her and went into her office. Katherine showed them her ring then she had to tell them everything. Her boss broke it up when he came in and told them to get back to work. Nothing could make Katherine mad today because she was in love.

Ashley was already in the office when Leroy walked in and watched while she studied the blackboard. "Have you got the case wrapped up?"

"Not yet, but I'm working on it."

"We have titles on those two cars and we need the tag office."

"Yes we do, but I have an idea. How would you like a new job working at the tag office? Thank you could handle it?" asked Leroy.

"What do you want me to do?"

Leroy explained, "We talk to the Supervisor at the tag office and get you a job in the tag office next to the girl selling the titles we have. You search the computer for our stolen cars."

"How will I know when I have one?"

"Check with the manufacturer of the cars and see if there is a car with those ID's. I would bet my next paycheck the numbers on the titles are phony. Look up the other cars and do the same with them."

"What else?"

"Watch every title the girl sells. We want to catch her in the act before we bust her."

"You think she is doing it for the money?"

"Yes, watch her hands as she does each title. She will probably get paid at the time she does the title. Her name is Ginger. She will be part of the ring stealing the cars. She is how they can sell the cars without questions being asked. She is very important to the ring and you can bet she gets paid well for her work."

Ashley called the tag office and told the Supervisor they were coming to her office. When they arrived they went straight to her office. Leroy explained what they wanted to do. Ashley would just be another employee in training. The Supervisor said she would let Ginger train her so she could keep a close eye on her. Leroy said it will probably take a long time to catch her.

The Supervisor laughed, "Then I get a free employee while she is here to help with the work load."

Ashley said, "I thought I would get two paychecks while working here."

They laughed at her.

"When do I start?"

"I will start you tomorrow with Ginger."

Back at the Police station, Ashley and Leroy went over their plan again. They had to come up with something soon. They decided to quit early and start again tomorrow. Ashley went home to Jim and Leroy went home to Katherine. Leroy cooked dinner while waiting for Katherine to come home from work. It was so nice for them to sit down to dinner together and then make love that night. They were two happy people.

Outside of Dallas at the Renaissance, five men were at a table playing cards, Jason Crow the leader of the pack, Allen Pen, Bryan Veal, Mark Owens, all were security guards for the Renaissance and Will Von the runner that got rid of the stolen cars. Willie was staring at the two women tied to racks on the other side of the dungeon.

Ann Mitchel was naked, bowed over on her back with her legs spread apart, bare feet on the floor, she was trying to sleep. Shannon Wilson was naked bent over face down with her legs spread apart with her bare feet on the floor.

She was whimpering, "Please let me go, I won't tell on you, I won't tell, please let me go."

"Shut your mouth or I'll shut it for you," warned Jason.

Willie lost the next hand and got up from the table. He walked over to the bulletin board where pictures were posted. They took pictures of all the girls they had raped and killed. All the girls were dead except for Ann and Shannon. Willie pulled a picture down and asked could he have it? It was a picture of Ann's hot box with the words (keep off the grass).

He laughed, "It's so cool."

Jason replied, "Why not, you can have it."

Willie thought he might as well go for broke, so he walked over to Shannon and slid a finger into her folds. "Can I have a piece of this one?"

"You can have her when we are done with her," replied Jason.

"Come on, let me have her, she has been here a long time."

"Ok, but you clean her up after you are done with her, someone might want a shot at her before we leave."

Willie didn't waste any time dropping his pants and shorts. He had a big erection. He grabbed her by her hips and slammed into her soft body. She begged him to stop and not hurt her. She had been raped several times by the four men and her body hurt all over. While he was banging her she passed out.

"The bitch quit on me."

With one brutal stab he shot his seed deep into her body. Willie was mad, grabbing a water hose he hosed her down. The cold water revived her and she started screaming. He hit her up- side the head and knocked her out. "You got to get rid of this one, she has had it." "We will as soon as we get another girl. Both these girls need to go," replied Jason.

The Renaissance was closed and it shut down their car theft operation.

"We may have to take a chance and car jack one in the area, but we need to find a nice young girl with a new car, 'explained Jason.

They had the perfect place to get girls and cars. They were the security for the Renaissance. They had found a secret dungeon in the Medieval Castle behind the regular dungeon.

The wall was thick enough to be sound proof so they could do anything they wanted even when the Renaissance was operating. The dungeon had an escape tunnel leading away from the castle, coming out in an old barn where they kept the cars they stole until they got a title. There was a deep hole in the dungeon floor with a cover on it where they dropped the dead bodies. They had it worked out. The guard where the traffic came in would spot a new car with a young girl driving. He would pass it on to the guard inside. The guard would talk her into going to the castle to show it to her. The fourth guard would make sure the dungeon out front was empty of people. As they walked by the dungeon door, he would push her inside where the other guard was waiting. They then took her through the secret door to the back dungeon.

There they stripped her and tied her to the rack naked. They then took turns raping her until she died or they got tired of her and killed her. They took her keys, got a phony title and sold the car. They did this over and over again with- out thinking of getting caught, but now they would have to car jack a car if they wanted a new girl and a new car or wait until they opened the Renaissance again.

Ashley reported to the tag office and was put with Ginger for training. She had her own password and showed how to do tags or a title. She called the manufacturer of the two cars and they were phony numbers.

Ashley called Leroy and told him about the two titles.

"You know what to do, watch Ginger."

"You got it. I'll keep an eye on her at all times."

Ashley searched the computer for the other cars and titles. It was slow doing her work and searching for the other titles. She was tired by the end of the day. Leroy ran the streets looking for a trace of where the cars were before they were sold.

Leroy and Ashley back at the office brain stormed on what they could do next to hurry things along. The only good lead was Ginger, but they didn't want to bust her until they caught her working a bad title.

Time rocked on, the New Year only two days off. They had one more day to work before everything shut down for the holidays. New Year's eve, everything was slow with the tag office closed at noon and would be closed until after the holidays. Leroy was a new Detective so he didn't know a single snitch, but he roamed the city trying to find one.

At noon Ashley called Leroy to meet her at McDonald's for lunch. While they ate lunch they tried to come up with something.

Ashley said, "I know something we haven't tried. We could check out the hookers tonight and ask them if they have heard anything on the street. I know several of them and I turn my head on what they are doing since I'm not vice. I leave them alone."

"It sounds like a good idea, but you know what tonight is?"

"Yes, but tonight is the best night to do it. All the hookers will be out tonight."

Leroy asked, "What about Jim and Katherine?"

She replied, "Why don't we get them to ride with us."

"Are you sure you want to do this?"

"Yes, we can use my car and leave our Police car at the station. Tell Katherine to bring her camera."

"She never leaves home without it."

"I'll call Jim and you call Katherine. We can make it like a date, eat out at six, work the streets until eleven, go to a club for a drink and bring in the New Year."

"It sounds like fun, I'll call Katherine."

Katherine was all for it. Ashley called Jim and it was ok with him. It would be something different. They went home to get ready for tonight.

Jim and Ashley picked up Leroy and Katherine at five twenty. They wanted to have a fun night.

"Let's go to the Crab Shack," suggested Leroy.

Ashley turned right and headed for the Crab Shack.

The Hostess showed them to a table in the main part. The room was large with decorations of fish, nets and pictures. Off to the side was an outside dining area where all the little kids got to play and sing songs. The staff was good with the kids so the adults could enjoy their meal.

The waitress came and took their orders. They all decided to order lobster and all the trimmings. They enjoyed watching the staff playing with the little kids. Some of the kids were dancing on the tables.

Detective Doug Masters and his wife Sara came in. Ashley waved at them and when they came over, she asked, "Do you want to join us?" They placed their order for lobster also.

Ashley brought them up to speed on the case and asked if they had any input on the case. They were working on another robbery case at this time. Doug said, "I can't believe you two are out on the town." Ashley looked at Leroy, "Actually we are working tonight." She explained what they were going to do when they finished eating.

"Not a bad idea," responded Doug.

Their food arrived and shop talk was over. The lobster was succulent dipped in butter. Everybody was hungry and it didn't take long to down all the food.

Leroy said, "Time to go to work."

Jim paid the bill with objections from everyone except Leroy who was broke.

Ashley drove and Leroy got out his notebook to take notes. She stopped when she saw a girl she knew. The girl came over to the car. She knew Ashley wouldn't bust her. Ashley asked if she knew anything about the car thefts. She didn't, but she called several more hookers over to the car. She told them it wasn't a bust and I was ok to talk to Ashley.

They thought they had struck out when a redhead with a mini skirt and a plunging neckline stepped forward. She told them she had turned a trick with a guy named Willie. She didn't know if he gave her his real name. He didn't give her a last name.

What got her attention was he talked about making a lot of money selling cars to used car lots. He also told he was doing a girl a couple of days ago and she passed out on him. He was real mad about it and he hosed her down. She thought he was a sick-o and got rid of him as soon as she could. Leroy asked her to describe the man. She thought about it for a minute.

"He was about five feet ten inches tall, maybe one hundred eighty pounds, black haircut short, around twenty eight years old and looked like his nose had been broken."

"Anything else you can think of that set him off?"

"He had a chain tattoo around his left arm, love on his left hand and hate on his right hand. He had on a short sleeve blue shirt and blue dress pants with black dress shoes. That's all I remember."

Leroy stared at her he couldn't believe she remembered so much. He thanked her for her help.

"If you ever need any help just call Ashley or myself. The only help we can't give you is if you get busted doing your trade."

She laughed, "I understand."

They drove around and talked to several more hookers. One other hooker remembered Willie, but didn't know his name. He told her about selling cars and making a lot of money. He said she was good and gave her one hundred dollars for her services.

As Ashley pulled back into traffic, Leroy joked, "Jim we could put our girls to work and we could take it easy.

The girls didn't think it was funny.

Katherine said, "How about we put you and Jim out for stud and escort service?"

Leroy and Jim answered at the same time, "Sounds good to me."

Ashley and Katherine were ready to kill both of them.

Leroy glanced at Ashley, "You did a good job tonight. I think we have the one that gets rid of the cars. I think he was stupid enough to give the girls his real name, but now we need a name and address.

Jim asked, "Are we still going to the club, it is eleven o'clock?"

"I'm ready for some fun," replied Leroy, Let's go to Forth Worth to Billy Bobs. All in favor raise your hand.

Ashley turned on I-30 and headed for Fort Worth. The club was located at the Stockyards. Ashley asked, "Do you think we can get in this late at night?"

"You bet," replied Leroy. "I called right after we decided to go out tonight. They told me they were sold out, but when I told them it was for Dirty Harry, they came up with a table so I guess it does come in handy sometimes to be called Dirty Harry."

It was getting cold out by the time Ashley parked the car. They entered the front entrance and told them who they were. A man escorted them to a table close to the dance floor. The Little Texas Band was playing and people were dancing the two-step. They sat and ordered drinks.

Katherine jumped to her feet and grabbed Leroy by the hand. ""I want to dance."

Leroy stood up, opened his arms and she went into them. They finished that dance and stayed on the floor for the next three before leaving the dance floor. Jim and Ashley danced a couple of times before they sat down. They ordered another round of drinks and talked while listing to the music.

When the waitress delivered their drinks she told Leroy the Manager said their money wasn't any good, everything was on the house. He was honored to have Detective Cooper and Lewis in his place of business. The Police Force needed more like them. Leroy and Ashley were shocked at what happened.

Katherine said, "You two are the best. Don't you know that by now? You make a big difference in this town. I should know since I write about you all the time. You are a household word in this town. You are always on the news."

"The clock struck twelve midnight, the noise was so loud you couldn't hear a thing. Leroy kissed Katherine and hugged Ashley. Jim kissed Ashley and hugged Katherine.

Raising his hand, Jim said, "A toast to us, friends forever."

Leroy said, "One more dance before we go."

He asked Jim if he could dance with his partner, Ashley. Jim replied, only if he let him dance with Katherine. They walked out on the dance floor together and joined the mob on the dance floor.

"We got lucky tonight. We are one step closer to closing our case, now if can get lucky tomorrow," Leroy said triumphantly. He was happy tonight.

It was one o'clock before Ashley dropped them off at their apartment. They got naked and went straight to bed, but they were too tired to make love. They curled up together and went to sleep. New Year's they didn't do nothing but rest.

The next morning the alarm clock went off early. They used the same routine they always used, Leroy fixed breakfast while Katherine showered and got dressed. After breakfast Leroy showered and got dressed while Katherine cleaned up.

They kissed and headed for work. They knew it would be a long day since they didn't get much sleep last night.

Ashley was standing at the blackboard when Leroy entered the office. She had added Willie to the board.

"I was just on my way out. I have to be at the tag office to clock in thirty minutes. What are you going to do today?"

"After I have my cup of coffee, I'll go looking for Willie. You know the description the hooker gave us matched the one the car lot owner gave us. I don't want to put out an APB on him yet. I would like to find him and tail him. Maybe he would lead us to the rest of the ring."

Ashley worked hard on the computer with the long list of stolen cars. She hit pay dirt checking all the titles Ginger had issued she found car after car. Ginger had been doing this for a long time. Leroy rode around all day, but didn't find Willie or anyone that knew him.

Ashley met Leroy at their office after she got off work at the tag office. She gave him the list of stolen cars she had found to put on the board.

"Wow, this girl should be rich by now. "I'll run a check on her tomorrow."

The next day Leroy ran a check on her bank. He couldn't believe she was using the same bank as the tag office. How stupid could she be? She had a large bank account so he checked where she lived. She lived in a high rise apartment that cost a bundle. Leroy sweet talked the girl in the office to let him in her apartment. As he expected it was furnished with high priced everything. The closets were filled with expensive clothes and shoes. She had a box full of real jewelry. She had enough jewelry to start her own jewelry store.

Leroy waited in the parking lot when Ginger got off work. She was driving a new Ford. Her pay didn't match her life style. Leroy was right, Ginger was getting a big piece of the pie and so was Willie. He wished he knew how many was in the ring.

Ashley met Leroy at the office where he told her about Ginger. He would keep looking for Willie while Ashley kept watch at the tag office.

Two long weeks went by and nothing happened and both of them were in a bad mood. Something had to happen soon or they would both go crazy.

Back at the castle, Jason told the others they needed a new girl and a new car. They would scout around and find one, then car jack it. Two days later they found a sixteen year old with the shape of a twenty-year old.

"I like that one. We need a young hot one to keep up with us," suggested Allen. That night they waited at her home until she drove into her driveway. She was driving a new Ford Mustang. As she got out of her car Allen grabbed her from behind. She bit his hand and screamed, but he hit her and knocked her out. He shoved her into the back seat while Mark got in the back seat on the passenger side to keep her quite. Allen got in to drive. Mr. Moore heard the scream and came outside just in time to see them drive off.

"We done it, we got us some fresh meat," said Jason as he pulled in behind the Mustang.

"Yeah man, now we can get rid of Shannon," quoted Bryan.

They drove south of Dallas to the Renaissance which wasn't open yet. They parked the cars in the barn and went through the tunnel into the dungeon. Ann and Shannon looked up as they came in. Ann still had some life left in her, but Shannon was almost dead already. Jason and Mark stripped Megan. Allen and Bryan untied Shannon and dropped her down the pit. She was dead when she hit the bottom of the pit.

Megan was tied face down and her legs spread. Jason licked his lips. Megan was five foot six, slender, a cute little set of boobs and cold black hair. She started to scream, but Jason slapped her on the buttocks and told her to shut up if she knew what was good for her. He reached under her and squeezed her nipples making them hard.

Jason dropped his pants and shorts, "Party time boys and I get to go first."

Ann glanced over at the new girl. She felt sorry for her, but there wasn't anything she could do for her and she knew she was next to go down the hole.

Jason grabbed her buttocks and slammed into her soft body. She screamed because it hurt. She was tight only having done it one time with a young boy. Jason was big and stretched her until it finally started to feel good, but he finished by planting his seed deep into her soft body.

He laughed, "Dam that was good. Who is next? Get her while she's hot."

Mark took her next followed by Allen and Bryan. After Bryan finished he hosed her down and dried her off.

"Honey you are good, we'll keep you a long time." He ran his hand over here soft body. She started crying softly as he squeezed her buttocks and ran a finger into her soft folds. "You liked every minute of it so shut up. If you're good I'll feed you."

When they did feed them they were hand fed and never were they untied from the rack. Ann had been there a long time and she was getting weaker every day. She was at the point she didn't care if they killed her so it would be over.

"I hope I live long enough to see you face Dirty Harry because he will kill all of you."

They laughed as they left for the night. Ann wasn't raped tonight because they had a new toy. She asked was she all right?"

"I hurt all over."

"You should be after being raped four times tonight. The pain won't be as bad next time. Just relax and let them do their thing."

Ashley went to work at the tag office while Leroy searched for Willie. About ten o'clock Ashley saw Willie walk into the tag office. He got in Ginger's line which had a lot of people in her line. While getting tags for a lady Ashley phoned Leroy.

"I'm on my way, don't let him get away."

Before Leroy got there Willie made it to front of the line. He gave her the money for the title and an envelope. While

Ginger was making change Ashley eased around the counter and came up behind Willie.

Ashley pulled her weapon from her ankle holster and motioned for the people behind Willie to move back out of the way. As Ginger turned around with his change Ashley said, ""Willie put your hands on the counter. Ginger move over to your right and put your hands on the counter. Both of you don't move a muscle.

"What is going on, can't a person buy a title?"

Ginger asked, "Why do you have me like this? I haven't done anything wrong."

Ashley let them talk while she stalled for time waiting on Leroy.

Leroy walked into the tag office, "Well, well, Willie you are a hard one to find."

Leroy cuffed him, read him his rights and searched him. Ashley watched Willie as Leroy turned his attention on Ginger. He picked up the title and scanned it.

"I'll bet my next paycheck this car is stolen and you just made a phony title for it." It was a Ford Mustang like the one stolen.

"Where is the girl Willie?" Leroy was in his face and he was mad.

"I don't know what you are talking about. I bought the car at an auction."

"Sure you did."

Leroy turned back to Ginger, "What's in the envelope?"

He opened the envelope and counted out one thousand dollars. "That's a good tip. I wish I could find a job like yours." Leroy turned to Ashley, "Cuff her."

Ashley went around the counter, cuffed Ginger, searched her and read her rights. She turned to her Supervisor, "I'm sorry I am leaving you short- handed, but don't forget to mail my paycheck to the Police Station.

They Supervisor laughed as they walked out the door. Leroy put the suspects in the back of the car and Ashley followed him to the Police Station. Captain Curry saw Leroy and Ashley bring in the suspects.

"Well what have we got here?'

Ashley replied, "We got two of the car theft ring and we want to interrogate them before they make bail. You know how fast they get out on bail. They go in one door and out the other."

"Not this time, as soon as you get them booked, put her in room one and Willie in room two. Leroy and I will take him and you take the girl.

Ashley laid a recorder on the table and told Ginger she was going to record. Ginger told her Willie was the only one she knew and that was all she would answer. She wanted her lawyer. Ashley told her she was in serious trouble by being linked to the car theft ring. They had probably killed several girls. She still wouldn't talk and wanted her lawyer. The Jailer took Ginger and locked her up.

Captain Curry told Willie he was in deep trouble, but if he turned state's evidence it would help him get a better deal.

"Willie told the same story, "I bought the cars at auction." He wouldn't give them the auction address and he wanted his lawyer. Finally after an hour they gave up on him. The Jailer took Willie and locked him up. Leroy and Ashley went into their office. They added the information to their blackboard. They now had Willie's last name and address. His last name was Von.

Leroy said, "They will probably make bail tomorrow. I want to follow Willie and maybe he will lead us to the rest of the ring. Let's call it a day. I think we have earned our money for today."

When Leroy walked in, Katherine told him he had a call from a classmate by the name of Gary Mitchell. He hadn't talked to Gary since he left home. He called right away.

Gary picked up on the second ring. "Well how is the big bad Policeman?"

"I'm trying to make a living."

"I thought you were going back to college."

"I think I will when I get some money saved or marry a rich woman. What have you been doing all this time?"

Nothing for a couple of years which is a long story, but now I am a Tracker. I have a Wolf that runs with me. We track anything for money."

"You mean a Wolf like an animal?"

"Yes, he saved my life and I don't go anywhere without him, but that is another long story."

"Are you going to be home long?"

"Yes if I don't get a call for help. I make big money at this job so I can take off awhile. It makes you feel good when you find a lost person and save a life. I take the job when everyone has given up and called off the search. Rich people or a company pays big money. I even hunt animals."

"That is really a strange job, but who cares if the money is good."

"If you ever need my help just give me a call."

They talked for another hour about old times in High School and old friends. "Have you called Rex? He is here in Dallas."

"Not yet, but I'll give him a call." Leroy gave him Rex's phone number and they hung up.

Katherine had dinner on the table, soup, a sandwich and tea to drink. "I don't want to get fat," murmured Leroy, "What's for desert?"

"Me," Katherine giggled. She left the room while Leroy was eating. When he finished eating he glanced at the door to the bedroom. Katherine was leaning against the doorframe with nothing on, but a black negligee. She giggled as she crooked a finger for him to follow her to the bedroom inviting further intimacies. Leroy chased after her into the bedroom. They made slow love for a long time before going to sleep.

Leroy met Ashley at the office the next morning. They waited until Willie made bail. He was out on the street by three o'clock, money talks. Someone wanted him out of jail in a hurry. Willie got his car out of the pound and pulled into traffic. Ashley and Leroy trailed him at a safe distance.

"Ashley said, "It looks like he is going home.""

Willie parked in front of his apartment and went inside.

"What do you want to do," asked Ashley.

"Wait and see what he does. Maybe he will lead us to the car theft ring."

Ashley and Leroy had never done a stake out so it was time to learn. They didn't notice a car parked across the street with four men in it. Jason picked the car phone and called Willie. He answered on the first ring. "What did you tell the cops?"

"Nothing Boss," he sounded nervous.

Mark glanced over at Jason. He was driving, "Time to go."

Mark pulled out into traffic, "Goodbye Willie," Jason said as he punched a small red button on a black box. Willie's apartment exploded in flying debris followed by fire.

"Damnation, what a way to go," murmured Leroy.

Ashley called it in. Fire trucks, Police and ambulances were everywhere. Willie's whole apartment was gone and so was Willie. They would have to pick him up piece by piece. Several other people were injured in the explosion that rocked the building.

"There goes our only lead," admitted Ashley, "They made sure of that."

"Yeah you're right, back to the old drawing board."

Leroy talked to the Police handling the crime scene. The Bomb Squad would be there shortly. They would try to find out what kind of bomb it was. They finally started to find pieces of Willie, very few, not enough to put a body together. Down in the dumps Ashley and Leroy drove back to the Police

Station. Captain Curry met them as they entered the office. They told them the bad news. They would have to start over. They went over their notes looking for anything to get them going again. The only lead they had now was Ginger, but she didn't know anything. The only person she knew in the theft ring was Willie and he was dead.

"Do you think they will do away with Ginger?" asked Ashley.

"No, she's not a threat, she doesn't know anything. She hasn't made bail. That tells you they aren't worried about her.

Leroy quoted, "They won't be stealing cars for now until they find a way to get rid of the cars. They are shut down for now."

Ashley said, "Let's ask the other Detectives about a snitch that might know something since we had good luck with the hookers. If we can find a whorehouse maybe we can find something there. Willie was throwing a lot of money around, but for now we are stuck so let's go home."

Katherine had covered the explosion, but didn't see Leroy or Ashley. When he came home she asked him what happened. He told her about Willie and Ginger. He told her why Willie was killed to shut him up.

"Now I want you to do something for me, along with the story ask the public if they knew Willie or anybody he ran with to contact us at the Police Station."

"I can do that."

"Now what's for dinner?"

Katherine had cooked a big meal, fried chicken, mushed potatoes, gravy, peas and biscuits with tea to drink. Leroy scanned the table, "Now that's more like it."

They ate until they were full. Leroy asked, "Now what do you have for desert?" Katherine looked at him and giggled.

"Not again, I don't think I could take it again."

"Poor baby, I'll take it easy on you tonight."

The phone rang, while he talked on the phone Katherine ran her hands inside his shirt and played with his nipples.

CHAPTER EIGHT

"Sorry honey I got to see a hooker about a man."

"Can I ride with you?"

"I don't see why not, let's go."

They took her car and she drove while Leroy told her the address. She knew the town better than Leroy. The address was on Gross Road in a large old house. Leroy pulled into the driveway where several other cars were parked. There were cars parked on the street also.

"Business must be good," commented Leroy. "Wait here for me and look your doors." He started to leave, but turned to look at her. "Do you have your camera?"

"You bet, never leave home without it."

Leroy went into the whorehouse showing the Madam his badge. He told her the girl in room five called him. He wasn't here to cause the house any trouble he wanted to talk to the man in with her.

"I'll call her for you."

"No I want to catch the man she is with so I'll just go up to her room." When he found room five he drew his colt 45. He slammed into the door and bounced back. The dam door must be made of iron. Leroy heard a lot of noise in the room. Bryan grabbed his pants and slammed through the window as Leroy hit the door again. The door gave way and Leroy ran into the room, The whore pointed to the broken window.

Leroy said, "I'll be back."

Katherine grabbed her camera as a naked man ran to a car across the street with his pants in his hand. She took pictures as he ran past her until he was in his car and burning rubber away from the cathouse.

Leroy came running out of the house his gun in his hand, "Where did he go?"

Katherine pointed down the street.

"Move over I'll drive." Turning around burning rubber he drove like a crazy man. "Tally ho there goes the fox."

Katherine hit him on the arm, "If you wreak my car I'll kill you."

They chased Bryan for a couple of miles before they lost him in traffic. "I think that he is one of the car theft ring, I'm going back to talk to the hooker." Leroy turned the car around and headed back to the whorehouse. "Did you get the pictures?"

"Does a dog have flees?"

"Great you got them."

"You bet, but they are R rated and I can't use them in the newspaper unless he had his pants in front of him. He was naked as a jay bird."

"Do not look Katherine," Leroy teased, using the song, the streak for effect.

Leroy pulled into the driveway at the cat house.

"Yeah I know, lock my doors and you will be right back. Don't sample the merchandise while you are in there."

Leroy hung his head, "You take all the fun out of going in the cathouse."

She teased, "You have a pussy at home you can pet all you want to."

The hooker was waiting for Leroy when he entered the front door. "Sorry about the window, I'll get it fixed."

The Madam said, "Don't worry about it she would take care of it." The hooker showed Leroy to a table and chairs.

"Tell me about the man."

"His first name is Bryan. I don't know his last name. He said he knew poor Willie and laughed about what happened to him. I thought that was sick. I know he is a security guard, but I don't know where he works. He said he comes here because he doesn't get his share of the women. I didn't know what he was talking about. He said he had cars to sell and if I was good to him he would get me a good deal on a new one."

"Anything else you can think of?"

"He was a bad trick, he likes to get rough and scream when he had a climax. I didn't like to turn a trick with him, but he paid big time. I made as much with him as I made with three john's so I would grin and take it."

"We got pictures of him as he ran to his car, but give me a description anyway."

She closed her eyes to think, "Let's see , he was about six feet, long hair in a ponytail, about one hundred eighty pounds that's for sure since I have so many guys on top of me I can guess within a couple of pounds of what they weigh."

Leroy laughed at that.

"He had what looked like a knife scar on his left cheek about an inch long. His face looked like he had a bad case of acne when he was a young man." She closed her eyes again. "I think that that's all I can remember."

Leroy stood up to leave, "If you think of anything else give me a call at the Police Station. Thank you for your help."

She looked Leroy over like she was shopping for a ham. Looking down her front, she said, "Would you like a free sample?"

"Sorry but I have a cat at home waiting to be petted, but thanks anyway."

She stared at him as he went out the door, she thought he was crazy. How many men would turn down a free piece?

Katherine was in the driver seat waiting for him.

"Don't you like my driving?"

"Get over it. What took you so long? Were you getting a free piece? What did you find out?"

Leroy told her she could use everything he found out in her newspaper. He wanted to flush out this guy and try to get a last name. He didn't care if his partners killed him. That would be one less to hunt down. Leroy went home to pet the cat.

And pet the cat he did. She wanted to him pet the cat not to kill it, but when he gave her a final brutal stab she knew the cat was dead. They kissed and went to sleep. Leroy teased Katherine as they got ready for work about the dead cat.

"See you tonight and we'll see if we can bring the cat back to life. Don't work too hard." She gave him a cold look.

Ashley was waiting in the office when Leroy walked in. He told her about Bryan and the car chase last night. Again they didn't have a last name to work with, but they had a good description of the man.

"We need to go over to the newspaper and get a set of the pictures Katherine took last night."

Captain Curry came in the office and they brought him up to speed on what was happening.

"We are on our way over to the Newspaper to get a set of pictures."

When they arrived at the Newspaper, Katherine had the pictures spread out on her desk. Her boss and several of the employees were looking at them. She had written the story and it was ready to set in print. Her boss was happy as a lark with the story. They had one picture they could use for the story.

Katherine handed Leroy a set of the pictures. He thanked her and said they had to get back to work. They went back to the Police Station where they laid the pictures on the desk and studied them. Ashley pointed to one of the pictures.

"He cut his body bad when he dove through the window. We need to check Doctors and Hospitals for this guy."

Leroy replied, "Let's check the Hospitals for this guy."

They went to their car and started making rounds of the Hospitals.

CHAPTER NINE

By lunchtime they had made several area Hospitals, but without any luck. Leroy said, "We will make the rest of the Hospitals, but I think we are barking up the wrong tree. This guy would only go to a Hospital if he were on his deathbed. We need to check bars and cat houses."

Meanwhile back at the dungeon, Allen was trying to patch Bryan up. Allen stated, "Bryan needs a Doctor. He is cut up bad."

Jason looked at them, "No Doctor, we can't chance it. Patch him up the best you can."

Ann glanced at them and smiled, she would bet her life Bryan had had a run in with Leroy. It gave her hope that she might get out of here alive. Megan glanced over at Bryan and back at Ann. Why was Ann smiling? She didn't see anything to smile about.

"Who was it that was after you?" asked Jason.

"I don't know, I didn't look back, but I know he was a cop."

Mark walked into the dungeon. "I can answer that for you," he laid a newspaper on the table. The front page told what happen last night with a picture of Bryan on it. "The man that was after you was Detective Cooper."

"So who is he, is he Just another cop?"

Ann laughed, "Not just another cop. This cop is the one called Dirty Harry. Do you know how many bad guys he has killed already? I'll tell you, try seven already that I know of and it may be more by now. You don't want to cross him or you will be dead."

Allen got Bryan patched up the best he could without stiches he would have a lot of scars.

Leroy and Ashley finished checking hospitals. They went back to their office. Ashley asked, "What do you think we should do now?"

Leroy studied the blackboard. "I think we should go out to the Renaissance tomorrow. I got a gut feeling the key to our case is at the Renaissance so why don't we drive out there and look around? Have you ever been there?"

"No, but it sounds like fun."

They called it a day and went home. Katherine was working late so Leroy fixed dinner. After he ate, he sat down and studied his notes on the case. Maybe he had missed something. Why did the Renaissance keep coming up in his thoughts? They had stolen all the cars in the parking lot except one and that was after the Renaissance had closed down. What happen to the girls? How could they get rid of the girls without someone seeing them with so many people around? Looks like they would have screamed and someone would help them or call the Police. It didn't make a lick of sense.

Finally Leroy got up and took a shower. It wasn't too late so he decided to call his Mom. She answered on the third ring.

"Mom I have been wrapped up in this case I'm working on that I can't remember if I called you or not. Katherine and I are going to get married." He waited for a lecture, but she was happy for them. She liked Katherine and thought she would make him a wonderful wife.

"When are you going to get married?"

"We plan to have it on Valentine day. We are going to keep it small, just family and a few friends. Be prepared for you and Dad to come to Dallas."

"I'm glad you found a nice girl and going to make a home for her. I guess you know I want some grandchildren."

"Yes I was sure of that."

"We will probably get a small church in Dallas. Everybody works so I hope you understand."

"I do and it will not be a problem."

"Thanks Mom I got to go."

Leroy called Mike and told him and Katherine was getting married. It didn't surprise him. "I knew you were hooked when you and Katherine visited us."

"How did you know?"

"I have been there and done it. The look on your face was a dead giveaway. You just didn't know it yet."

"Would you, Linda and Cindy be in our wedding?"

"You know the answer to that, of course we will."

"The wedding will be on Valentine Day."

"Sounds good, we will be there."

It was getting late when Katherine finally came home. She was tired to the bone. Leroy wanted some loving, but he knew she was too tired so she ate the dinner he had made. They got ready for bed, cuddled up together and went to sleep.

For once Leroy beat Ashley to work and was staring at the blackboard when she came in. "Anything new on the case?"

"No, I went over my notes, but I couldn't come up with anything. If we could get a last name for Bryan it sure would help.

Ashley said, "Are you ready to go to the Renaissance?"

'Yes, let's be on our way."

Ashley drove, pulling out into traffic and heading south. They arrived at about nine o'clock. They went into the Renaissance to look it over.

They started on the right side to work their way around. They would go in a circle and end up where they started. There were also things in the middle. The first place was a bakery. They were open to feed the staff that was working on different projects to get the Renaissance ready to open. It would be opening soon to the public. They had coffee and donuts.

They checked out the Black Horse Pub, moved on to the Queen's Kitchen and on to the Archery Range. The owner let them shoot some free arrows while he was getting the place ready to open. Leroy had a bow at home so he did well, but Ashley had never shot a bow and didn't do so good.

They moved on down to the Jousting Area. They checked out the building where the horses were kept. So far there were no clues and they pushed on. They checked out more pubs and games of skill. They checked out places where they had stage shows. Leroy would like to see the show with the belly dancers.

"You dirty old man," Ashley teased.

They checked out more pubs and stage shows. They checked an area just for kids, rides, stage shows and games of skill for little kids.

Leroy said, "Now who would watch a turtle race. It has to be so slow."

"I'm hungry, let's find some food and drink," said Ashley.

They found a kitchen open. They got hot dogs, potato wedges, chips, and cokes to drink.

"This is a big place," commented Ashley.

"Yes I know and we are only half through the place. It will take all day and we will still miss places. There are so many storage places here.

They rested, before pressing on. They checked out the mud pit stage and storage. Next they checked the Monster Museum. They checked out more pubs and stage shows. One stage had a band and dancers practicing for their show. When they quit for a break, Ashley asked about the girls. They didn't remember seeing any of them.

Leroy said, "Let's go look some more."

They checked more storage spaces. They walked up to the old castle and went inside. It was like going back in time. They found steps leading down into the dungeon. They looked around at all the machines used for torture. Racks were used the most. People were tied to the rack, whipped, beat, cut, hot irons put to the body, eyes poked out or stretch the body. The place was a living hell. They looked the place over from top to bottom. They looked for storage rooms, but couldn't find a thing.

As they left the Renaissance, Ashley said, "Well we wasted a whole day with nothing but sore feet to show for it. What do we do now coach?"

CHAPTER TEN

Meanwhile back at the dungeon, Jason said, "We got to get rid of the Mustang. Mark you find a chop shop that will take it."

"I'm on it." He left by way of the tunnel. He put stolen plates on the Mustang and went to search for a chop shop. Things were starting to fall apart. He was nervous driving a stolen car around Dallas.

Two hours later he found a chop shop that would take the Mustang. They didn't want to pay much for the hot car. They finally paid him three thousand dollars for the car. Mark called Jason to pick him up.

When Leroy and Ashley got back to the Police Station they looked at the blackboard to make sure they had covered all the leads.

Ashley asked, "What happen to the last car stolen?"

They had forgotten about the Mustang. They couldn't sell it without a title so that left a chop shop.

Leroy said, "We better check chop shops tonight. It's not dark yet so let's get on the road."

They were tired from all day at the Renaissance, but they pressed on. The car may already be in little pieces, but some of the big pieces may still be whole. They found two shops on the eastside of Dallas. They took their time looking through parts of all the different cars. They bought wreaked cars, stripped them and sold off all the parts. The trouble was some of the shops bought stolen cars, stripped them and cut up the body selling it for scrap metal.

It was hard to catch them doing it. Most of the chop shops were honest. They didn't care if Leroy and Ashley went over their parts, but there is always one bad apple in the barrel.

Ashley said, "Can we stop to eat? The last we ate was at the Renaissance and I'm hungry."

They stopped at Kentucky Fried Chicken. They each had a full meal deal with cokes to drink. They started looking on the south side of Dallas at an old chop shop. They found the color of the Mustang, but it was cut up so they couldn't tell and they gave up looking.

Katherine's boss called her into the office. He wanted her to go to the Renaissance and do a story about a new section they were adding on. She picked up her camera and notepad. It was about an hour drive. Pulling into the parking lot she looked it over. She remembered what Leroy told her about the missing girls and missing cars. He thought this was where it took place. She felt a cold chill go over her body. What was her problem? It was daylight and the sun was shining, but she still had a bad feeling something was going to happen.

Katherine found the person in charge and he showed her the new section being added. It was designed for the little kids, rides, games and shows. She took pictures and notes. She finished early and decided to look the whole place over. She walked around for an hour and then headed for the exit.

There were a few people around getting the place ready to open. She walked up to an old castle. She was curious about the castle and the dungeon so she went inside. She walked around until she found steps leading down. She walked down the steps into the dungeon. It had shackles on the wall with a dummy in the shackles for effect. There was a wrack with a dummy on it. There were all types of torture items.

Mark saw Katherine enter the castle and followed her. He wanted to be sure she was by herself. Katherine took some pictures and made notes. She was ready to leave this sick place. She couldn't believe people were tortured like that.

Katherine started up the steps and stopped. Mark was blocking the exit.

"What's your hurry?"

"I have to get back to Dallas."

"Let me show you the rest of the Dungeon. I think you will find it interesting."

"I have seen enough."

"Have you ever seen live torture? It is far out."

"Let me out of here."

Mark walked down the steps as Katherine backed away. "You shouldn't have come down here, now you will see what torture is really like."

She tried to get around Mark, but he grabbed her and pulled her toward the back wall, punching something and the wall opened up. Mark dragged her inside and closed the wall.

"Welcome to your new home." Mark turned around to face the dungeon. Three men got up from a table where they were drinking beer and playing cards.

Jason said, "What have we here? Where did you find this pretty little piece?"

"She was out in the other dungeon taking pictures. I think she works for the newspaper."

Katherine glanced over at the two girls on the racks and back to the three men. Mark said, "I told you I would show you torture, but you will enjoy this type of torture."

"I don't think so, you are sick."

He slapped her across the face leaving his handprint. "You learn to keep your mouth shut and you don't get hurt."

She stared at Bryan, "I know you. You are the one I took pictures of as you ran naked from the cat house. You were a funny sight."

Bryan walked over and slapped her, "You think it is funny now. I'm going to enjoy doing you and you will beg me to stop."

Katherine laughed, "I don't think so. According to the hooker you were a sorry john."

Bryan slapped her again busting her lip, "You better learn the rules or you won't live very long. See the pit over there, that's where you will end up when we are tired of playing with you."

Katherine turned white as she stared at the pit, then it hit her and she knew where all the missing girls were. They were dead and she could be next.

"I thought that would take the wind out of your sails," laughed Bryan. He reached over and laid a hand on her breast. She didn't move.

"Now that's more like it."

Katherine was scared to death. If Leroy was here he would kill them all and she would cheer him on as he did it.

Jason said, "We will save this one for later, strip her and put her on the wall in shackles."

Katherine was embarrassed to death, but she stood there and let them undress her. Mark and Bryan then hung her on the wall in shackles. They stepped back and starred at her. Mark reached over and touched her opening, then ran a finger in her soft body.

Katherine said, "I'll see you all dead."

They all laughed at her. Jason smiled, "She is a wild cat, but I will enjoy taming her."

Ann smiled, "You don't know who you have?"

Jason looked over at her, "Yes we have another toy to play with."

"She is Dirty Harry's woman and he will kill all of you."

Jason didn't look so brave anymore, "Bring him on, there are four of us."

Ann laughed, "He killed two men at a grocery store trying to rob it. He killed three more at a bank robbery. Leroy and his partner killed five in another bank robbery. Do you want to face him? I think not, back shoot would be more your speed."

Jason stared at Ann, "Shut up or you will be next in the hole."

They went over to the table and talked. Jason told them not to be out in public, stay at home or out here in the dungeon. He told Bryan not to leave the dungeon. They had plenty of food and drinks stored in the dungeon. Bryan liked the idea of staying in the dungeon with three women to play with, but Jason told him not to touch them, only when they were all there. Jason wanted his turn first.

Jason, Mark, and Allen left for the night. They were nervous and didn't rape the girls before they left. They didn't like Dirty Harry on their trail. They thought about dropping the girls down the hole and leaving Dallas, but Jason told them they could take Dirty Harry. They had made a mistake and left Katherine's car in the parking lot.

Meanwhile back at the dungeon, Bryan told the girls if he could bang them he would be nice to them if they wouldn't tell Jason on them. They told him to go to hell. He got mad and flashed them. He told them they didn't know what they were missing. The girls just laughed at him.

CHAPTER ELEVEN

Leroy and Ashley had been checking bars all day. They found one bar that knew Bryan, but didn't know his last name or where he worked. Back at their office they decided to work the hookers again. They had good luck last time with the hookers so why not try them again?

They made the rounds again and were lucky. One girl remembered Bryan from his picture. It seems he likes a lot of different girls. They decided to call it a day and drove back to the Police Station.

"Another day, another dollar," said Leroy.

When Leroy got to the apartment, Katherine wasn't home. It wasn't unusual for her to be late if she was tied up with a story. He decided to fix dinner. He fixed a salad and a sandwich for her. He fixed soup and a sandwich for himself.

Leroy took a shower and went to bed. At four in the morning, he woke up and she still wasn't home. Now he became worried. She should have called if she was going to be this late coming home.

Katherine didn't come home all night. Leroy called the Newspaper. After talking to one of the girls he asked to speak to her boss. He told Leroy she went out to the Renaissance to cover a story and didn't come back to the Newspaper. He thought she was late getting back and would write the story in the morning.

Ashley was in their office when Leroy stormed into the office. He was fit to be tied. "What's wrong?" she asked.

"Katherine went out to the Renaissance yesterday on a story and didn't come back."

"Oh no not Katherine, we better get out there now."

Leroy burned rubber out of the parking lot as Captain Curry was pulling in. He wandered what was going on. He went inside and asked, but nobody knew why they had left.

Leroy turned on the overhead lights and broke all speed limits. He pulled into the parking lot and saw Katherine's car. He checked the engine and it was cold. "Ashley I'll stay with the car and you go look for Katherine."

She went inside and worked her way around the Renaissance. Finally she found the people Katherine had talked to the day before. They told her Katherine took pictures and notes. Then she left. Ashley went back to the parking lot and told Leroy she had gone back to Dallas.

"No she hasn't, her car is still here. I know she is being held or her body is here."

"What are we going to do?"

"We are going to take this place apart until we find her."

"Do you want to call the Police Station for help?"

"No way, they have to follow the rules."

Leroy picked up the phone and called Ann's boyfriend. "I need as many bikers as you can get right now at the Renaissance."

"Man we are on our way."

"I got one more call to make." He called Gary Mitchell. He answered on the second ring.

"They got my girlfriend here at the Renaissance, but I can't find her. I got a gut feeling I know she is here."

"I'll be there in two hours if you will pay my speeding ticket."

"I got you covered, please hurry. I don't know how much time we have before she will be dead."

Bikers streamed into the parking lot. Leroy never knew there were that many bikers in Dallas. He told Ann's boyfriend to stay with him and Ashley.

Leroy explained, "I want twenty guys inside looking for her. The rest of you surround this place. I don't want anything going out until I give the word."

He gave some pictures of Katherine to all the bikers. Leroy left a biker with the car and everybody started to search for Katherine. They searched each booth, storeroom, stage, dressing rooms, closets, bars and barns where animals were kept. Anything that was locked they cut the lock off.

After two hours Leroy went back to the parking lot. About ten minutes later Gary Mitchel drove into the parking lot. He opened his door and got out followed by a huge Wolf as he walked over to Leroy. Leroy starred at the Wolf. He couldn't believe his eyes.

"Is this your partner you talked about?"

"Yes he is. He is the best and I never go anywhere without him."

Leroy stared at the Wolf and he stared back. Gary asked, "Have you found her yet?"

"No, I don't know what to do, I'm lost, I know she is here. She has to be."

Gary said, "I'll take over and you follow me. Do you have some clothes she has worn?"

"No, I would have to go back to Dallas to get some."

"Is her car here?"

"Yes it's over there."

They walked over to the car. It was locked. "Open the car."

Leroy took a lock cutter and smashed in the driver window. "She's going to kill me for this. What am I saying?"

Leroy opened the door. Gary said, "Wolf" and pointed to the seat.

Wolf smelled the seat and turned to Gary. "Wolf, go and find the girl." Wolf ran inside the Renaissance. Ashley and the biker came out to the parking lot.

"Did you see that big Wolf?"

Leroy asked, "Aren't you going to follow him?"

"No I don't have to." He closed his eyes and leaned back against the car. "I see what he sees, I don't understand, but I can, I see what the Wolf sees."

"Leroy asked, "Where is he now?"

"He is on the back side working his way around that side. He is hot on her trail."

They watched Gary finding it hard to believe what was going on. "When I open my eyes and look at you Wolf can close his eyes and see you through my eyes."

They thought Gary was crazy. Gary closed his eyes again. Wolf was on the south side working his way toward the front. Gary said, "She must have looked the whole place over." They waited as Wolf slowly worked his way toward the front. When he came to the castle he stopped and put his nose to the ground. He went into the castle. He went down the steps in to the dungeon, going to the back wall, he stood up on his hind legs on the wall and scratched.

Gary said, "Wolf has found her, follow me." They hurried to the castle and went inside.

Ashley asked, "Where is Wolf?" Gary ran down the steps with the rest of them on his tail. Wolf was stranding at the back wall.

Gary said, "She is behind this wall. I see a fine crack here."

They searched for a way to open the wall, but couldn't find a way and the wall was several feet thick.

Leroy said, "We need some C-4 to get in here."

Gary said, "Well I just happen to have some in my backpack."

"You crazy, I can't believe you carry C-4 in your backpack."

"Always, I never leave home without it."

Now where had Leroy heard that expression? Katherine always carried her camera with her. Gary took his backpack off and reached in a pocket. He came out with a block of C-4.

He placed the C-4 so it would blow outward. He reached in and got a fuse. Gary stuck the fuse in the C-4.

"Everybody get over to the side out of harm's way." He lit the fuse, "Fire in the hole."

Meanwhile in the dungeon on the other side of the wall, Jason said, "It's time to party." He moved up behind Megan, dropped his pants and shorts then slammed into her soft body.

She cried, "Please don't hurt me."

Mark moved into position in front of Ann, dropped his pants and shorts. He leaned over her, put his arms around her waist and slammed into her body.

"May you die today," Ann said as he slammed deep inside her. Mark and Jason laughed.

CHAPTER TWELVE

All hell broke loose as the C-4 blew the wall out. Leroy charged through the wall with his Colt 45 in his hand followed by the biker, Ashley, Gary and the Wolf. Jason went for his gun on the floor in his pants. Leroy fired and hit Jason in the chest. He was dead before he hit the floor.

The biker charged Mark while he tried to reach his gun on the floor with his pants. The biker snapped Mark's neck like it was a twig and dropped him to the floor.

Allen was at the table. He reached for his gun, but Ashley fired first, on target and Allen dropped to the floor.

Bryan turned and ran down the tunnel. Gary glanced at Wolf. "Wolf you can have him."

Wolf charged down the tunnel after Bryan. A bloodcurdling scream came from the tunnel and Wolf came back to Garry's side. Gary knew Bryan was dead.

Leroy said to Ashley, "Now you know why I didn't want the Police to help. It's all over now except cleaning up the mess."

The biker untied Ann and put his coat around her. She kissed him and hung on for dear life. Gary went over and untied Megan, put his coat around her, hugged her close, "It's all over, you are safe and they can't hurt you anymore."

Megan clung to him crying, "I want to go home."

Leroy fished around in Jason's pants pockets until he found the key to the shackles. He unlocked the shackles rom

Katherine's hands and legs. She fell into his arms. "Ann said you would find us. What took you so long?"

She kissed him with her naked body flat against him. He put his coat around her body. Katherine looked into his eyes.

"You have killed all the bad guys and kissed the girl. Can we go home now?"

Leroy smiled down at her, "Very soon now."

Ann pointed to the hole, "You'll find all the missing girls, our clothes, and garbage down in the hole."

Gary went over, pulled the lid off and looked down the hole. "It's too deep, you can't see the bottom."

Leroy said, "Ashley would go find the girls some clothes. The people working at the Renaissance should have some while I call Captain Curry. Gary, would you stay here while I make the call?"

Captain Curry came on the line, "What you got Leroy?"

"I got good news and bad news. The good news is the case is closed on the car theft ring and the missing girls. The bad news is the girls are all dead but two. Megan Moore and Ann Mitchel are alive to tell their horrible story."

"Dam, dam, I was afraid of that. Do you need an ambulance?"

"No sir, just a meat wagon."

"I take it all the bad guys are dead."

"Yes sir, they are all dead."

"Your crime scene people are going to have a hard time. The girls are down a deep hole in the dungeon. They raped the girls over and over again until they were tired of them. Then they dropped them down the hole and got a new girl."

"Oh my God," Captain Curry grimly said.

"I don't know how many girls are down the hole, but probably one for every car that was stolen."

"Why didn't you call for backup?"

"I had plenty of backup, just not your normal type."

"I'm not sure I should here this."

"When you saw me burning rubber out of here, I just found out Katherine was missing. She had gone out to the Renaissance for a story. When I got there and found her car I called for backup."

"And who did you call for backup?"

"I think all the bikers in Dallas, plus Gary Mitchel known as the Tracker and Wolf."

"You mean Wolf like an animal?"

"Yes sir a big Wolf. His name is Wolf. He found the girls and Katherine was with them. It will all be in my report when I get back to the Police Station."

"The girls will need a rape kit done on them at the hospital."

"I don't think we need to do that and embarrass them anymore. They were rapped many times by four different men. The four men are dead. Got to go and I'll see you back at the station."

Leroy called Mr. and Mrs. Moore and told them Megan was found and would be home shortly. He went back to the dungeon where the girls now had clothes on. Katherine was looking around the dungeon.

"Found it." She held up her camera. I want a picture of all of you. After she took pictures Gary said, "I'm taking Megan home."

Ann thanked them and she and her boyfriend left. Katherine started taking more pictures and asked Leroy for his notepad. This story will read like a horror book which is was. It would be a big story and she was in it. She would tell the story the way life was.

The crime scene people arrived and Leroy showed them the hole. The meat wagon came with body bags to pick up all the bodies. Leroy didn't want to be around when they started bringing bodies up out of the hole. He was glad he wasn't the one going down in the hole.

Katherine took pictures of the crime team. She had her story and what a story. When they got back to the parking lot she demanded, "Who broke my window?"

Leroy laughed, "Ashley did it."

"I did not."

Leroy told her why he broke the window. "The Wolf did what?" Katherine got her spare key from a box under the frame.

"I'll drive my car home. I need to go by the Newspaper, drop off my pictures and write my story. I'll see you at home."

Ashley drove her and Leroy to the Police Station. Captain Curry was waiting for them in their office. He was reading their notes on the blackboard.

"I see the two of you have been busy. Not the normal way Police work, but you sure do get the job done."

Captain Curry went into his office and waited for the report. He wanted to read it before he went home. He knew it would be some story. He wanted to know how all the car ring died. He would get a shock when he finds out Leroy only killed one of the bad guys.

Gary stopped on the way back to Dallas. He bought Megan some food because she was starving. When they drove into the driveway at Megan's home her Mom and Dad were outside waiting on them. Gary had her by his side and Megan had her hand on Wolf as they walked up to her Mom and Dad.

"Mom and Dad this is Gary and Wolf." She put her arms around Wolf's neck. "Wolf found me and saved my life."

Mr. and Mrs. Moore stared at Gary and Wolf. They had never seen anything like it. Gary was six feet tall wearing buckskins, boots and an old beat up hat. He wore a ponytail and had a rugged complexion. The Wolf was huge. They shook hands and thanked Gary for bringing their daughter home to them. He started to leave. Megan hugged him and Wolf.

When they were back on the road Gary had tears in his eyes for Megan and what they had done to her. He was glad they were all dead. If they had lived they would have had a fancy lawyer and might have figured a way to beat the system.

Gary went to Katherine and Leroy's apartment and waited for them to come home. About thirty minutes later Leroy pulled in. Katherine finally got home from the Newspaper. Her boss couldn't believe what happen to her. He looked at her arms where the shackles had made them raw. She showed him her legs that were raw also.

Katherine wanted a beer. The phone rang and she picked up on the second ring. Ashley wanted them to come over for a party and wanted them to be sure to bring Wolf.

There was more room in Gary's truck so they piled into his truck and drove over to Ashley's house. Gary was looking very sad as he stared out the windshield.

"What's wrong with you?" asked Katherine.

"I was thinking about Megan. She has to go back to school and you know how mean kids can be. They will call her names and the boys will try to hit on her. When she tells them no you know how they will be to her. If she can't take it she will try to commit suicide."

Katherine said, "I'll take her under my wing and spend as much time as I can with her. Maybe I can get her on part time with me at the Newspaper. I'll try to get her mind off what happened. What about Ann?"

"Ann is as tough as nails, she will be fine."

Gary pulled in the driveway at Ashley's house. Jim opened the door and told them to come on in. Ashley served a ton of finger food and beer. She asked if Wolf could have sweet food.

"He eats anything. When I fix dinner or eat out we eat the same food."

"Good, I got a treat for him. He saved the day and without him we would never have found the girls."

Ashley went to the refrigerator and pulled out a large cake with Wolf wrote on it. She cut slices for all of them and gave the rest of the cake to Wolf. He looked at her with love in his eyes, his tail wagging he ate all the cake.

Jim came in with cards in his hand, "Time to play cards and drink beer."

They played cards until midnight and then called it a night. Back at Katherine and Leroy's apartment Gary was going to a motel, but they wouldn't let him.

After breakfast Gary and Wolf left for home. Leroy thanked him for all his help and told him if he ever needed him just call.

When Katherine got to the Newspaper her boss was waiting in her office. "I can't believe how you always come up with the top story. How do you do it?"

She laughed, ""It's very simple, I hang around with Leroy Cooper and trouble always follows him. He is my boyfriend as you know and my future husband. He asked me to marry him and we set the date."

"He is getting one hell of a woman."

Katherine smiled, "You could say the same about him. He is one hell of a man. A man you don't want to mess with."

As soon as the boss left Katherine was covered up with all the girls wanting to know what happened. The boss looked back, let them talk, work could wait a few minutes. He couldn't believe that a short time back Katherine was a no-body and now she was the top reporter in Dallas. He was sure lucky to have her working for him.

Captain Curry was waiting in their office when Ashley and Leroy arrived. "You two sure do like to break the rules. Now I know why you didn't want to use the Police as a backup. The bikers went into all the places taking them apart, cutting locks and kicking in doors. You knew we would have to have a search warrant to search each business, but all the bikers look alike and they just did it. The owners were mad at first, but after you found the girls it was ok. Do you know how many bikers were involved?"

"I think every biker in Dallas was there. The parking lot was full of bikes."

"Which biker broke the scumbag's neck?"

"I can't remember, like you said they all look alike so I put it in my report the biker and the scumbag is dead. Who cares who killed him?"

"You didn't try to stop him?"

"No sir, the scumbag was raping a girl when we broke through the wall."

Captain smiled at Leroy, "This case is closed. You and Ashley did a great job now take the rest of the day off."

"Thank you, sir."

Captain Curry watched out the window as Leroy and Ashley walked to the parking lot. What a pair they made. Ashley was just like Leroy now, but he wouldn't take any ten officers over them. They made things happen and got the job done.

Ashley walked into the Newspaper office and looked for Katherine's office. She found her office and walked in.

Katherine looked up, "What are you doing here?"

"I came to get you and go shopping. You are getting married and I'm going to help you plan it. Tell your boss you want the rest of the day off."

"I don't know, but I will ask him."

"After what you went through you need some time off."

Katherine's boss told her to take the day off and more if she wanted to. She grabbed her purse and coat. They went up, up and away.

They shopped until they were ready to drop finally finding the wedding dress she wanted. She had to have shoes and dresses to take on a honeymoon. She ran her credit cards to the maxim limit, but what the heck a girl only gets married one time she hoped.

EPILOGUE

Katherine and Leroy sent out a few invitations to their family and friends for the wedding. They picked out a small Baptist Church in Garland. The wedding was to take place on February 14th, Valentine Day at 4:00 pm.

"What do you want to do about the Police and my Newspaper," asked Katherine

"I don't think very many will be off to come so just put it on the bulletin board and anyone who wants to come is invited."

Ashley gave Katherine a wedding shower at her home. She received everything you would need for a home. Some gave her baby things. Was that a hint or did they know something she didn't.

Jim gave Leroy a bachelor party at Hooters. There were lots of food and drinks and hooters. Leroy thought if Katherine could see him now she would kill him. Jim had a girl rub on Leroy and show off her large hooters. After they left Hooters they went to a topless club. Rex wanted to dance on the stage with the strippers. They had to hold him back from going on the stage.

The day of the wedding Leroy was nervous as a cat on a hot tin roof. Katherine laughed at him and told him to cool it.

The wedding march turned out to be a sight to see. Jim Lewis was best man in a suit. The grooms were Rex Johnson in a suit, Punky Wilson in his Navy dress uniform, Mike Love in a country western suit, Gary Mitchel in buckskins and Wolf as himself.

Ashley Lewis was maid of honor in a beautiful long red dress. The bridesmaids were dressed in short red dresses. Her bridesmaids were Ann Mitchell, Megan Moore, Linda Love and Cindy Love.

The church was decorated in red for Valentine Day. Red flowers were everywhere. Leroy took his place dressed in in a suit. The bridesmaids and grooms took their place. Ashley whispered to the bridesmaids, "Now all we need is a bride. I hope we don't have a run-a-way like in the movie." The girls giggled.

The wedding march sounded and all heads turned to the back of the church. Leroy couldn't believe what he saw. The church was full. Police, Newspaper people, and family filled the church. What happen to the small wedding?

Katherine's Father escorted her down the church isle and gave Leroy her hand. After the wedding vows, the exchanging of rings and kissing the bride it was time now for the food and drinks. They went in a back room for that. A newspaper took pictures of the whole weeding.

Leroy and Katherine wanted to get out of the reception as soon as they could. They ran for the front door of the church.

As they came out the door the walk was lined with Police in dress uniform, "Present sabers." Leroy and Katherine walked under the sabers.

Mike pulled up in a good-time van as they reached the end of the sabers. People stormed them throwing rice on them. Mike tossed Leroy the keys to the van.

"I thought you would have more fun on your honeymoon with a ride like this."

Leroy handed his car keys to Mike, "Take care of my old Thunderbird."

"I will and you two have a fun honeymoon."

Katherine kissed Mike on the cheek, "Thank you."

She turned and tossed her bouquet over her shoulder and Ann caught it. She stared at her biker.

"We'll see what we can do about it." Ann opened her arms and he went into them.

Leroy pulled out into traffic and headed south. They were on their way to San Antonio.

Leroy glanced at Katherine, "Do you want to stop at the next rest stop and make love?"

Katherine giggled, "Yes it's a long way to San Antonio. We may have to stop at a lot of rest stops along the way.

XXXXXX